"DEAR REBECCA. YOU ARE SAFE HERE, SAFE ALWAYS WITH US, FOR AS LONG AS YOU WISH. WE WILL NEVER LET ANYONE HARM YOU."

Maria spoke the words over and over in a soft monotone. "We love you, Rebecca, and we want you. Want you to stay. Want you to be with us. We want you. *I* want you to stay. Do you understand?"

There was a long pause before Rebecca answered softly, "Yes."

The count stepped out of the shadows, his sinewy body lit by the fire's glow. He took Rebecca into his arms and felt her weaken. He bent his head forward, placing his mouth on Rebecca's neck, measuring her readiness. He pulled his head back and looked into her eyes.

"You are going to let go completely now, Rebecca," he whispered in her ear. "Come fly."

the
Kiss

KATHRYN REINES

AVON BOOKS NEW YORK

**VISIT OUR WEBSITE AT
http://AvonBooks.com**

THE KISS is an original publication of Avon Books. This work has never before appeared in book form. This work is a novel. Any similarity to actual persons or events is purely coincidental.

AVON BOOKS
A division of
The Hearst Corporation
1350 Avenue of the Americas
New York, New York 10019

Copyright © 1996 by RNK Enterprises, Inc.
Published by arrangement with the author
Library of Congress Catalog Card Number: 96-96172
ISBN: 0-380-78347-9

First Avon Books Printing: October 1996

AVON TRADEMARK REG. U.S. PAT. OFF. AND IN OTHER COUNTRIES, MARCA REGISTRADA, HECHO EN U.S.A.

Printed in the U.S.A.

RA   10   9   8   7   6   5   4   3   2   1

PROLOGUE

The train left them alone on a wooden platform in frigid darkness.

Almost as though it were eager to be gone from this place, *Richard thought as he watched the red lights disappear down the tracks.*

There was a single station building, which was empty. Its tiny office was closed, and a naked light bulb hanging over the locked door offered the only illumination. The cold night air quickly wrapped itself around them.

Richard studied a timetable that hung in the window. "Well, it says 1938 on the schedule, so at least that means it's current and people come and go from here. But apparently the trains only come through once a day."

Richard looked back at Rebecca and saw a tear threaten to spill out of her left eye. "Rebecca, I'm sorry," he said.

She shook her head. "No. I'm just tired. It seems like we'd been on that train forever."

He stroked her face once and kissed her, then took hold of her hand and nodded to the east. "I'm tired, too.

But we can't stand here all night. There has to be a town nearby, probably down that road. We'll get help."

Rebecca looked around her. The ancient, craggy mountains that surrounded them seemed to add to the gloom. "Okay," she said, "let's go."

They put on gloves, picked up their suitcases, and began walking. The unpaved road twisted sharply right and left, but eventually the lights of a small village shone in the distance. The night wind blew harder, drifting dead leaves around their feet as they walked. They held hands, but neither of them spoke.

They had walked about a quarter of a mile when a long, black Mercedes appeared on the road in front of them. It stopped a few feet away, shining its bright headlights in their faces. For a moment nothing happened, and then the front door on the driver's side opened and a tall man got out.

He spoke to them in a foreign language that they did not understand.

Richard tried speaking in German. "Where are we?"

The man answered in German, but with a heavy Slavic accent. "You are from the train?"

"Yes."

He nodded, and his voice sounded sad. "Ah, then we have missed it." He turned around and spoke to someone in the automobile.

Rebecca hugged her coat tighter, and Richard put his arm around her. Finally the man turned back and faced them again.

"You do not know where you are?"

"No!" Rebecca snapped. "Are you going to tell us?"

The man stared at her, then looked again at Richard. "You are just outside the village of Boleslaus, at the *easternmost edge of Bulgaria. Romania is right over those mountains."*

"Is there an inn in this village where we can stay?"

The man leaned back into the car and spoke again, and this time the side door opened. As Richard and Rebecca watched, a woman climbed out and walked around the front of the car. At first she seemed invisible, a shadow in the shadows of the night. But as she came closer her slender figure and her thick black hair slowly became apparent. When the beams from the headlights caught her features, Richard's eyes widened.

She was astonishingly beautiful. Her high cheekbones and narrow chin seemed carved in perfection. Her lips, Richard saw, were painted bright red, their fullness accentuated against her white skin and black hair. But her most remarkable feature was her eyes. Dark and luminous, they dominated her face, and the strange thought came to Richard that those eyes must see everything. He glanced at Rebecca and saw that she was staring at the woman also.

The woman smiled. "My name is Countess Maria Viroslav. And this is Gregor," she said, indicating the tall man. She spoke German better than her driver, but still with the same trace of Slavic intonation. "We were just going to the train station ourselves."

"I am Richard Anderson, and this is—"

But Rebecca did not wait to be introduced. She stepped forward and held out her hand. "I'm Rebecca. Rebecca Bittan."

The sensuous smile on her painted lips evaporated, and the countess studied Rebecca for a long moment while nobody spoke. *It is her presence,* Richard thought, that makes us hesitant.

Finally she smiled again and said, "I'm afraid you

will not have much luck finding a place in the village. There are very few accommodations, and those that do exist are quite primitive. But please come with me and be my guests. My husband and I do not live far from here, and you will be more than welcome."

A gust of cold air blew through the canyon and Rebecca shivered. "It's very kind of you," she said. "We've come all the way from Berlin, and we've been put off the train because we ran out of money."

Richard's mouth dropped open at what Rebecca said, or more so at the way she said it. She had sounded like a small child. He looked at her in surprise, unsure of why she had spoken like that, why she was telling this strange woman their plight. He could see the exhaustion on Rebecca's face, and he worried that she was falling apart. Then he thought of the last days in Berlin and the madness there that had almost destroyed them.

He looked back at the countess. It was his fault that they were stuck here. The invitation was welcome, yet even though he knew they needed rest and time to plan, Richard hesitated. "Well . . . "

Now the countess turned to him, almost as if seeing him for the first time. "Oh, please say you'll come. We have more than enough room for both of you. You will be much more comfortable, and we do enjoy meeting people from beyond our rural world."

Richard glanced at Rebecca, but she was still staring at the countess. Apparently she felt none of the apprehension that had momentarily overcome him.

The countess smiled at Richard, and again he was filled with something close to awe at her beauty. He wanted to fall into those fathomless eyes.

"You must be exhausted," she said.

It was true. A wave of exhaustion came over him. Steam rose off the car's engine and swirled in the *headlights. The idea of continuing on foot suddenly seemed insane. He glanced at Gregor, then back at the countess. They were all waiting for him to respond.*

"We do appreciate your hospitality. . . . " he stammered.

Rebecca turned to him. "Oh, let's accept her invitation, Richard. It's the nicest thing that has happened to us since we left Berlin."

The countess took Rebecca's arm and said, "Wonderful! Come along, then, and get in the car. It is a very cold night for October. And those trains are not very nice, are they?" Both women got into the car.

Gregor took their suitcases and put them in the trunk. Richard stood in the cold night air and watched the tall man move silently around the car. He was so tired he could not think straight. When at last Gregor finished his task and climbed in behind the steering wheel, then he, too, climbed in. He sank into the rich black leather that covered the backseat and pulled the passenger door closed behind him.

I

Count Viroslav bent an aristocratic finger and pulled a conical-shaped plug from the wall. He dropped it onto the top of an ancient, hand-carved Egyptian table and then leaned forward and peered through the hole into the next room.

In the adjoining bedroom he saw a young blond woman holding a tiny black dress against her body and studying herself in a full-length hanging mirror. She turned right and then left, and chewed lightly on her lower lip.

"Charming," he said. "Where did you find her?"

"Them," his wife corrected him. "It was not only she. Her boyfriend is with her. I found them this morning just before dawn on the road from the train station. They've come all the way from Germany. They were very tired, so I told them to rest all day, and they were quite happy to do so. They are Americans, Alexander. Fleeing the Nazi madness in Berlin, they say."

"You do not believe them?"

"I'm not sure. The girl is hiding a secret or two; I can see it in her."

"Well, at least I can practice my English. What is this one's name?"

"Rebecca."

Rebecca seemed to make up her mind. She reached for a hanger and draped the dress over it, then hung it from the edge of the mirror. With an unaware innocence she reached for the top button of her blouse and undid it. The count watched as her throat was bared, her fingers moving rapidly downward, pulling wooden buttons through tiny holes, releasing the tension imposed by the white cotton stretched tight across her chest. When the final button was loosened and the lapels fell free, a piece of brilliant white lace flashed in the mirror.

The count's eye widened perceptibly.

"So you approve?"

He looked at his wife. "She wears decent lingerie, at least. The last one had on something like a hair shirt."

The countess smiled, and he turned back to the hole. "Denyse, you mean," she said. "A peasant girl. But as I recall it had been a very long time."

"Yes. It had been a long time." He watched Rebecca shrug out of the blouse and toss it out of his view. Now her back was bare except for the straps of her brassiere. The count's nostrils flared slightly.

Next, Rebecca unzipped her skirt. She put her hands on the waist of the garment, and was just about to pull it down over her hips, when suddenly she stopped and turned around toward the wall. Her eyes searched the room suspiciously and she frowned. The count smiled. It was not the first time his presence had been felt. But he knew she would never find the peephole in the elaborate design of the cubist painting that housed it.

"And the boy?" he said. "How did you find him?"

"He was with her."

"That is not what I meant."

The countess' eyelids raised a little and her chest expanded slightly as she took a deep breath. "He is tall, blond-haired, and boyishly good-looking. He reminds me a bit of the young Marquis de Sade the year we met Napoléon. His name is Richard. He has a small scar on his left hip. Otherwise, perfect."

Again the count pulled back from the mirror and turned to regard his wife. "How did you get him to undress completely?"

She shrugged, pleased with herself. "I spilled some tea in his lap and then sent him to his room."

"They did not wish to sleep together?"

"Perhaps you have forgotten what year it is. It is no longer the eighteenth century, Alexander. In this new century things are done quite differently."

His eyes narrowed coldly, and his voice took on an edge. "I have not forgotten what century it is, my dear. But regardless of what age, a young man and a young woman should want to sleep together."

Maria hesitated. "I'm sure they did, but I gave them the impression we were terribly proper. It was the only way they would not be afraid of coming here."

He looked back. Rebecca had already removed the skirt and was stepping into the black dress.

The count swore silently, but as she stood up straight and began pulling the shoulder straps upward, he held his breath. Her breasts, he was delighted to see, were firm and perfectly proportional to her body, the nipples large and erect.

"Has she changed yet?" the countess asked.

Rebecca pulled the zipper up the back of the dress and examined herself in the mirror. She looked smashing, and she knew it. The count saw a slight smile cross her face.

"Yes." He stepped back from the wall and replaced the plug. Then he walked over to his wife. "And what are you going to wear, darling?" he said.

"All white, of course." She put her arms around his neck and kissed him.

2

At the knock on the door, Richard glanced around and watched the knob turn, then Rebecca entered. "I love the way you look in a tuxedo," she said.

"Thank you. I love the way you look in a tiny black dress. Is that really what she gave you to wear? I thought they were prudish."

Rebecca beamed at the compliment. "I've never really dressed for you. It's been all studies and grades. I almost feel nude with this on, but isn't it a beautiful dress?" She twirled around. "I feel very risqué."

"What do you have on underneath?"

"Just the most divine silk. It was laid out next to the dress, so I put it on."

Richard reached for her hand and pulled her to him. He kissed her mouth. She melted against him, then broke off the kiss and giggled when she realized how hard he had become.

"Really, Richard! Sometimes you should appreciate my body just as though it were a statue or painting, and worship it."

5

"I'll put you on a pedestal and strip you. You'll have to stand there naked all day long."

She laughed. "You're terrible." She looked around his room, then back at him. "Really, what do you think of the countess?"

"I'm grateful for the haven. Her? I think she's a little horny."

"Richard! She's a wonderful woman. So beautiful; she must not be even thirty, and I thought countesses were always these ugly old women. But besides that, she is so elegant, so cultured and worldly. To be here with them, in their very own castle, it's fabulous!"

He nodded thoughtfully. "Yes, it's a pretty soft place to land. The Nazi police were right behind us. I thought we were cooked." He went to the window and looked out.

Rebecca watched him. "Do you think we're safe?"

He turned his head and stared at her thoughtfully. "Yes. Your boyfriend won't follow us all the way here."

"He's not my boyfriend. Don't say that again!"

"But he was," Richard insisted.

"Yes, but that's all over now."

"Then why did you go see him again?"

"To tell him to leave us alone." She looked down at the floor, not wishing to take the discussion further.

"You still have not told me what happened."

Rebecca put a fingernail between her teeth, then quickly pulled it away and dropped her hand onto her lap. "Must we discuss it?"

"I need to know, Rebecca."

She sighed. "I told him I loved you now, and that I did not want to see him anymore."

"And?"

"And he said he would not accept that. That he would have you arrested as a spy."

"But that's ridiculous! I've never done anything wrong."

"You were seen talking to the wrong people, Richard."

"Only talking."

"It doesn't matter. He was looking for any excuse to remove you from my life."

"He is obsessed with you, Becky. It was crazy to go back to him."

She nodded quietly, thinking that Richard would never know just how crazy it had been. She was being coy with Richard and did not like herself for it, but she could not see any other way. Richard was right about one thing: Eric was obsessive and very frightening. "Yes, of course you are right. I guess I underestimated his reaction."

Richard came back into the center of the room. "We've been invited to stay the night. I'll find a telegraph or phone tomorrow. We're in Bulgaria now. It's only a matter of time before the Nazis come here; I'm certain of that. But there's no war yet, and even with reciprocity and political pressure, I think we have a few days. Don't worry, we'll get out in time."

"Promise?"

"Yes. They're not going to send the whole army after us, anyway. They've got bigger fish to fry."

She stood up and smiled, happy to see the effect she had on Richard when she took his arm and turned toward the door. "In that case, I think we should go down to dinner and enjoy this experience. I must say, I never thought when I left

Philadelphia that I would be having dinner in a castle with a real count and countess!"

They stepped out into the hall onto a long, narrow rug, and Rebecca immediately shivered. The blazing fire in the fireplace had made Richard's room cozy, but the hallway was much cooler and her dress left more uncovered than not. Rebecca put her hand through Richard's arm, and they walked closely down the hall toward the stairwell, admiring the various paintings and sculptures that adorned it. At the end of the hall Richard stopped to examine a rich tapestry.

"I wish the light were better," he said, leaning forward under a dim bulb. "This lady looks a bit like you."

Rebecca squinted and realized it was a scene depicting the fall of Constantinople. In the tapestry there were hordes of women fleeing the invaders in terror. Most of the women were either scantily clad or completely naked, and very few, it appeared, would successfully escape. She looked at the woman Richard indicated.

"No, she doesn't," Rebecca said, tugging at his arm. But she had not really been truthful. The figure in the painting did look like her, and it disturbed her. She did not wish to look at it. Richard still had not moved, so she tugged again. "Shall we go on down to dinner?"

They moved on to the stairs and stepped onto the cylindrical staircase. Twenty-five steps and a complete circle brought them down to the main floor of the castle. They stepped out onto a highly polished wood floor, then stopped for a moment to stare at the opulence of the great hall.

Giant stuffed heads of game adorned the walls from fifteen feet up, and battle axes, swords, and guns filled the thick oak panels in between. At the opposite end of the hall, the rounded cut-glass panes over the huge doors were dark, signaling that the sun had completely set.

"We were supposed to meet them for drinks in the music room," Rebecca said, whispering self-consciously.

"I know," Richard whispered back theatrically, mocking her.

She frowned at him and returned to normal voice. "Where's the music room?"

They stood still and listened. A piano was playing. Richard frowned and cocked his head slightly. "Chopin?"

"Yes, it's *Ballad*. That way." Rebecca pointed toward the opening of a large, dark hallway to the left, and they went down it in search of the music's origin.

There were no electric lights in this wing. Large, tapered candles mounted on ornate holders sat every ten feet to guide them. Arched, lead-lined windows on their left allowed some light from a rising full moon, but the overall effect was mystifying, and they stepped through pools of darkness unaware that they were holding each other's hands very tightly. Gradually the sounds of the piano grew louder.

A door at the end of the hall opened into a relatively small room, and from inside they could hear the piano. They walked in and stopped.

An expansive fireplace filled almost one entire wall and a roaring fire poured its light and heat into the room. A shining black grand piano stood against the adjacent wall opposite Richard and Rebecca, surrounded by at least thirty candles. The countess sat at the bench playing the piano, her fingers never missing a note. Rebecca stared at her, as overwhelmed by the serenity on the countess' face as by her brilliant playing.

Richard gaped at her, and when he realized this he forced his jaw closed. She was dressed in white, a long gown that seemed to shimmer in the candle and firelight. Her raven black hair was swept up onto her head, showing a long, narrow neck that in turn accentuated the beautiful lace front of the gown. It dipped across her breasts and formed a deep décolletage. The effect was more than startling, and Richard swallowed hard. He was not sure whether she was angel or devil or even the same woman he had met on the dark road, and for a dangerous moment he had completely forgotten Rebecca was standing next to him.

The countess finished playing and looked up, smiling. "There you are," she said in German. "I am sorry I did not give you directions to the music room. I can see, however, that you are resourceful. That is good." She stood up and placed her left hand on top of the piano. "May I present my husband, Count Alexander Viroslav."

Rebecca had not even noticed the huge chair off to one side, but the count began to rise and her eyes widened as she watched him. Richard was tall, and certainly at six feet two inches he was above average in height, but the count was at least two inches taller. *He's magnificent!* she thought.

It was impossible to judge his age, but by his posture and nearly black hair, she doubted he was even forty.

"I am so glad to finally meet my guests," the count said, smiling. He bent forward, took Rebecca's hand, and kissed it. His eyes did not leave hers for several seconds, then he turned and smiled at Richard. "I am so pleased to make your acquaintance."

Richard found his voice first. "We are very grateful for your hospitality, Count Viroslav. I'm afraid two Americans in Bulgaria, especially these days, that is . . . Anyway, we appreciate your help."

The count watched him stammer, and a thin smile played across his lips. "It is our pleasure, Richard," he answered, "to be able to be of assistance to you and, of course, to Rebecca."

"We really are grateful," Rebecca said. She felt his eyes on her and was surprised to find that it pleased her. Getting herself under control, she put these unexpected sensations out of her mind and turned to the countess.

Rebecca was almost as impressed as Richard at the way the countess looked. And, she admitted to herself, a little envious. "You play magnificently, Countess."

She switched to English. "Thank you, Rebecca. My, that is a lovely name. It has always been one of my favorites."

"Thank you."

The count spoke, also in English, though his accent was slightly more pronounced. "Would you like a glass of wine? I'm afraid we do not drink a lot of spirits here, but the wine is quite good. I should really not say that, of course, since it is from our estate, but it has won several awards."

Richard saw their hosts glance at each other. He felt slightly uneasy, but he was not sure why. Rebecca spoke quickly.

"Yes, that would be wonderful. Your own wine, how interesting."

The count smiled at her and nodded slightly, and his eyes again raced over her figure. Rebecca blushed under his gaze, feeling as though she stood naked in front of him. To cover herself, she turned away from Richard and walked to the piano.

"It's beautiful," she said, running her palm across its top. "I'm afraid I'm not much of a player. It's Dixieland jazz, and the new swing in the States, and I've not really practiced anything classical for years."

"Well, you'll have to play us some of this Dixieland, then, Rebecca. Perhaps after dinner," the countess said.

A morose-looking man stepped through an almost hidden door, carrying a silver tray with crystal wineglasses. He handed one to the count and one to the countess, then brought the tray to Rebecca. With a start Richard realized it was Gregor, the chauffeur. But instead of the cold strength he had shown last night, he now looked very much the humble servant.

Richard thought it rude not to serve the guests first, but he decided it was perhaps a cultural oddity. He took his glass when offered, and the four of them touched the crystal together in a toast.

"Very nice," Rebecca said. She was anything but a wine connoisseur, but she did not want them to think her too naive. "Very nice indeed. It has a most distinctive taste, rather like a burgundy, yet not."

The count smiled, never taking his eyes from

her. "It is, I guess you would say, simply a 'Viroslav,' since it was made here."

They all took another sip, and Rebecca felt a strange warmth flow into her, making her feel happy and safe.

Richard felt a calming sensation, relaxing him and making him, too, feel comfortable.

And the count and countess, who were not drinking wine at all, felt the blood in their veins begin to simmer with excitement.

3

In the dining room, Gregor seated Rebecca by pushing the chair gently against her knees. Rebecca sat up straight and carefully placed her napkin across her lap. Gregor then seated the countess, who floated into her chair as he pushed it forward. Richard and the count seated themselves and Gregor went around the table, filling their plates with steaming meat and vegetables served from antique silver serving bowls.

"What a marvelous dinner," Rebecca said, her voice light as she surveyed the many plates that lay before her. "How wonderful to see such food so elegantly prepared."

"You mean this far from the great cities of Europe?" said the count.

Realizing that he was teasing her, Rebecca laughed. "Well, it is a little out of the way."

"Gregor does us proud," the countess said.

Across from her, Richard agreed. "It is certainly better than what we might have expected, given our rather abrupt departure from the train."

When Gregor finished with the count's plate,

he poured wine for everyone and bowed out of the room, pulling the doors shut behind him as he went.

The countess pretended to eat while engaging them all in conversation. In the shadowy light of the candles she would pick up her fork and lift food onto it, then deftly drop it into a hole in the table whenever the attention of her guests was diverted. She and the count worked together, asking a question or eliciting a response back and forth, and thus made it look as though they were eating the same food as Richard and Rebecca.

"Tell us about America, Rebecca," the countess said. "What part do you come from?"

"I'm from Philadelphia; Richard is from Cleveland. As I told you, we met in Berlin—we're both studying European history on scholarship."

"Indeed," said the count. They had been switching back and forth between German and English; he decided to stay with English. "How intriguing. What era do you find most interesting, then?"

The candlelight danced across the pale bare skin of Rebecca's upper chest and arms as she answered his question. She spoke of the early Renaissance. The count widened his eyes and let himself be absorbed in her response. He enjoyed the way the shadows danced between her breasts over the top of the low-cut gown. For a minute he imagined what her body would be like without the dress and he gripped the side of the table fiercely.

"What was that?" Rebecca said, hearing the strain of the heavy oak. She turned her head right and left to trace the sound.

The count forced himself to release his grip. "I do not know, my dear. It must be this old castle, constantly settling. It is more than five hundred years old."

"How wonderful!" Though she had not actually caught him at it, Rebecca had felt his eyes on her, exploring her, caressing her. It was extraordinary the way he kept her gaze yet seemed to see all of her. Her heart pounded heavily in her chest and she felt warm. She reached for her glass of wine and took a sip from it. Instantly it righted her mood. Again she was happy, enjoying herself. She sneaked a glance at the count and saw that he was watching Richard talk to the countess.

One might be almost flattered, she thought.

It was the dress, of course. Really, she felt quite naked. Deliciously naked. She took another small sip of the wine, was again rewarded by its warmth, and set the goblet decisively back on the table.

I must eat or I shall become quite drunk.

Richard was telling the countess about football. "It's a bit rough, I guess. We have a team of eleven who go against another eleven, trying to move a ball against them one hundred yards."

The countess regarded him with her large, beautiful eyes. "A contest of flesh and will, then," she said.

For a moment Richard felt trapped in the power of her eyes. He had heard a trace of irony in her voice, and it confused him. "Er, yes, I suppose you could describe it like that," he said. He swallowed and forced his eyes away from her own. But he made the mistake of looking downward, taking in her long neck. His gaze fell to the top of her gown and suddenly his throat was dry again. He picked up his goblet and without thinking drained the last of it.

"Your wine is excellent," he said.

Her sensuous lips curved into a smile. "Thank you, Richard. We are so glad that you like it. But you have finished your glass." She turned around, and instantly Gregor was there with a decanter, filling Richard's glass again.

"Thank you," he said, and he took a sip from it, peering over the rim of the goblet at the top of her gown.

It rode the crest of her shoulders in a straight line and was covered in tight circles of delicate white lace. The circles grew subtly larger as they descended across her chest, successfully drawing his eyes downward even farther. The countess' delicately perfect skin promised wondrous delights as it pressed apart the tight silk held together by the narrowing V of lace.

"Do you win these games often, Richard?" The countess was amused, pretending not to notice that her gown was having its desired effect on the young man seated across from her.

Richard shook his head to clear it. For a moment he had actually forgotten where he was, and he raised his eyes guiltily to her face, relieved that she had not noticed his stare. It was hypnotic, the atmosphere. The candles, the wine, the intoxicating beauty of the countess. He was having trouble thinking. Quickly he glanced across the table at Rebecca, who was talking to the count, then at the count himself, who likewise was not looking at him, and breathed a sigh of relief that neither of them had noticed his temporary lapse.

Richard relaxed. *I must stay off that wine. Or at least ease off it. This woman is amazing.*

"Are you feeling all right, Richard?" the countess asked softly so the others would not hear.

"Yes," he said. "I'm fine. I was just lost in thought, I guess."

She smiled and patted the back of his hand with her long, tapered fingers. "I do that sometimes, too," she said, her voice happy and as musical as the piano she had been playing earlier. "When I am relaxed and content. Are you relaxed and content, Richard?"

He looked at her and used all his will to hold her gaze. "Yes, I guess I am. This is a wonderful meal, and I'm having a wonderful time." Then he put his head down on the table and passed out.

"Oh! Richard!" Rebecca had been so caught up in her conversation with the count that she had not noticed Richard's wavering attention until she heard his head hit the table. Alarmed and feeling a little guilty, she looked wide-eyed at his slumped form. "Richard! Are you all right?"

"I'm sure he's fine, dear," the countess said quickly. She stood up and motioned to Gregor, who appeared from the shadows by the door and came over to help. "He's just had a tiny bit too much wine, perhaps, and is exhausted from your trip and all the excitement. Gregor, would you please help the gentleman up to his room?"

When Rebecca heard the servant's name, it occurred to her that this was the first time she had given him any real notice. Even in the car driving here she had paid no real attention to him. Now she realized that she had never known anyone with that name, and for some reason she immediately thought of Kafka's story, *The Metamorphosis.*

Gregor, meanwhile, stood behind Richard and pulled his chair back from the table as though it weighed nothing, then lifted Richard's right arm and put it over his shoulder. With a smoothness of motion that belied his size, he lifted Richard to his feet.

Rebecca stood up also. "I should not leave him. . . ." She watched Richard being carried toward the doorway and a burst of fear spread through her. But as she got to her feet, the room spun, and though she had intended to go after Richard to make certain he was all right, she hesitated. She blinked several times, suddenly not quite sure exactly what it was she should do.

The count stood. "Please don't worry, Rebecca," he said. The picture of cordiality and panache, he tossed his napkin onto the table beside his plate and came around to her. "Richard will be fine. We've all had a bit too much wine at one time or another, haven't we?" Then he fixed a piercing stare on her. "And as Maria has said, it is just fatigue. Really, let him get some rest, and in the morning you can tease him just a little, no?"

Rebecca felt very confused. The brilliance of the count's stare was overwhelming. She turned toward the doorway, where Richard was already being carried out of the room by Gregor, and hesitated again. She tried to think what she should do, but it was becoming more and more difficult.

"Richard . . ." she said toward the empty doorway. Her voice faded, lost in the huge room.

The countess was watching Rebecca closely. Sensing the timing, she glanced at her husband, then went to Rebecca and put her arm around her. "It is fine, Rebecca. There is nothing to worry about. Alexander is right. Your Richard will be fine after he has had a night's rest."

Rebecca was vaguely aware that the tone of her hosts had become familiar, even intimate. She nervously picked up her goblet and took a sip of wine.

The countess kissed her lightly on the cheek. "The night is young," she said with a smile. "And we have so enjoyed your company. Really, it has been too long since we have had such a delightful evening. Please," she went on, taking Rebecca by the arm and guiding her gently from the table. "Come into the music room and play for us that Dixieland music you mentioned."

"Well . . ." Already Rebecca felt better, more calm. She took one more sip of the wine. It really was just drunkenness, she decided, that had made Richard pass out. And it was a bit irritating. Rude of him, embarrassing her like that. Sometimes Richard was really such a bumpkin. Her worry faded. The countess was right. The night was young, and she felt wonderful. She, at least, would be the good guest. "All right."

"Wonderful," her hosts said in unison, and then laughed together.

"Bring your wine and let us go into the music room," the countess said, and again she took her arm and gently but firmly guided Rebecca toward the adjoining doors.

Rebecca sipped from the goblet as they walked. The count lingered for a moment behind them as his wife maneuvered the young woman into the music room.

"You really do look stunning in that dress, Rebecca," the countess was saying softly in Rebecca's ear. "I thought it would suit you earlier; that is why I had Gregor lay it out for you. I am pleased to see that my choice was correct. Richard is a very lucky young man."

Any worries that Rebecca felt were instantly banished, and her spirit soared. Contrary to what had happened to Richard, Rebecca did not feel drunk at all. Instead she positively glowed with energy and goodwill toward her hosts, who were so kind and generous. For a moment she was so infused with emotion and gratitude that she nearly wept. "Oh, thank you, countess," she said. "That is so very kind of you."

They entered the music room.

"Please, Rebecca, let us not be so formal tonight. Call me Maria."

That a countess would allow herself to be called by her first name! It was too amazing, and yet, Rebecca thought suddenly, it was somehow right. And natural. She giggled.

The countess giggled, too, and lightly touched her bare shoulder.

A wave of sensual awareness poured over Rebecca each time she felt the other woman's hands on her arms and shoulders. She felt a sensation of pressed flowers or velvet, exquisitely soft and dry, and then just as quickly Maria lifted her hands and the sensation went away.

Rebecca stared in wonder at the room they had entered. It was filled with candles. Where there had been one or two dozen before dinner, now there were literally hundreds, blazing so brightly as to almost eclipse the fire in the fireplace. The room was wonderfully warm, and Rebecca's tiny dress seemed just right for the occasion.

"So many candles! The room looks like Christmas," Rebecca said. Then added, "Maria."

"And why not? We are having fun tonight, are we not? And so we shall pretend it is a holiday. It is so nice to have someone young and beautiful with us in the castle again. Sometimes I feel a bit lonely, I'm afraid," she confided.

Rebecca looked at her in surprise. For the first time she saw a sadness in the countess' eyes, and again her own mood swung dramatically, making her almost want to cry.

"Oh dear," she said, "could you be lonely in this wonderful place? That is so sad!" She turned her body a little too suddenly toward the countess, spinning into the woman's arms and almost falling against her.

The countess caught her without making it appear awkward. Rebecca put her arms around the countess, hugging her and at the same time steadying herself. Immediately Rebecca perceived that strange, heightened physical sensation that had raced through her a few minutes earlier. She smelled perfume, subtle and light, and felt the slight brush of soft hair against her cheek. The press of Maria's body against her own breasts was strangely erotic. Startled, Rebecca did not move for a moment, until the countess suddenly released her.

"You must play for us now," the beautiful woman said, smiling. "This ragtime, no?"

"Play ragtime?" Rebecca said a little breathlessly. "Oh, yes, of course. You'll like it, I'm certain. It's silly and fun."

Rebecca turned around to go to the piano and saw the count standing by the fireplace. She had not heard him come into the room at all. A tiny sense of disquiet touched her and she reached for the wine. She took a sip, enjoying the taste. Then another until the glass was drained. Once again it did not fail her. The disquiet left and, now filled with excitement, she sat on the piano bench.

The count and countess sat on a love seat nearby and watched her attentively. Rebecca glanced up at them and inexplicably became filled with sadness. There was something about them that seemed both terrible and fascinating. She stared at them, wondering what it was that made them seem tragic.

Suddenly she realized they were watching her, and she blushed. When they smiled at her Rebecca took a deep breath, then put her hands to the keyboard and played the first thing that came into her mind, "St. Louie Blues." Her fingers danced over the keys, and as she found the rhythm her confidence increased. She finished with a flourish and they applauded wholeheartedly.

"Wonderful!" the count said. "I enjoyed that. Do you know any others?"

She played "Tiger Rag," "The Entertainer," and a rag version of "Amazing Grace."

"Magnificent! Brava!"

"Yes, that was wonderful, Rebecca," the countess said. "This is remarkable music, so light and enjoyable."

Gregor stepped out of the shadows with more glasses that he had filled and distributed them.

"To the pianist," said the count, holding his glass up. They drank to her, then she toasted the countess' playing, modestly saying that she could not compare to the performance given by her hostess.

"How kind you are, Rebecca."

"She has a good ear, Maria," the count said. "And you are accomplished."

The countess gave a small curtsy.

"Perhaps you would play another waltz for us, Maria," the count said, as though the idea had just occurred to him. "I do so love them, and Rebecca and I will dance while you play."

The countess smiled, then sat down on the bench and began to play.

Before she knew it, Rebecca found herself dancing lightly around the polished floor in the arms of the count. They danced well together, she thought as they ended up next to the piano when the countess finished the first waltz. The count spun Rebecca around in a grand flourish, keeping hold of her hand and bowing to her. Breathlessly she smiled at him and curtsied dramatically as she had learned in ballet class. She looked up and opened her mouth to speak, but the countess began to play another waltz and suddenly off they went again.

Rebecca was astonished at the count's strength. She had never known a man whose arms held such unwavering power. Around and around they went, but no matter how fast they spun Rebecca never felt his arms slacken. She began to feel quite certain that they would not let her go no matter what. Without quite realizing it, she began to dance higher and higher on her toes, lifted by the steellike arms. The room spun and the candles blurred and still they danced faster, urged on by the lightning speed of the countess' fingers across the ivory keys.

They had no sooner finished the waltz when another one began. This time Rebecca's feet left the floor, and she did no more than hang on to the count while he twirled her around and around. The wine that had lightened her mood earlier now coursed through her veins and into her brain. It lifted her ever higher, giving her a superawareness of her body while at the same time robbing her control of it. She felt herself become not one person but two, dissolving into a sensuous nymphet on one hand and on the other an ethereal spirit that watched uninvolved.

Perhaps I am dreaming, she thought. *Yes, yes, that is what it is. How strange that I am dreaming and yet know that I am dreaming. How wonderful and unusual.*

She was certain now that it was true, because otherwise there was no explanation for what happened next.

Rebecca was aware that the countess had quit playing the piano. When exactly she was not certain, but she was now draped across the arms of the count. Gregor had appeared again, pushing a wide table to the center of the room in front of the fireplace. When he had it positioned, he went through the room extinguishing every other candle, leaving a diminished light that was both soft and mysterious. He worked his way to the door and then turned and bowed and pulled the door shut behind him.

Rebecca drifted through the air, feeling the count's strong arms carrying her to the table.

✻|✻

4

With the wooden table underneath her, Rebecca lay on her back, feeling the warmth from the fire spreading over her. Her arms lay away from her body, hanging over the edges of the tabletop. Her feet were slightly apart and she was vaguely aware that the bottom of the little black dress had risen all the way up her legs and that the straps had fallen against her upper arms, leaving her shoulders completely bare.

She wondered if anybody noticed. Her feet felt very warm.

It's from the fire. What happened to my shoes?

She looked down, saw the top of her dress, saw her breasts pushing against the deep-cut front, and felt the silk on her nipples.

Incredible.

"How are you feeling, Rebecca?" The voice, female, came from far away. Rebecca did not recognize it.

"She's all right," said another, this one male.

There were fingers on her forehead, brushing away her hair, caressing her eyebrows. Someone kissed her lips, and she closed her eyes automatically.

A different kiss.

Rebecca tried to focus her eyes, but everything seemed so far away.

There was another kiss. The lips trembled against hers slightly.

"Undress her." The second voice came, familiar somehow.

Rebecca felt fingers on her neck, gliding downward. Soft and knowing, they slid on her skin and somehow made the material open outward. The fingers moved down her front quickly, unfastening everywhere, releasing everything, revealing all of her. In seconds the dress was opened all the way and both sides of it slid away magically. Her modesty fell over the edge of the table.

"Remove the rest."

The gentle, knowing fingers slid across her stomach to the elastic of her silk chemise.

The rest.

Rebecca breathed in sharply as the silk slid down her legs and across her ankles. She blinked and suddenly she could see again. But her vision was distorted, as if she were looking down a long tunnel or looking backward through a telescope.

The countess leaned over her and kissed her on the lips. She smiled at Rebecca. "It is good, no?" she said quietly into Rebecca's ear and ran her fingers slowly across Rebecca's breasts. She put her lips down where her fingers had been and sucked on the hardened nipples. Rebecca squirmed. The countess slid a long, red fingernail across her stomach, leaving a trail of fire. It moved on, going lower, burning into the soft skin above her fine hairline and touching her most intimate parts. Finally it slipped inside her, and Rebecca gasped. She shut her eyes tight.

"Is she ready?" the other voice said. Rebecca knew the voice now. It was the count.

"Yes." The countess stepped away from her.

Rebecca felt humiliated and yet also excited that he would know. She opened her eyes and saw the two of them kissing, though only their lips touched.

The count broke the kiss. "Strip," he said.

Not taking her eyes from his, the countess slowly put her arms up and unfastened the clasp at the back of her neck. The white lace fell forward, freeing her breasts. She put her hands to her waist and gave a slight push across her hips, and the gown fell to the floor. She wore nothing underneath it.

The count stared at her naked body, and Rebecca heard herself moan. He began to remove his own clothing, pulling off his shirt and trousers. Finally he exposed a furious erection.

Rebecca tried to move, but could not.

Now the count and countess put their arms around each other and kissed, long and deeply. A wind came up outside, whistling through the top of the fireplace and rustling the leaves outside. Inside there was only the crackling of fire in the fireplace.

Rebecca managed to lift herself an inch but could not sustain it, and she fell back panting.

The count put his hands under the countess' arms and lifted her above him, then slowly lowered her onto himself. They kissed as they joined.

Rebecca watched wide-eyed and her body betrayed her excitement. The count lowered his wife slowly and their shadows danced in the firelight. The countess put her hands around his neck, and he moved his hands under her thighs to support her. His huge biceps contracted and expanded over and over.

Countless times he lifted and lowered his wife, then placed her on her feet next to Rebecca. The countess breathed deeply and her eyes widened as she placed her hands on the table, fingertips touching Rebecca, looking at her. As the count entered her from behind, she closed her eyes and groaned.

Rebecca looked up into the beautiful face and watched it change with passion. She felt each stroke as the count pushed the countess against the table and watched the countess' face contort with the intensity of her pleasure. They made love nonstop for what seemed like a long while. Rebecca was beside herself, her own body aching with need and frustration. Finally the two of them broke apart and stared at her.

"You should go into her now," the countess said, staring down at Rebecca. "You are both ready."

The count stood panting, his erection undiminished. He looked from his wife to Rebecca, then nodded and went to the side of the table. He bent down and stroked Rebecca's cheek and kissed her, then looked deeply into her eyes.

Rebecca felt what was left of her will drain away. She shut her eyes, surrendering. With a deft move he crawled onto the table. He pushed her legs apart even wider and touched her, feeling her wetness. Then he moved forward.

"You are beautiful," he said.

He lay across her, and she accepted his weight. She felt him move his hand down across her side, and then he guided himself into her.

As she realized how large he was, she cried out. He opened her wider than ever before, impaling her. When he moved, withdrawing slightly, she gasped, and gasped again when he reentered.

He began a steady rhythm in and out of her. Her pleasure was so insurmountable as he slid into her that when he withdrew, however temporarily, she felt abandoned. Over and over she cried out helplessly. She began slipping away into a whirlpool, knowing that he controlled her like no other ever had, and she wept.

Rebecca heard his voice in her ear. "You will feel a slight pinch," he said, "and then nothing but wondrous pleasure."

Rebecca wanted to tell him that she was already feeling wondrous pleasure. The count lowered his head to her neck and licked. He made the area warm and wet with his tongue.

She could not speak.

Suddenly she felt a sharp pain that made her contract heavily against his continuing thrusts. Something hot and sticky trickled down her neck, and as she realized it was blood Rebecca thought she would cry out, but did not. She felt his lips on her neck, felt the gentle, insistent sucking, and she began to glow with warmth and a strangely erotic pleasure.

His thrusts continued deep into her, but now the pleasure came from two directions, meeting in the middle. When the orgasm hit her, everything went black.

The count withdrew slowly, still breathing hard. His wife stared at his face for a moment, and feeling her gaze he turned his head toward her and nodded. Then he climbed from the table.

"Call Gregor," he said.

She nodded and reached for a long, ornate rope that hung along the wall. She pulled on it, ringing a bell in the distance. Gregor came immediately.

"Take her to her room, Gregor," the countess said. "Make everything all right."

Gregor went to Rebecca immediately. He picked her up into his arms and carried her from the room.

"I love to watch you," the countess said. "I was so happy for you. It has been so long."

His breathing gradually slowed, and the count sat down in a large chair by the fire. He picked up a brandy glass that Gregor had brought in earlier and sipped from it.

"She was receptive," he said.

"Perhaps?"

He shrugged his shoulders. "Perhaps."

He stared at the fire for a few minutes, then smiled and raised his eyebrows. "I find myself hoping she can make the change."

Maria's face was a mask. "She is young and strong."

"What do you feel?"

"About her?"

He nodded.

"She is beautiful and full of life. She will please you for as long as you wish, if she can make the change."

His eyes narrowed. "But you do not like her?"

"I do like her."

"Then what bothers you, Maria?"

She shook her head and turned away from him. "Perhaps it is the game itself. With the others . . . well, it was different. I enjoyed the sport."

"And with her?"

"She is full of lust, it is true. But there is an innocence about her that is surprising. She is not a child and not a virgin, and yet she seems vulnerable. It almost makes it unfair."

Alexander burst out laughing. "Unfair? Don't be ridiculous. She won't think it unfair once she makes the change."

"If she makes the change."

He shrugged his shoulders. "You saw how she enjoyed it tonight."

Maria considered. "Yes. She could be entertaining, I suppose. As much fun maybe as Denyse, even. Perhaps it is just me."

Alexander stood up and walked to her, then turned her around slowly and stroked her cheek. "Perhaps you just need some fun. You grow morose in this castle, I think, when it is too long between times."

The countess nodded, but again her face was unreadable.

"Shall we get dressed and go see how Richard is doing?" he said.

A few minutes later the count took his wife's hand and the two of them walked out into the hall. As they left the room Maria saw Gregor standing in the shadows, but she walked by him without acknowledging his presence, and he said nothing. Maria and Alexander went to the stairs leading down to the castle dungeon.

5

Richard opened his eyes, momentarily confused. He was lying on a table in the center of a large room. Shadows created by torches and a huge fire danced demoniacally on the walls and beams around him. He tried to sit up, but he was pulled down immediately by cuffs attached to his wrists. His ankles were also restrained, and he realized he was stretched spread-eagle on the table. The surprise turned to embarrassment when he saw that he was completely naked as well.

With a determined grimace he struggled desperately against the chains that bound him. His biceps and triceps, honed from years of weight lifting, erupted across his arms and his pectorals bulged across his chest. But it was in vain. The chains that bound him were short, and he could not move either his arms or his legs more than a half inch. Humiliated and feeling like a wild animal chained against its will, he roared with frustration. He took a deep breath and tried again and again, but the chains held, and finally he was forced to admit to himself that he was helpless.

A light sheen of perspiration covered his body, and it glowed in the firelight. He panted hard for several seconds, thinking, and then the panic came again and he shouted at the top of his lungs. "Help!"

The countess had been watching him from the doorway behind his head. Now she spoke. "Richard, you disappoint me. You struggled so valiantly, and now you give up and call for help?"

Her icy words pricked him, making his heart pound violently as a chill went down his back. Following the sound of her voice, he bent his head to the right. Still he could not see her.

"Countess?"

Her voice changed, becoming soothing, even unctuous. "You have a very fine body, Richard. It excites me to see such a well-developed body struggling so hard. Isn't that what you were telling me about earlier? The game you play. A contest of flesh and will?"

"Not like this!" he shouted at her. "We play fair!"

She moved closer to him. "Ah, but Richard, you are such a big, strong young man, and I am but a slight woman. A contest of strength would not be fair, would it?"

"I don't want a contest." In spite of himself he knew he sounded petulant.

"Richard, you're whining. All life is a contest, dear boy. All life and all death. I've seen too much of it, you see. There is nothing left for me now but this contest. I believe in this contest, Richard, revel in it, actually. My pleasure now is in your submission.

"I simply removed the unfairness of physical

strength. Removed it from the contest, that is, but not from my vision. I love to see your power harnessed against your will."

She scared him. "What do you want?" he said.

He had not heard her move, but suddenly he felt her breath on his left ear.

"A contest of will, Richard," she whispered. Her tongue stabbed the center of his ear and he jerked his head away from it.

"Why are you doing this?" In spite of himself he had felt the first stirring of an erection. It terrified him and yet thrilled him to be in her power.

I've got to concentrate on my predicament here, and not . . . not on the other.

"You enjoyed looking at me this evening, didn't you, Richard?" Her voice came over his right shoulder now. Her movements were too fast to follow. "You wanted to see me, see all of me. You wanted to have me, maybe, Richard? You wanted to undress me and make love to me, Richard?"

He jerked his head to the right, but saw nothing. "No."

Now her voice, soft and musical, was directly behind his head. "You're lying, Richard. But irony is so delicious. And practically indispensable in a contest of wills, don't you think, my dear, naked boy?" Her laughter was like the tinkling of bells.

He felt her fingers in his hair, the sculpted nails scratching his scalp and twirling his locks around and around. "You're a naughty boy, Richard. You wanted to do naughty things to me, and now you're in trouble for it."

"No." He felt himself losing control, felt the flesh of his penis roll across his thighs as it hardened, and he was ashamed at displaying his lust even as he raced headlong into the web of desire that she spun.

"Ah, but yes, Richard. Very much yes. I know you all too well. You wanted me even though your lover Rebecca was sitting across the table from you."

It was all too true. Everything she said condemned him. He was reminded of Rebecca. "What have you done with Rebecca!"

She laughed again, but this time the sound of it was cruel. "At last he remembers his beloved," she mocked.

"I never forgot her!"

"You did. Admit it." She pulled hard on his hair, and he cried out in sudden pain. "Didn't you! Didn't you!"

He heard the wildness in her voice. "Yes, yes, I'm sorry. But you're so beautiful," he answered.

She let go of his hair, spoke softly again. "Thank you, Richard. I'm glad we understand each other, now. No more coyness. Even though coyness can work sometimes in a contest of wills."

Richard took a deep breath. "What do you want?"

She laughed. "Men always want to know what a woman wants. I can *see* what you want, Richard."

His face grew bright red.

"Close your eyes now, darling. That's right. You wanted to see me without any clothes on, did you not? Did you not want to have sex with me?"

The aching in his balls was driving him mad.

"Even though your very beautiful young girlfriend was right next to you, still you wanted to have sex with me. I should be flattered, I suppose, Richard." She moved silently away again. "What would you think if I told you your Rebecca was as lusty as you? Even more so. What would you think, Richard?"

"No, it's not true." But as soon as she said it, his mind followed the path and he could not stop it. He saw Rebecca, naked and sexy, then the countess, also naked. His member jerked up and down, and he felt a tiny drop ooze onto his lower stomach. The battle was being lost.

"It is true, Richard. She was incredibly hot. I know, I saw her, Richard. I kissed her lips. Did you know that she liked that, Richard?"

"No. She wouldn't have." His voice sounded weak.

"What do you think of that, Richard? Would you like to see me kiss your Rebecca, see her respond to it?"

"No. No, please, she's not like that." But in his mind's eye he saw Rebecca being kissed by this other woman. He heard the countess moving behind him, heard the rustle of material.

"You may open your eyes, Richard," she said. "I've undressed for you. You may open your eyes and behold me, as you wished earlier this evening."

"I won't." Though he knew he would.

"I'm standing here, next to you."

Richard felt her fingernails scrape his erection. He moaned, feeling like crying.

"Why don't you look at me, behold the beauty you spoke of, Richard?"

The fingernails scraped him twice more. He

ached with the need she was giving him. Her fingers moved down, grabbed his balls, and squeezed hard. He cried out.

"Open your eyes, Richard." It was no longer an entreaty. "Open them now."

A purple shot of pain flashed under his eyelids. He opened them quickly, ready to do anything to stop her from torturing him further. She let go of him and smiled, and he moaned softly at the radiant beauty she displayed, that she gave to him.

Her breasts stood full against her narrow frame, the nipples hard with excitement.

"Why are you doing this to me?" he asked, his voice a hoarse shadow.

She bent forward and kissed him on the lips. "Because, Richard, it excites me to see a beautiful young man helpless under my grasp."

Richard stared openmouthed at her as she crawled up onto the table. She knelt across his chest, letting the coarse curls of hair between her legs scrape his nipples. She laughed out loud, then slid down his front and held his face in her hands while she kissed him.

"Because it excites me, and I have not had a beautiful young man in my grasp for a very long"—she kissed him again—"long . . . time."

Her scent was intoxicating. He was frightened of her words and more terrified of her eyes, yet he could not lose his erection.

She knelt over him and lifted him into her with her fingers. Then slowly she lowered herself onto him and gave a long sigh of satisfaction. She smiled at him and kissed his eyes.

Her muscles were working on him, making him

lose thoughts of anything but the nearly insane pleasure she was giving him.

For several minutes she teased him, bringing him ever closer to orgasm but without allowing him release. She tortured him sweetly until his body was shaking.

"Did you want this, Richard?"

"Yes."

"Did you want this all along, in spite of your love for Rebecca?"

"Yes."

"You do love Rebecca, don't you, Richard?"

"Please, don't . . . don't do this to me," he gasped.

She smiled. "Don't do what, Richard?"

"Don't make me . . . make me talk about Rebecca while you're doing this to me."

Maria whispered in his ear. "But Richard, I am excited, too. Why can't we talk about Rebecca? I don't mind if you love her. You can still lust after me. It excites me. And that is what you wanted, is it not? To have me excited?"

He moaned.

She continued to move up and down on top of him, and whispered again. "I'll tell you something, Richard. I can do something to you that your Rebecca has never dreamed of. I can give you a pleasure that will drive you nearly mad. A pleasure that she just now experienced for the first time, though she does not understand it. She will learn it and be able to give it. You will learn it now from me, though you will never be able to give it. Close your eyes, and let me show you."

She pulled her lips away from her teeth and her twin sharp fangs slid out. With infinite care she placed them against his throat and sunk them into his neck. He screamed as the intensity of what she had been doing with her body suddenly increased tenfold. She sucked hard, and as her saliva mixed with his blood they came together.

Richard was out only a few seconds, but when he came back to consciousness the countess had already climbed off. She stood by the table, contemplating him. He looked back at her, feeling exhausted, almost faint.

"Richard, you look like a rabbit caught in a snare as the hunter approaches."

"Is that what I am?"

She smiled, and again he heard the sweet tinkle of her laughter. "Perhaps. Perhaps that is what you are, Richard."

"What are you going to do with me?"

"Richard, you can be told, but I should not be the one to tell you. My husband can do a much better job. Alex?"

Richard gasped when he saw the count step from the shadows. "Count," he said, "please, I had nothing to do with this, I mean . . ."

Count Viroslav lifted a finger to silence him. "Richard," he said, "you do not understand. Why should you?" He shrugged his shoulders.

The countess disappeared from view and the count came over to the table. Richard was embarrassed at being thus bound naked in front of another man, especially with the evidence of his lust and his adultery shining wetly across his abdomen.

The count, though, did not seem upset. He regarded Richard for a moment, then drew a breath and began to speak.

"Richard, listen and understand. Your only

means of survival at this point is acceptance of the fate that has befallen you."

He hesitated for a second, raising his eyebrows to ask if Richard was still listening. Suddenly seeing fathomless cruelty in the count's eyes, Richard felt his skin grow cold. He nodded.

"Good," said the count. "I watched you making love with my wife, saw how much you enjoyed it. Just as she watched me with Rebecca."

"You didn't! You bastard!" Richard shouted in spite of himself, before he considered his tenuous position.

The count pointed his long index finger at Richard's mouth and jerked it once. "Richard," he said, "you will not speak to me such again. In fact, you will not speak to me again at all unless I give you permission."

Richard's jaws clamped shut and his lips locked together as if glued. He regarded the count now in silent panic.

"As I said," the count went on, "I saw how much you enjoyed making love to my wife. I could be fully justified in killing you. It would be the normal thing to do, and perhaps it is what I would do, if I were a normal man.

"Of course, as you may have realized, I am not a normal man. Some time ago I had the opportunity to explore the limits of pleasure and decide that if it suited me, I would make it the focus of my life. I did choose it, as has everyone I have ever met who was given the opportunity. Maria chose it. She chose to become my wife, knowing full well what I was and what I could give her. And of course, the price of it."

He snorted out a small, cynical laugh. "Gregor chose it, even though he knew he would never become one like me or his beloved Maria. Rebecca has chosen it, too."

He saw the nearly mad look on Richard's face. "Oh, it's true. She may not realize herself yet that she has chosen it, but she has. I know she has, because over the years I have seen others respond in the same way she did tonight. Yes, Richard, she has chosen it, and soon she will choose to become one like me, like Maria."

Sweat was pouring down Richard's face. "You may speak, Richard, but remember, be kind or I will shut you up again." He pointed his finger at Richard's mouth and jerked it once.

"What do you mean? What have you done to her? She is good and pure. She would not throw her life into debauchery willingly."

"Oh, she may be good, Richard. If there is such a thing. But pure, well, I don't think so. Certainly not any more. Not since she has experienced real pleasure."

"But you cannot change her into whatever it is you are."

For the first time the count smiled. "What is it that you think I am?"

Richard's eyes widened again, warily but with dawning comprehension. "You are some sort of monster."

"Richard, my wife and I are vampires."

Richard remembered the bite he had received from the countess and the burning sensation against his throat.

"I myself have lived for more than five hundred years. Five hundred years, can you imagine? Maria has lived two hundred and twenty-seven. I met her at a fair outside Budapest and instantly fell in love with her. And she, too, loved me. At the time I was searching for a wench to fuck and kill."

The count's sudden vulgarity mixed with his normal sophistication made Richard shudder.

"But as soon as I saw Maria, I knew I did not wish to kill her. Instead I wanted her desperately. I pursued her for several nights, finally getting her alone in the woods. I explained who I was and told her that I loved her. I promised her pleasure beyond anything she had known, and then to prove it I made love to her. I seduced her, Richard, with my incredible sexual prowess. I did not make her become a vampire, but seduced her into it. She agreed to become a vampire. It was the last time she and I ever orgasmed together. For you see, Richard, vampires can only have an orgasm when they use the innocent and the vulnerable, the human who lusts against his or her will. Which is not to say that we do not give each other pleasure. We make love for years, even decades between orgasms. It draws us ever closer together, until we are almost mad with lust. Then, when we find someone who is right, we use them to achieve the orgasm we cannot have with each other. It is tremendous. Sometimes we make that person into a vampire, other times we just use them."

Richard lay back, pondering. "Will I become a vampire?"

"Oh, no, Richard." The count laughed. "You can only become a vampire if another vampire wills it. That can only happen if you are brought to the absolute pinnacle of mad lust under a vampire's spell, and then at that moment of climax you are filled with the semen of that vampire at the same time his saliva is mixed with your blood. That, of course, I will never do."

Richard closed his eyes in disgust. He breathed deeply several times before being able to speak. "What will happen to me, then? Will you let me go?"

The count stared down at him, his face filled with an expression that Richard could not interpret. "Just because you will never become a vampire does not mean you cannot be kept alive by a female vampire. Her body's fluids can keep you preserved, just as Maria has kept Gregor alive. He never wanted to leave his beloved Maria, even though his position was that of servant to us. Vampires can use good servants; they are so hard to find."

He laughed at his own joke, but the sound of his laughter was malignant.

"Let you go? Richard, I will not keep you. The truth is, like Gregor you will not want to leave. I have seen the love of this pleasure in your eyes."

6

It was late morning when Rebecca awoke. The sun had climbed nearly to its early October zenith, shining down out of a brilliant blue sky. There was a window open in her room, allowing a soft breeze to bring in the scent of pines from the mountains. It was a beautiful, end-of-the-summer day.

Rebecca did not appreciate it.

As soon as she felt the warmth on her eyelids, she opened them, then blinked painfully. Her head ached and her body felt stiff. She groaned and put the back of her right hand across her eyebrows.

What had happened last night? Her memory of it was dim, as though it had been no more than a dream. There was something disturbing, though. Rebecca tried to remember, but even as she thought about it everything faded like a long-lost childhood experience. Except that whatever had happened, there had been nothing childlike about it. Of that she was certain.

More troublesome was the fact that she could not remember even when or how she had gotten to bed. Yet the feeling stuck with her that she had been involved in something very wicked, or maybe made a fool of herself at dinner. It was the wine, she thought, the count's own wine. It had to be.

Rebecca peeked through her fingers at the blue sky outside. She looked down and saw that she was still wearing the little black dress. That was a relief. It meant that whoever had helped her to bed had not undressed her.

But the dreams!

Images came back to her, disconnected, nonsequential, yet strong enough to make her want to close her eyes tightly in embarrassment.

What a bizarre unconscious I must have!

Rebecca considered herself to be very sophisticated when it came to sex. She had readily given up her virginity at age nineteen to a college professor who spoke to her of Keats. She had allowed herself to be seduced by her father's business partner in his office the following summer, and she hadn't even felt bad about it when it went sour. He had talked her into having an affair, though it had not taken a great deal of effort on his part. Eventually his wife had found out about it and made a terrible scene. The partnership and the business were threatened, and the family's position in Philadelphia society was diminished as gossip became more and more vicious. Finally Rebecca was sent off to Germany to live with her grandparents in Berlin. They told everyone at home that she went there to study and work on her German. But the story had been a falsehood, one that she had told first to Richard and now to the count and countess.

But nothing had ever happened to her to make her have dreams like that.

An image of the count and Maria swam up through her consciousness again, as if to tease her. She saw them both standing nude over her. It flashed quickly, leaving a comet's trail of erotic longing, and made her tremble slightly. What was the matter with her?

Rebecca groaned and took her hand away from her eyes. She stared at the ceiling, pondering the thoughts that had taken root in her mind, and again asked herself where they had come from.

Things were good with Richard. Their lovemaking had been satisfactory. No, she corrected herself, it was better than satisfactory. It had been good. Really good. Richard had been eager, perhaps a bit too eager at the beginning, but willing to learn how to please her.

The count knows how to please without being told.

Rebecca shuddered again. That had only been a dream. She decided it was time to get up, put on some fresh clothes, and have something to eat. Also, she needed to find Richard and see about his plans—no, their plans—for the day.

She pushed herself up onto her elbows, surprised at how much effort it took. Again she was aware of how heavy and stiff her body felt. She remembered dancing with the count for what seemed like hours. Drinking and dancing all night long. She could not quite remember what had happened after they danced. Nothing except the dreams, which were only dreams. She pushed the memory back down and forced herself to sit upright.

Rebecca tried to swing her legs over the side of the bed. To her alarm they refused to budge. For a terrifying second she lay inert and helpless. In a panic, she became convinced that she was paralyzed. She slapped frantically at the unfeeling calf muscles and hit both legs as hard as she could. This time she was rewarded with a tingling sensation.

She tried wiggling her toes, and to her relief that worked. Forcing herself to work them back and forth for several minutes, she gradually became aware of feeling returning to her legs. Eventually she was able to move them and get them over the side of the bed.

Panting with the effort and feeling sweat break out across her brow, Rebecca leaned against the bedside table and attempted to stand up. She almost fell forward, but she righted herself at the last minute and forced her left leg forward. The right one followed, and then the left one again. With tremendous effort she slowly worked her way around the room.

Exhaustion forced her to stop twice and rest, but bit by bit sensation and strength returned to her muscles, and by the time she reached her bed again her ability to walk normally and have control over her movements had returned. Feeling absurdly victorious, she caught her breath and walked almost easily to the window.

That, Rebecca admitted to herself, had been too scary. It had to be that she must have slept wrong, crossing her legs awkwardly in the deep sleep that she had experienced. She reached down and stroked her legs and decided there was nothing wrong with them anymore. Overcome with relief, she wiped her brow with the back of her right hand and studied the grounds outside.

It had been dark when they came in, and she had not really been able to see much. In the light of day, however, she could see that an expansive yard and gardens surrounded the old stone castle for a hundred yards in all directions, coming to an end only at the edge of the forest. There was one straight, unpaved road cutting a brown slash through the green lawn. As Rebecca watched, a long black car emerged from the woods and came quickly toward the crescent drive that led to the castle entrance.

A small flag was attached to the front fender, fluttering wildly in the self-created breeze. The black car pulled into the drive and stopped, and the lightning red and black of the swastika became completely visible.

The side door opened and a young man in uniform with blond hair, highly polished black boots, and a riding crop climbed out. To her astonishment she found she could see every detail of his face with perfect clarity, even though he was quite far from where she stood. Two other men, one in German soldier's uniform and the other in civilian clothes climbed out a moment later.

It must be the clear mountain air here.

His left eye was blue with green specks in it, and his right eye was green with red. Rebecca gasped as she recognized him.

The Nazi soldier regarded the castle for a moment, his eyes sweeping across its battlements, and Rebecca backed quickly away from the window to avoid being seen. Below her the large front door of the castle opened and Gregor stepped out. Rebecca heard Gregor greet them and she turned her head slightly, listening intently yet still careful to remain out of sight.

"I am Captain Eric Stryker," the man said. Rebecca peeked around a heavy curtain and studied him. "I have come all the way from Berlin searching for a young man and woman. Americans who have stolen certain valuable items and are attempting to escape with them."

Once again his eyes briefly flashed upward to the windows of the second story, and Rebecca jerked her head back. How could he have tracked them so quickly! Rebecca held her breath and waited for Gregor to reply, knowing that her fate and Richard's relied on his answer. "We have no visitors here," came the flat reply, and Rebecca breathed a sigh of relief.

"Really?" By his tone, the Nazi made it clear he thought Gregor was lying. "I know they were put off the train at the station here because they had no money to travel any farther. They did not stay in the town, and I have searched the entire area for them. Everywhere except here."

He turned his head as he spoke and surveyed the grounds.

Gregor said nothing and for a minute there was an uncomfortable silence. Finally Captain Stryker turned back to Gregor and spoke quickly.

"Perhaps I might speak with the countess herself? It is very important."

"The count and countess are out for the day."

"I see. When will they return?"

Gregor paused before he answered, and when

he did he made his scorn obvious. "You do not have jurisdiction here, young German."

The captain bristled. He stared menacingly at Gregor for a second, looking as though he might physically attack him. But just as quickly he seemed to think better of it and relaxed. His thin lips curved upward, and even from where she stood Rebecca shuddered at the viciousness in his smile.

"Yes, that is true, we do not have jurisdiction. Yet. We will soon, though. And when we do it will be a great advantage to have friends with jurisdiction, my man."

Gregor seemed to consider what he had said, and again Rebecca held her breath. "I will tell them you called, sir," he said finally.

"I could wait."

Rebecca could not see Gregor's face, but she caught a slight sneer in his voice as he repeated, "I will tell them you called."

The captain stiffened, then turned on his heel and climbed back into the car. The door slammed shut and the long black automobile turned slowly around and went back down the road, finally disappearing into the forest.

Rebecca watched it go and leaned back against the wall, letting out a long breath. A multitude of disparate sensations, thoughts, and fears suddenly swept through her, leaving her breathless. She told herself that she was glad Eric was gone, and yet she could not deny that even though she feared being caught by him, it had occurred to her to run out of the castle and into his arms. There had been a time when she had done that willingly. Then she remembered what he was, and what he stood for, and frowned. *No matter what happens*, she promised herself, *I will never go back to him.*

She turned and started for the door, then remembered that she still wore the short black dress and decided to change before going down to thank Gregor. She placed her fingers on the front of the dress to undo it, then dropped them, puzzled.

Now why did I do that? The zipper is always in the back.

She reached behind her and found the zipper and pulled it down her back, then stepped out of the dress and laid it across the bed. She went to her suitcase and retrieved a brassiere, a clean blouse, and a skirt, and put them on and went to the mirror. Her hairbrush was where she had left it, and she picked it up and straightened her hair as best she could. Then, satisfied that she was at least presentable, she replaced the brush and walked out into the hallway.

The door to Richard's room was slightly ajar, and Rebecca walked over to it. She pushed it open and stepped inside. The room was empty and neat. She had not really expected to find Richard there, but she was a little surprised at how tidy it was. The bed was made as tightly as it had been yesterday, and none of his clothes were lying about. She stepped back into the hallway and pulled the door closed behind her, then walked toward the stairs. Again the scene woven into the tapestry of the sacking of Constantinople caught her eye and she hesitated, staring at the beautiful naked women fleeing their pursuers. As Rebecca looked into it, entranced, it almost seemed as though the figures moved. This time she saw more in the picture. The woman Richard had pointed out last night did indeed look like her. But standing on a rampart was a tall dark man who looked rather like the count. She shook her head.

It can't be. My eyes are playing tricks on me.

But when she looked again, she saw Eric, then Maria in the crowd. Maria wore a transparent dress that flowed in the wind around her voluptuous body, and Eric was dressed in a toga of some sort, with a determined look on his face and carrying a whip. Rebecca put her hand over her mouth to stop a scream and ran down the stairs.

At the bottom she stopped and caught her breath. She had half expected to find Gregor or the count, but the great hall was deserted. Suddenly afraid again, she hesitated.

"Gregor?" Her voice echoed on the stone walls. "Richard? Count Viroslav? Maria?"

For a few seconds she stood silently, listening, then walked down the hall to the dining room. The kitchen was to the right. Rebecca decided she should try to find something to eat. Strangely enough, she was not really hungry, but she felt that she should eat something anyway. She made for the large double doors leading to the grand dining room, conscious of the sound of her footsteps clattering loudly on the tiled floor.

The grand dining room was empty. Rebecca walked past the long table where they all had eaten last night. Images sprang up in her mind, dark, erotic images of naked men and women calling to her. Shivering with fear, she ran to the kitchen, gave the door a shove inward, and walked into a huge, well-equipped cooking room.

She panted for breath as she closed the door behind her. She put her hand to her chest. The images were gone. They had been fleeting and yet so real. She took a deep breath and tried to put them out of her mind. She looked around and realized she was in the kitchen.

Sunlight poured through the windows, making the room cheerful. There was a huge stove, three sinks, and even a refrigerator, something Rebecca thought must be pretty rare in these parts, even in 1938. Rebecca walked over to it and opened the door. It was well stocked, she found, with fresh produce and meats. She found a plate in the first cupboard she looked in and helped herself to some fruit and cold cuts. Then she sat down at a small table in one corner and picked up a fork.

Rebecca cut a piece of meat with her fork and lifted it to her mouth. To her surprise, it was completely unappetizing. In fact, as she put it between her lips she was suddenly overcome with the smell of it and felt almost nauseated. She removed the fork and inspected the meat, but she found nothing wrong with it. It had not smelled bad, either, before she tasted it. Determined to eat something, she held her breath and forced herself to swallow the food. She could only get down a couple of mouthfuls, and the food did not make her feel any better. Finally she gave up and dumped the remainder of the food in a garbage sack and cleaned her plate. Then she turned and walked back to the great hall.

For the first time she noticed how few windows there were. Again she called out and again received no reply. The warmth of the sun beckoned to her through the cut glass above the large entrance door, so she went to it and pulled on the metal handles. The heavy wood moved reluctantly, but she pushed harder and it finally opened. A burst of sunlight flooded the darkened hallway.

Rebecca blinked painfully at its brilliance, surprised that her eyes were so sensitive. "It's the darkness of this spooky old place," she muttered. She waited until her pupils adjusted and then she stepped outside.

It was a perfect day. The warmth was framed by only the smallest hint of autumn. Though the lawn in front of the castle was still the deep, rich green of summer, it seemed the trees in the forest were just waiting for a frost to help them explode into color. Rebecca sat down on the granite slabs that led up to the doorway. "If no one is here," she said aloud, "then where are they? Where is Richard?"

She thought again of Eric, of his arrogance and maliciousness, and shivered. She and Richard had to get out of here soon. Of that she was certain. She hoped Richard had gone into the village to try and wire for some money from America. It had been an exciting adventure, narrowly escaping across the border. As soon as the two of them got out of Europe and back to America, they would tell the world what these Nazis really were.

Rebecca leaned against the granite railing that bordered the wide stone steps, thinking of everyone's reaction in Philadelphia when she returned.

She yawned.

Gradually she became aware of how quiet it was. No sounds of birds or animals anywhere.

Her eyelids were becoming very heavy. It must be from the late night of dancing, she thought. She lay down, expecting the stone to be uncomfortable, but she was surprised at how the warmth radiating up from it into her legs and arms actually relaxed her.

She yawned again, and closed her eyes. Sleep had never been sweeter.

7

Rebecca floated downward into sleep until she was deep inside her subconscious, and then began a long dream. In spite of the heaviness of her sleep, she became aware that she was dreaming. The sequence of events within her dream happened so quickly that she could not wake up, pulling her along through worlds where she both did and did not belong. It began with an awareness of lying on the flat stone outside the entrance to the castle, but as her perception shifted the light faded and it seemed as though it was night.

Rebecca heard a sound, a strange noise that at first was confusing to her. A long, deep humming seemed to rumble through stone. As she listened to it, though, she gradually recognized a pattern. A half dozen different pitches were repeated, though so slowly and over such a period of time that if she did not concentrate, she lost track of where in the pattern she was.

Making an effort, Rebecca listened carefully and placed the origin of the sound as coming from below and inside, or under, the castle. After several iterations of the routine, Rebecca found that she could anticipate when the notes would change and the pattern begin again. After the third round she discovered something else in the sound. Behind the deep, masculine drone, which she had identified as some sort of chant, were other voices. Voices that were much more subtle, hidden in the texture of the bass, yet very definitely present.

Higher male voices became apparent first, tenors rising out of the male choir, then altos and sopranos gradually making themselves heard until Rebecca could discern an entire chorus singing in the stone beneath her ear.

Fascinated, in her dream she rolled over onto her stomach and lay her right ear on the stone slab. She closed her eyes and listened. Again it took several minutes to quiet her thoughts and get into the sound in the stone, a sound that almost seemed to be more mental than aural, though it disappeared if she took her ear from the step.

The music made by the choir was strange and beautiful, but somehow terribly sad. To her surprise it sang to her, calling her by name in its slow rhythmic chant. So perfect was the harmonization that after awhile the many voices became as one, calling to her as one, encouraging her to join them.

> *Rebecca, Rebecca, come to me*
> *With me try harder*
> *Try harder*
> *I need you, I want you*
> *Your song must join mine*
> *If you will stay with us.*

Listen harder, Rebecca
Leave everything else
Come into the stone
Let me show you how I want
You to come here inside
Your song must join mine
If you will stay with us.

Rebecca let the siren song draw her inward deeper and deeper. Her heart slowed, then her breathing, and then . . . she . . . was . . .

Suddenly inside the stone. Except it was not stone. It was a thickness surrounding her, making her move slowly, as if she were underwater.

She sensed others around her. Rebecca felt their eyes on her, though she could not actually see them. She wondered if she had gone blind.

The singing stopped and it became quiet again. Rebecca felt herself suspended in time. She lost sensation of everything except this strange void.

"Rebecca."

With the sound of her name, Rebecca's perceptions changed again, and what had been a void now established form.

"Rebecca, come here." The voice was beautiful, full and rich. A singer's voice calling to her, its trained inflections thrilling her and intriguing her.

Rebecca saw light and made her way toward it. If she could just find the source of the voice, she thought, all would be well.

"Here, Rebecca."

Rebecca adjusted her perspective slightly and suddenly she was in a room full of people. She stared at them in surprise and saw them to be elegantly dressed men and women. There was a party going on. Someone handed her a goblet.

"Rebecca, so glad you could come," a silver-haired man said above the noise of the surrounding conversation. Several others turned and smiled at her.

"Yes, how wonderful, Rebecca," a woman said, her face wreathed in delight.

She heard a familiar voice say, "Feeling better?"

Rebecca turned and saw Richard. "Richard! Where are we?"

He grinned, then winked at her and turned back to the small group around him. She shook her head in wonderment and moved forward through the crowd. As she walked she heard various languages being spoken and again wondered about this place.

They were ancient languages. She was sure of it. Or at least languages that had lost their prominence in the world. She heard words in Greek, Turkish, Persian, and Russian. All of which struck her as odd, since she knew exactly what everyone was saying, even though she could speak none of those languages.

Rebecca stopped in the center of the room. She sipped from her goblet and looked around curiously. The ceiling was high and decorated in a gold leaf. Mosaics adorned the walls, and high arched windows let in the cool night air. Rebecca continued walking past marble columns toward the windows.

Outside the lights of a large city glimmered for miles around. She stuck her head out the window and saw that the building was huge, several stories high and a hundred yards or more long. They were inside a palace, Rebecca realized, on a hill with a breathtaking view.

"The amir has done a tremendous job, don't you think, Rebecca?" someone said behind her.

Rebecca spun around and looked into the startling eyes of a beautiful young woman.

"Hello, Rebecca," she said. "I'm so glad you came. We've all missed you."

The woman looked maddeningly familiar, but Rebecca could not remember her name, though she searched her physique for a clue as to her identity.

Deep black hair was swept up on the woman's head, held in place by gold bands. Jeweled earrings hung from her ears, gracing her long and slender neck. She had blue green eyes that looked at Rebecca in amusement, obviously realizing Rebecca's torment at not recognizing her and yet not about to give away the secret.

But she was so familiar! Rebecca even recognized the gown, though from where she could not say. It was Etruscan by design, a light gold and green that swooped down across her chest and displayed most of her breasts, then hugged her narrow waist and flared out all the way to the floor.

The beautiful woman laughed, her voice a melody. "You do not remember me, do you, Rebecca?"

Desperately Rebecca searched her eyes. She knew this figure of beauty and yet could not name her.

"Shame on you, darling. I am the goddess of wine, do you not remember?"

The goddess of wine? What did that mean? Rebecca searched for a clue but found nothing.

The goddess looked out the window. She took

a sip from her own goblet, then turned back to Rebecca.

"You can see the entire city from this site. They say the emperor himself was upset that our amir managed to acquire it."

Rebecca looked out the window at the night sky. It was familiar, too. Everything about the place called to her yet hid itself from her recognition.

"Where are we?" Rebecca started to ask, but the goddess did not appear to notice.

"I've got them all drunk here tonight," she confided, leaning forward and whispering into Rebecca's ear.

Rebecca looked around the room. It was true, she thought. Everyone seemed very tight. There were red noses everywhere, and gales of laughter broke out constantly, spreading outward like waves across the room. The noise level in the room seemed quite loud, with even the musicians in the corner straining to keep up.

A fat waiter stopped by with a silver tray of delicacies and waited for her to take one. His eyes insolently raced over her body, and then he moved on.

"He's rather rude," Rebecca said.

The goddess smiled at her. "Well, he is uncultured and so of course is out of his depth. But really, if the entire crowd here wasn't so drunk I cannot guarantee they would not have gawked at you as well. I told them what you were going to do and prepared them all for it. Suggested that it was the fashion and reminded them that you were the most notable fashion expert of us all. Then I handed them my wine and they all gulped it down."

"What are you talking about?"

The goddess of wine smiled. "Coy on top of everything. How so very like you. Charming and daring. Well, of course if I had a body like yours, I might take the plunge myself. I think that's why half the crowd professed to be shocked when I told them you were coming nude tonight."

Rebecca looked down and saw to her shock that she was, indeed, completely naked. She gasped and stared wide-eyed around the room to see if people noticed, and what they were thinking.

"Very daring, Rebecca," the woman went on. "And clever, too. If you pull it off we shall all save a fortune in clothing. Though I imagine some of the fat old sows around here will never consent to looking as horrible in public as they do underneath their expensive garb."

Rebecca felt horrified. Why had she done it? "I hope everyone is taking it well," she said, trying to appear calm.

Her companion was not fooled. "Don't be embarrassed, dear. Not now. I tried to talk you out of it earlier, but you insisted. Now all you can do is pull it off with style."

"But . . ."

"Anyway, half the people here have seen you nude before. Just not at the amir's ball. If he was not in love with you I hesitate to think what might happen, but no one attending tonight will dare risk his wrath. So relax and enjoy yourself. Show off that magnificent figure and make them all jealous. Why, if I were a man I would scarce be able to control myself."

Rebecca stared at the men, and saw for the first time that they wore togas. Suddenly she remembered. "It's Constantinople," she said.

"Out there it is, Rebecca, but in here it's the elysian fields."

"No, I mean, I know now where . . ."

"Of course," the beautiful woman went on, ignoring Rebecca's stammering and peering more deliberately through the arched window, "it won't be for long."

Rebecca paled. "What do you mean?" she said, even though she already knew.

"The armies of the night, dear child. They have breached the walls. They will be here soon."

Rebecca turned and looked, gasping at the sight of an invading army crashing through the gates and setting fire to the city.

"We must do something! Sound alarms, call for help!"

"There is no help," the goddess said dryly. "This is where it all began for you. For you and the amir. Don't you recall? It is Constantinople's last night, the night when he first saw you."

"What are you talking about?" Rebecca cried, suddenly fearful of age-old memories that were beyond comprehension, memories that she had never known, but now recalled. Memories that terrified her. "Who saw me?"

"Why, the amir, Rebecca," the goddess said. Then the goddess looked intently at her with large dark eyes. "Alexander."

Rebecca backed away from her. Why could she not remember who this woman was? "No," she said. "No, I do not belong here. This is all wrong! I want to go back, to wake up. This is all wrong!"

"But Rebecca, it is you who have found your way here. I have only come after you, to see what you are doing."

Rebecca put her hand over her mouth and her

eyes grew wide. "No, what you say is not true. It cannot be. I do not wish this. Take me back!" She spun around and searched the room. "Where is Richard? Take me to him."

"Richard is partaking of pleasure in his own way, Rebecca."

"No," Rebecca said. She cried out, trying to make her voice heard over the noises of the party. "Richard, where are you?"

But the revelry had increased, and when she again looked through the windows, she could see the invading armies coming up the streets.

"You had best flee these invaders, Rebecca. Who knows what would happen if they captured you."

Rebecca knew she was right. But she did not want to leave Richard. She looked around wildly.

"Step through this doorway, Rebecca," the goddess said. "Quickly!"

Rebecca turned and saw her beckoning from a narrow door nearly hidden behind long, flowing curtains. The woman motioned, her gestures becoming more insistent. Once more Rebecca looked for Richard, but he had disappeared. There was a crashing sound from the floors below that could only have come from the invaders breaking down the doors to the palace. Rebecca had a brief and terrible sense that all was lost, and then she obediently walked to the door and stepped through it.

8

When Rebecca stepped through the door, she was no longer in the palace, but instead in a garden. Confused at the sudden change and frightened of its implications, she looked around just as the door closed behind her and disappeared into darkness.

The warmth of the palace was gone. It was cool and damp here. Heavy gray and white clouds hung a few feet over her head. Wisps of fog swirled around her feet in slow-moving currents, and the many leaves on the plants and shrubs around her dripped water.

A diffuse light shone in the distance, its beam broken by narrow iron tubes on a fence that marked the perimeter of the garden. Several statues were placed, almost randomly, throughout the grounds. The nearest one was set on a fat square of concrete only a few feet from where Rebecca stood. She walked over and looked at it.

Although the pedestal was still in one piece, the sculpture on top had decayed into a shapeless mass. Rebecca touched it with her fingers and brought away grainy pieces of wet clay. She looked down at the plaque on the side of the pedestal, but the markings on it were faded, worn away by time and weather.

A pebbled path wound through the garden from one statue to the next, and Rebecca followed it to a statue that was in better condition. This one was of a young woman, tall and graceful, whose lines were as clean and smooth as if carved from alabaster only a short time ago. She stared up at it, marveling at the artist's skill in re-creating the feminine form.

The model had long hair, rich and thick. Her face, beautiful in its subtle bone structure and full lips, seemed so real that it was almost frightening. Rebecca brought her eyes farther down, studying the Edwardian dress that was very flattering to the gentle voluptuousness of the girl. The dress ended in folds that graced the concrete pedestal. Rebecca followed them downward to the plaque on the pedestal's side, and by running her fingers across the engraving could tell that this time the lettering was intact.

Black shadows denied immediate awareness, but working with fingers as well as eyes, Rebecca spelled out the inscription.

DENYSE FANCHONE
Beloved of Count and Countess Viroslav

Rebecca stepped away from the pedestal and again looked up at the statue.

"What is this place?" she said. "Everything here is alive, and yet it is a cemetery."

The fog swirled heavier around her legs, but she was not cold. She looked up at the statue again.

"Impossible," she said out loud.

The statue's right hand was between her legs, touching herself. It had not been like that before, she was certain of it.

"Rebecca!"

It was the countess, whispering to her through the fog.

"Come here, Rebecca!"

Rebecca blinked and went toward the dark feminine form. "How are you, Maria?" she said, then felt stupid for asking.

The countess ignored her question and demanded, "What are you doing here?"

"I'm not sure."

"You mustn't be here. Come, let us go." The countess grabbed her wrist and began pulling her along.

"Why? Where are we going?"

"Out of here. Back to Constantinople."

"But didn't you just bring me here?" Rebecca was certain the countess had guided her to this garden.

"Not here. You were not supposed to come here! Come along. We must go back now."

"But what is this place?"

Rebecca felt the cool fog moving between her legs like a soft, wet tongue. She breathed deeply.

"It's where Alexander and I will bring you, but only when you are ready. You must not come here yet. Come! It's dangerous here!"

A creeping sensation of erotic longing filled

her. The inside of her thighs burned with a cold heat. It built quickly, making her ache with a desire that frightened her.

She was breathing hard. "All right."

"Close your eyes and let me touch the lids. Then open them."

Rebecca felt Maria's fingertips graze her eyelids ever so slightly, and then she opened her eyes and found herself standing in a large bedroom, dressed in a light robe. Beside her stood two handmaidens, and Maria. She felt strangely glad to be in this room, though something was different.

"You won't really, will you, darling?" Maria was saying. The handmaidens giggled.

Now it made sense. It was an act that she and Maria were playing out. Rebecca remembered her lines. "Why not? It will create an effect, don't you think?"

Maria laughed. "Most certainly. But do you dare?"

Rebecca laughed also, then flipped her wrist in the air in a gesture of indifference. "Why not? It will make the men helpless with lust and the women helpless with rage."

"That is your wish? You play with fire, Rebecca."

Rebecca turned away and looked out the window to hide the slight smile that crossed her lips.

"What about the amir, though?" Maria went on.

"You mean Alexander, don't you?" She felt bold, daring.

Maria studied her. Apparently this had not been part of the script. "He is the amir."

Rebecca laughed.

"He is quite mad about you," Maria went on. The handmaidens went back to giggling. "And flaunting your body like that might just infuriate him."

"He does not own me."

"He seems to think he does. Ever since you came to this city you have teased him and taken gifts from him, too, I might add."

"So?"

Maria stepped close to Rebecca and put her hand on Rebecca's shoulder. She motioned for the handmaidens to leave the room, and when they had she whispered into Rebecca's ear.

"A word of caution, darling," she said. "He is an extremely powerful man. It is said even the emperor gives him leeway."

An icy thrill raced through Rebecca. "But he loves me. Does he not? This will make him love me more."

"Or hate you. With the passion you inspire, one is never far from the other."

Rebecca turned and put her hands on Maria's waist and searched her eyes, then her look became mischievous again. "It is his power that makes me love him. He must give me some of it if he wants to have me."

"It is a very dangerous plot you hatch."

"Will you help me?"

Maria moved her long fingers to Rebecca's forehead and gently brushed back a lock of hair. "What do you want me to do?"

"Brush my body with the powder that will make it glow and shimmer."

For a second Maria did not understand. Then she smiled. "If one is to dream-travel through another's unconscious," she said, "one must be prepared. "If that is your wish," she went on. "Take off your gown then, and I will begin. When I am done you shall be even more beautiful than you are now. But be warned, raising such beauty will give you a power of attractiveness that will be beyond anything you can imagine. It can be dangerous."

Rebecca reached to her own shoulders and undid the restraints of her robe. It fell to the floor, leaving her completely nude.

Rebecca turned away from Maria and stared at herself in the mirror. "I want there to be no one at the party tonight who does not desire me."

Maria let her eyes float once over the beautiful nude body in front of her. "I'm quite certain you will succeed," she murmured.

Finding a bottle of gold powder and a soft brush, Maria quickly painted Rebecca's body. Rebecca moaned softly.

"Now come, let us return," Maria said.

Rebecca felt a sudden wave of anxiety. "How?" she asked. "What will happen?"

"Let us see." Maria touched her once on the forehead.

✳

9

Rebecca was by herself, running down a hall. From all sides came screams of terror and the relentless noise of soldiers invading the palace.

A shout came from somewhere not too far behind her, and Rebecca ran faster. When she came to a juncture where the hallway split and turned in two directions, she quickly chose the left branch and raced around a corner. Momentarily the noise down the hall receded, and Rebecca leaned against a wall and tried to catch her breath. In front of her was a mirror, and she stared at her reflection. To her relief she saw that the figure gazing back was dressed in a light blue gown. How or why she was no longer nude was a mystery, but not one on which she could dwell. She peered back at where she had come from, wondering what had happened.

Almost immediately the noise grew louder again. Shouts echoed down the long, marbled hallways, sounding death and worse for the survivors. Shadows reflecting on the wall foretold the coming of soldiers. She began running again, not knowing where the hall led, but feeling she had to keep away from the noise behind her.

The Byzantine architecture allowed for a maze of hallways and stairs, and Rebecca ran through them blindly. She stopped in confusion at another intersection of halls, then looked right and left through opposing narrow doors. A shout from her left made her take off to the right, and she caught the hem of her gown on a sharp corner of a statue. It ripped along the side all the way up the curve of her thigh. She ignored it and continued on.

A steep flight of stairs lay ahead. She bounded upward, hoping to find shelter on a higher level. But the torn garment caught underneath her feet on the steps, causing her to nearly trip. She reached down and ripped the hem off just above her knees, then dropped the blue gossamer material and continued on upward two steps at a time.

As she climbed higher her lungs felt as though they were on fire. She realized with alarm that smoke was coming from below. At the top of the stairs she broke into a coughing fit and stumbled into a long, narrow room. For a few seconds she pounded her chest and hacked painfully. But as soon as she regained control of her breathing, she looked around the room and blinked in amazement.

Alexander and Maria were sitting calmly in the corner, watching her.

"It's the invasion!" Rebecca said, feeling stupid as soon as she said it.

Alexander nodded. "I suspected as much."

"I believe you're quite right about that," Maria agreed.

"But . . . what can we do? The army is under us now! It won't be long before they find this room."

Alexander and Maria looked at each other and nodded in unison. "Once again you cannot be faulted, Rebecca," he said.

"Interesting costume, Rebecca," Maria noted. "Have you switched to the ragged look, then?"

Rebecca looked down at herself. "My clothing is unimportant. Can't you see that we're in serious trouble?"

Maria got up and went to look out the window at the city burning below. "I believe I'm beginning to understand," she said.

"Understand?" Rebecca was beside herself.

"What is it, my dear?" said the count.

"Why she brought us here."

"I didn't bring you here," Rebecca wailed.

He ignored Rebecca. "I was here, long ago. It was before I met you, Maria. Long before you were born." He became pensive. "Yes, yes, there was a girl then."

He stared at Rebecca, studying her in a way that made her feel cold. "There is something familiar."

Rebecca felt the same thing, yet she was unsure what it was that was familiar.

"It was the tapestry," Maria said.

"Yes. It has worked before."

"What do you mean!" Rebecca shouted.

Alexander turned toward his wife. "She saw Constantinople in the frame. Denyse saw Rome, if you recall."

"It was Rome in its pre-Christian madness that touched Denyse. Just as apparently it is Constantinople for our Rebecca."

"Yes."

Maria now looked at Rebecca. "Was she there, Alex?"

"Perhaps. I remember one like her. So much like her." He put his fingers under Rebecca's chin. "Would you like to stop this ever-turning wheel of incarnating, my dear?"

She backed away from him, now terrified. "What do you mean?"

"Leave her alone, Alexander. She is trying to show us something that will help us to make her become one of us."

He nodded and turned back to Maria. "Indeed, my dear. You feel something is going to happen in this room?"

Maria nodded. "Soon, I should think. It will explain what we need to do. I hear soldiers on the stairs."

Rebecca looked wild-eyed from one to the other, then twirled around in horror and stared at the doorway just as three large men in blood-splattered soldiers' garb burst in the door.

"It's her," the first one said. "The one he wants."

"Yes, it has to be," answered the next. Then he said to Rebecca, "Are you the one they call Rebecca?"

Her eyes widened. "No," she said, backing away. She looked desperately to the corner, but instead of Alexander and Maria she saw two small bats hanging upside down, watching her.

The men stepped forward and grabbed her.

"Wait."

The voice came from the doorway, its timbre so authoritative that the soldiers froze.

Rebecca looked and saw Eric. Long blond hair

framed his face, and in spite of her fear she thought that he would have been quite handsome except for those cold, cruel eyes. One was blue with green specks in it, and the other was green with red specks.

The officer stepped forward and the soldiers parted around her, though they still held her arms behind her.

"Rebecca, it is you, is it not?" He came closer, studying her. His eyes roamed from her neck to her legs, and she looked away. "Yes, it is; I would know you anywhere. I have searched long and hard for you."

"Why? What do you want?" she said.

He smiled and stroked her cheek. "You are the favorite of the amir now, they say, and the scandal of the court. I can see why. You are very beautiful."

Without turning his head he told the men to restrain her. He watched, his colorful eyes brimming with lust and hunger, as she was tied by her wrists to a rope. The rope was quickly hung from a wooden beam in the ceiling, then drawn up tight.

"Leave," the officer commanded, and the men backed out of the room.

"What do you want?" she asked again, her voice hoarse.

He put his hands on the torn gown and yanked, shredding it once down the middle so that it hung in two folds along the sides of her breasts. He slowly put his hands under the folds of the material, slipping his palms under her breasts, then kissed her hard on the lips.

"You," he said. He unbuttoned his sleeves, then

undid the buttons down the front of his shirt, watching her all the time in silence.

"I want you," he said again. He shrugged off his shirt and stood in front of her bare-chested. "I'll follow you anywhere you go. You cannot escape me, Rebecca. I want you. I'll have you."

"Maria!" Rebecca cried into the silence of the room. "Alexander, help me!"

Eric put his hand around her neck and pulled on her hair, forcing her to look up at him. He kissed her again, then broke the kiss and slapped her face. "There is no one here but you and me, my sweet."

Her cheek burned where his palm had connected. "Bastard."

He put his hands on her shoulders, grabbed the remainder of her gown, and ripped it from her, leaving her hanging naked. Then he smiled. "I'm going to teach you what happens if you run away from me."

She saw with astonishment that he had a whip in his hand. He backed away from her slowly, and with the same cruel grin he raised the whip over his head.

Rebecca screamed as loud as she could. "Alexander, help me!"

Count Viroslav and his wife stood at the base of Denyse's statue, looking up at it.

"A great pity, all the more so because she would have made a magnificent vampire," the count said.

A red tear dropped from Maria's right eye, slid across her cheek, and fell to the ground. She wiped its trail from her skin and nodded.

"Perhaps, but she was missing what she needed to carry her over into our world."

"She was passionate."

"True, but she loved the pleasure too much and the anguish not enough."

They eventually turned to each other.

"Shall we go in, my dear?" Alexander said, almost gently.

"Yes, let's do."

They walked together through the fog, knowing the way instinctively out of the garden. When they reached the door it opened automatically and they went inside. It closed silently after them.

Gregor stood in the great hall, waiting. "There's a fire in the music room," he said.

"Good. Come, Maria, let us go in there for a bit."

Two chairs had been pushed up to the huge fireplace, and between them stood a small Victorian wine table with two crystals of red liquid. Alexander sat on the left; his wife sat nearest the piano bench. Each picked up a glass and drank the entire amount, then set it back down and stared at the fire.

"Why did you leave her with that man, darling?"

Maria shrugged. "I learned what I needed to know. She'll wake up in a moment."

"Will he hurt her?"

"It's her dream. She is creating the plot."

"Does she crave pain, do you think?"

Maria looked into the fire, then turned to her husband. "She is manufacturing an emotional intensity all on her own. An anger, I believe, unlike any she has ever known. She has an enormous talent for becoming one of us, Alexan-

THE KISS ✿ 81

der. In fact, I might say she could almost do it on her own."

"No one can make the transition by themselves, Maria. You know that."

"All I am saying is that it won't take much. Just the right stimulation at the right time. Her sensuality and her fury swirl within her like volatile chemicals waiting to mix. I do believe this man we have just seen is the catalyst for the change."

"Then we will bring her to the peak of passion tonight, and tomorrow to the peak of rage."

They watched the fire burn and crackle in front of them.

"She is enjoying herself in her little dream," Maria said after a while. "It has been fascinating to watch."

"I agree. Splendid unconscious imagination. I do think she could almost put you to shame."

"Shame it would be, too." Maria laughed.

"It's good to hear you laugh, my dear. It seems you have grown morose these last few years."

Maria looked into the fire and said nothing. Gregor appeared silently and refilled the glasses, then backed away into the gloom.

"I crave her, you know," Alexander said.

"Yes, I know."

"You're not jealous?"

Maria shook her head. "No, are you?"

"How could I be? The night you agreed to become a vampire and be with me, I knew you had made me the most solemn and dedicated promise possible."

A smile played enigmatically on Maria's lips.

"What are you remembering?"

"That night, when you took me in the woods away from the fair in Budapest. When we made love, and afterward when you told me who you were and what you were."

He nodded. "Ah, yes, that night is one I, too, shall never forget. I call up the image sometimes when I am thinking of you. Why, I'm not sure, except that when you looked at me, after I had told you, the look on your face was extraordinary, and I knew from that moment that I loved you more deeply than anyone I had ever loved before."

She took his hand in hers. "What was the look?"

"Surprise and amazement, I think. Maybe even fear. But you were not terrified. Not panicked, as I would have expected. Your eyes, those magnificent large eyes, shone with excitement. It astounded me."

"Really? Still, it was not without some fear that I gave myself to you that night."

"I could not tell, then or now. You are an incredibly strong woman. But would you . . ." He hesitated, yet had to ask, "Would you do otherwise now, change two centuries together, knowing what you know of the vampire's existence?"

Maria turned her head slowly from the fire to her husband, smiling. As he watched, the smile became broader and bolder. Maria stood up and walked to the center of the room. She hesitated, then rose into the air and hovered a few inches off the ground, continuing to stare at him with her large, exquisite eyes.

"Never let me forget, Count Viroslav, vampire!" she cried suddenly.

Without looking away from him, she reached for the stays on her gown and loosened them. The dress she had been wearing fell away from her body in a slow, floating spiral to the carpet below her, leaving her completely nude.

She raised her hands into the air, splaying her long fingers. With a sudden twist of her head, she sent her long black hair flying down over the creamy skin of her bare shoulders. Then she brought her arms back slightly, causing her breasts to jut forward. The hard, round nipples stabbed the air in front of her, and her small, flat belly shook with a laughter that rattled the windows high overhead. With the same determined movement she pushed her hips forward, showing the narrow black strip of soft hair that grew at the juncture of her legs.

"Show me again what it means, Alexander!" she sang. Her voice rang with melody and force. "Come to me and make me glad I'm your vampire! Make love to me now and forever!"

The count was already on his feet. He strode toward her hungrily, his eyes on her breasts, his nostrils flaring.

She laughed louder even as her own eyes took in the wide, flat pectorals that framed his muscular body and his narrow hips and waist. Already he was hard, so large and thick that she thought it must be painful.

"Take me!" she screamed.

He rose off the ground and into her arms. She spread her legs as he took her breasts into his mouth and received him into her. They rose to the ceiling, turning slowly around and around, over and over, and then descended nearly to the floor only to begin to rise again in their heated vampiric lust.

Gregor watched from the shadows, in awe and envy at the sight of the two vampires making their own love, oblivious and indifferent to everything and everyone.

Rebecca sat up in a stunned awareness that she had been dreaming again. Only this time the dream had been even more intense than the one last night. She put a hand to her damp forehead and closed her eyes.

And saw the evil man with the huge, erect penis, aiming it at her, sending it toward her. . . .

She shook her head and opened her eyes. *I am surely going mad with these incessant thoughts of sex!*

Her throat was dry and her body ached with an insistent longing that was so strong it was making her cross. She looked around at the darkened lawn in front of her, realizing she had slept away the afternoon.

The trees in the distance were black with shadows, and yet surprisingly she could see into the shadows quite well. She looked to her right and left, realizing that the gloomy features of the ancient castle were not hidden in the coming twilight as she might have thought.

The dream was beginning to fade, which made her feel better. She stood up slowly, aware not of a creakiness in her joints, as she might have expected after falling asleep on unyielding stone, but instead of a stickiness between her legs that almost demanded she touch herself.

Rebecca walked across the entrance and pushed open the great doors. It was darker inside. The great hall was steeped in shadows.

"Gregor?"

There was no answer. Rebecca sighed and walked back to the dining room, stopping at the door. She looked at the small silver watch on her wrist and saw that it was past five. Really too late to have been left alone this long.

Remembering the images she had seen earlier in this room, Rebecca hesitated, then decided to go to the music room instead. She would play some music while she waited for someone to show up.

She walked across the ancient stone floor and pushed open the doorway to the music room, then stepped inside and pulled it shut behind her.

"Maybe some Joplin," she said out loud, mainly because she was tired of the oppressive silence that clung to the walls, floor, and ceiling of the castle.

"That would be nice," Gregor said.

A terrible, bone-chilling shiver shook her from head to foot. She had not seen him, nor felt his presence. "Gregor!"

He smiled, though his eyes remained as flat as ever. "Yes, Miss."

"I . . . I didn't see you."

"I am sorry to have frightened you."

"You didn't frighten me," she said too quickly.

"You wish, perhaps, to see the count and countess?"

"Yes. And Richard. Where is Richard?"

Gregor stared at her for several seconds. "He went out," he said finally. "Something about some business he had to attend to in the village. I am certain he will be back soon if he has no problems with transportation, or . . ."

"Or what?"

"Nothing."

Rebecca grabbed his arm. "Gregor! Where is Richard?!? I must know!"

He looked down at her fingers. She let go.

"I'm sorry, Gregor, but I must know what has happened to him. He should have returned by now, and I'm very worried. I tried to find someone this afternoon to tell me what had happened, but no one was around. I saw you briefly from my room. . . ."

"You saw me? What else did you see?"

"I saw the Nazis come earlier, Gregor. Thank you for not telling them we were here."

He never took his eyes from her, nor did he respond.

"Do you think Richard is in danger from the Nazis?"

"No."

"Oh. Good." She walked to the piano, putting some distance between herself and Gregor. "When will the count and countess return?"

"Soon."

The conversation was not exactly scintillating, she thought. "Gregor, may I ask you something?"

"Yes."

"How long have you worked here for them?"

He paused before answering. "A long time."

"Do they . . . do you think they are all right?"

"What do you mean, Miss?"

Rebecca searched his eyes, then looked away. "Oh, nothing. I don't know. I'm just worried, I guess. Everything seems so strange."

He stood silently for several seconds before speaking again, and then it was in the same flat voice.

"May I bring you something to drink? Some wine, perhaps?"

Rebecca laughed self-consciously. "That wine makes me feel very strange, Gregor. I don't think . . ."

"I am so sorry you did not like it," the countess said, emerging from the shadows.

Rebecca spun around. "Countess! I did not hear you come in."

"I did not mean to frighten you."

"Oh! No, you didn't. That is, I'm glad to see you. No, the wine was excellent."

"Then perhaps you would like some more. Gregor?"

"Yes, ma'am."

"Bring us a glass of wine, and we shall enjoy . . . Joplin, did you say?"

"Yes, Joplin. But . . ."

"Yes, Rebecca?" The countess raised an eyebrow imperially, and the last of the setting sun accentuated it.

"Nothing. Really, nothing." Rebecca sighed. "Yes, some Joplin."

⁕⁑⁕

10

Richard lay stretched out on the hard wooden rack. The medieval torture device kept him spread-eagled, pinching his wrists and ankles and stretching his muscles painfully. Again and again he fell into unconsciousness and awoke with a start, convinced momentarily that what had happened so far had only been a dream. Yet each time he was forced to admit that the dream was reality . . . and reality was a nightmare.

The torch hanging from the stone wall last night had long since burned itself out. The only illumination in the dungeon was whatever sunlight could find its way through a single narrow window at the top of the wall behind his head. Even that ray had faded, telling Richard that it must once again be night. He groaned.

There was a sound of footsteps descending on stone, coming to the dungeon. Wincing with pain, Richard gritted his teeth and twisted his body to the left, straining to see the entrance to the dungeon. Only the top of the arched doorway was visible.

"Good evening, Richard." It was Gregor.

"Gregor! What is happening? Have you come to torture me as well?"

Gregor walked to the rack and put a bowl and some towels down. He picked up a ladle and dipped it into the bowl, then brought the ladle to Richard's lips and allowed him to drink cold water. Richard drank greedily, spilling at least half of it down his chin. When he had had enough he let his head rest back on the wood.

"Thank you," he said, grateful in spite of himself.

Gregor nodded without comment or interest, then picked up a towel and soap and began washing Richard's body. He did it so clinically that Richard was not embarrassed. When he was finished Gregor picked up his things and began to walk away without speaking.

"Gregor!"

Gregor stopped without turning toward Richard.

"Please. Don't go."

Gregor turned slowly around, but he said nothing.

"Gregor, what is going on here? Is Rebecca all right?"

"Better than you are, I should think, Master Richard."

Richard let out a relieved sigh. "Where is she?"

"She dines with the count and countess."

He frowned. "Why doesn't she come to me?"

"She does not even know you are here."

"Why not? What have they done to her?"

Gregor put the items he was carrying on the floor and returned to stand next to Richard. "It's not what they have done to her, Richard. It's what they will do," he said.

A coldness crept over Richard that had nothing to do with his nakedness. "What do you mean?"

"Did the count not explain to you that they are vampires?"

"Yes. But I didn't think . . ."

Gregor nodded. "I did not think so either, at first. So very long ago."

Richard swallowed hard. "What are you talking about? Aren't you in league with them?"

Gregor considered. "I suppose I am," he said.

"You won't let me go, then."

A thin smile crossed Gregor's lips and was gone. "No."

"You're not a vampire, though, are you, Gregor?"

Gregor shook his head. "No."

"Then why are you here? What do they have on you that makes you want to stay with them?"

Gregor stared at him, and Richard guessed. "It's the countess, isn't it? She's worked her magic on you, too. I can see it in your eyes. I understand; she made me go mad, too. But it's not right, Gregor! We cannot allow it to go on! You must let me free and help me save Rebecca and—"

"Be quiet, you fool!"

Richard stared in surprise at Gregor, who had never shown even the ability to express emotion before. "But . . ."

"How long do you think I've been here in this castle, being the servant?"

"I don't know. When did you come here?"

Gregor smiled sardonically. "You cannot imagine how long it has been. Look at me; do you think I am older or younger than they?"

Richard studied him for the first time. "You look about the same age. But he said that they are old. Ancient, in fact. Hundreds of years old!"

"As am I."

Richard stared at him, now as frightened of Gregor as he had previously been of the count. "You're not a vampire, though."

"No. They would not make me one. But that does not mean I cannot go on living indefinitely, serving them, staying near the one I love."

"That's insane!"

"Really? It is possible. She can keep me alive through her kiss. The kiss of a vampire. When she takes my blood and mingles it with the disease in her saliva, she keeps me alive."

"You want this kind of existence?"

"You fool. Do you think I have enjoyed this life?"

"Why do you stay?"

Gregor said nothing for several minutes. "I was her first love, her only real love. I loved her more than anyone has ever loved anyone before. I saved her from a wasted life and took her from the clutches of a debauched aristocrat. I gave up my birthright and risked everything when I took her out of my homeland. I had thought then that I would make a new life for us in France.

"That was my plan. But then we ran into *him*. She was young, and he was everything that would turn a girl's head. I failed her one night, argued with her over money and our future, and he was waiting.

"He caught her alone, in the dark, and raped her. She was only a girl! Then he . . . he did to her what his kind has done for centuries to the innocent, and turned her into one like him."

Richard watched Gregor and was astonished to see the man's eyes momentarily brim with tears.

Gregor's voice became stronger as it filled with passion. "But she loved me even then. She still loves me."

"Why have you not killed him before now?"

Gregor's eyes became small and hard. "She would not allow me to do it."

Richard saw the madness that had taken over Gregor's thoughts. He was unsure what to say.

Gregor went on unbidden. "We were going to leave him last night, when we found you. We had been planning it for weeks, but he was suspicious and delayed us, and we missed the train."

Richard thought he saw an opportunity. "You and the countess were trying to leave here? Where would you go? How would the two of you live?"

"We could survive anywhere."

"When did you come here?"

Gregor looked wary. "In 1738."

Richard's jaw dropped. "In 1738," he repeated. "You've been here ever since?"

Gregor nodded, eyeing him.

"It's a different world out there, Gregor."

Gregor seemed to consider that as if for the first time. A wave of sadness filled Gregor's features. "Perhaps you are right," he said.

Richard feared he may have said the wrong thing. He decided to try to be more positive. "You will need help."

Gregor backed away. "I've told you too much."

"No, wait, Gregor!"

Gregor shook his head. "No, you do not understand anything. You're a fool. You speak the truth and do not know it."

"Gregor, stop! I can help you."

"You can help me? Look at you. You cannot even free yourself from the rack. No, I think you were right before. The world is changing, and there is no place away from here for me or her. Our time to escape has long passed."

Richard saw his opportunity dissolving. "Gregor, don't give up. I can help you. You and Maria. Rebecca and I can, if only you'll give us a chance."

"I've dreamed of escaping him for two centuries yet have not ever been able to do it. So has she. But it was only a dream. Once he took her for his unholy bride, that is what she was forever. There is no hope, except . . ." Gregor paused thoughtfully.

"Except what?"

Gregor looked at Richard and shook his head. When he spoke, his voice had a dangerous tone of resolve in it that Richard had not heard before. "There is no real hope for you, Richard. Your lover is being taken from you and nothing can stop it. You'll see. I will try to get you out of here, but it is too late for Rebecca. There is no hope for her—any more than there is for Maria. And only oblivion for me."

He began to walk away.

"Gregor! No! Stop, Gregor. Come back, please." Richard called toward the sound of the retreating footsteps until only his own voice remained, echoing against the stone.

11

Rebecca was teaching Dixieland tunes to the countess, who laughed with delight at the syncopated rhythms. Rebecca enjoyed showing Maria something new. She felt mildly superior when she explained the style, since it really belonged to the twenties. Rebecca wondered if Alexander and Maria ever left this place.

Alexander watched the two women for several minutes, then left the room. It was not unlike him to leave his wife early in the evening sometimes and slip away into the night. He would feed alone just after sunset, flying long distances from the castle and descending on a lone hiker or a small house deep in the woods. When he did, he would kill or not, depending on whom he found, sometimes draining them of all blood, sometimes only puncturing a delicate neck and leaving the body weakened. When he flew away the victim would often as not feel weakened but strangely unsatisfied. She would awaken as from a trance, longing for a tall, handsome stranger she had never met and not sure why. Such times were amusements for Count Viroslav, small adventures to whet his appetite until he went again later with his wife for more.

Out of the corner of her eye Maria saw him step back into the shadows of the music room and then disappear. She assumed he was raising his desires for Rebecca's blood and body. It promised to be quite a night, she mused. Then she turned back to Rebecca and played the haunting melody of Chopin's "Nocturne Number 2."

But Maria's assumption about her husband's intentions was wrong. Intrigued with the results of the dream search, he had become interested in the man who had followed Rebecca all the way from Berlin. Gregor had told him that a Nazi had visited the castle that afternoon, but that the Nazi had only said he wanted to see the count.

Under Count Viroslav's instructions, Gregor had searched Richard's luggage but found nothing that would cause a German officer to travel hundreds of miles in pursuit. Such inexplicable behavior warranted further attention. Alexander had not lived seven hundred years by not being cautious.

"Who is he, Gregor?" he had asked when Gregor had finished going through Richard's things.

"A member of the Nazi police, lord. They are the new ruling class in Germany, from what I gather."

The count nodded. "I shall be gone for a little while, Gregor. Take more wine in to them. Tell Maria I will meet her in the observatory in an hour."

"Yes, lord."

Within minutes Count Viroslav was standing in the forest at the edge of the village.

Pietre, the village constable, stood at the door of the small building that housed the jail and his office, listening patiently to the admonitions of the German officer. It had been a long day and now promised to be an even longer evening. All the constable wanted was to get home and have some dinner.

"Yes, Herr Captain Stryker," he said in his heavily accented German when the other man had finally stopped long enough to draw a breath. "I understand completely. I have instructed the driver to return at seven-thirty. We will leave then and return to the castle."

The man with the strangely colored eyes regarded him with obvious disdain.

How rude they all are, the constable thought.

"That is acceptable, Herr Constable. I shall return to the inn now and expect you in"—he glanced at his watch—". . . one hour."

"Very good, Herr Captain." It was demeaning, but what could he do? Instructions from headquarters had been quite specific about helping this arrogant bastard and maintaining good international relations with Germany, whose growing power was felt everywhere in Europe and was beginning to be feared, even in these mountains so far from Berlin.

The constable watched Stryker step down onto the dusty street and stride away toward the inn. He sighed, then pulled the door shut behind him and went in the opposite way toward his own house.

The man was crazy, he was thinking. Going out

to that castle after dark was asking for more trouble than even the Third Reich knew how to handle. He himself dreaded it. The constable pulled his coat tighter around his shoulders. A fog was filling the street, and its dampness made his shoulders ache.

As he walked he thought about the situation. For countless aeons the people of this area had lived in mortal terror of the nightly wanderings of the castle's inhabitants. No one dared venture out at night, for those who did often were never heard of again. Especially young girls. These wild mountains, which covered most of southeastern Europe, were untamable by even the most determined kings, czars, and dictators, and the people who lived in them were left to make their own way.

They had, too. The legends and tales spread across Europe, causing interest that generated unwanted focus. Though change was not made, the castle's inhabitants became more circumspect. They were willing to reach a compromise to protect their anonymity against the coming of the new age, they said.

It had been the constable's own grandfather who had made the "understanding" with the count, and for two generations none of the towns-people had been bothered. No one was to speak of the count or in any way draw attention to his existence; in return, the villagers would be left alone. It was tantamount to complicity in whatever unspeakable crimes the monsters up there were involved in, but what choice did they have? If they had not agreed, they would all have been dead long ago. Or worse.

Yet now even this fragile compromise was

threatened. The ostentatious young fool in a fool's costume had come, full of hot air and nonsense, upsetting the balance. It would serve him right, the constable thought as he rounded the corner of the last building on the street, if . . .

He gasped in sheer terror and froze in his tracks. There before him, nearly hidden in the thick fog, stood Count Viroslav himself. No one had even seen the old one for more than twenty years. Most of the villagers had even allowed themselves to believe he had gone away or died, though Pietre had done his best not to let them become complacent. His father had made certain he understood the importance of that.

But now here was the monster, standing huge and staring down at the constable with eyes that burned, as though they came from hell's own furnace.

"Good evening, Constable." The voice was as cold as a grave.

The constable stammered, "My lord Viroslav!"

The vampire regarded him for several seconds in silence, and Pietre felt his spine encased in ice.

"I would have a word with you, Constable," he said finally.

"Yes, of course, sir."

Count Viroslav put a cold, heavy hand on the constable's shoulder and pulled him into the damp blackness beyond the village boundaries.

"Why were you at my estate this afternoon?"

The constable swallowed hard. "I was with a German, sir. It's politics these days. He has come looking for a criminal. Two criminals, actually. He thought . . . that is, well, that they might be hiding on your property."

"I look after my own property." The voice oozed threat into the night. "You know that."

"Yes, yes of course. It's just that, well, this has become an international incident, my lord. If we don't stop it now, attention will be brought to the village and . . . and your estate."

Count Viroslav was silent for a moment, and Pietre had to force himself to remain motionless even though his desire was to turn and run as fast as he could.

"Who does the German seek?" the count finally said.

"A young woman, sir. And her boyfriend."

"He seeks the girl?"

"Well, he claims the boyfriend stole something and the girl is his accomplice."

"And what else did you think of him?"

"It's just that he asked more about the girl than the boy."

"Perceptive of you, Constable. What are his plans?"

"He went to the telegraph office when we returned this evening. Now he insists that we come out to the castle tonight, sir. To meet you. Your man told him you would be back after dark," the constable added, then saw the expression on the vampire's face change and immediately wished he had not said anything.

The vampire's eyes turned from fire to ice and back again. "He knows my movements?"

"Only that you were out this afternoon, lord."

"He stays at the inn?"

"Yes, my lord."

"Say nothing of seeing me, Constable."

"Of course not, Count Viroslav."

Alexander stared at the constable, thinking for several more seconds, then stepped back into the fog and vanished. The constable wiped his brow and hurried home.

The next person the count visited was the telegraph operator at the train station. He opened the door and slid in so quietly that he was standing behind the old man before his presence was known. But the telegraph operator, a veteran named Sergei who had lived in the village for more than fifty years, felt his gaze and turned around quickly. He took one look at the tall apparition, grabbed his chest, and fainted.

The count watched him fall to the floor, then stepped over him and went through the papers on his desk and in his files. It was a quiet office, so it did not take long to find the dispatch he was seeking. He unfolded the yellow paper and read it.

TO CAPTAIN ERIC STRYKER STOP RETURN TO BERLIN ON THE NEXT TRAIN WITHOUT FAIL STOP BRING PRISONERS IF YOU HAVE THEM STOP

"If you have them?" Alexander muttered.

He left the telegraph office as quietly as he had entered and stepped quickly through the dark and deserted streets to the back of the inn. Then he paused for a moment to concentrate, and lifted off the ground and onto the roof. He peered into each room, finally discerning which one was occupied by the German officer. It was empty, and he slipped in the open window.

Moving quickly, he sped through the room examining everything. Inside Stryker's briefcase he found a yellow folder and some photographs. He glanced at the pictures, then pulled out the contents of the folder and began to read.

Dear Eric,

As I told you last evening, I want nothing more to do with you. After what I found out about your job, I know I cannot respect you, and certainly not love you. This may be difficult for you to understand, but as an American and as a human being, I simply cannot accept the necessity, much less the correctness, as you call it, of the Gestapo. It is not an organization devoted to the better-ment of anyone but its own members.

The letter went on for a page and a half, criticiz-ing the Nazi party and the German society that accepted it. Alexander scanned it quickly, slowing when the tone changed.

When I first met you, Eric, I was new in Germany and without friends. That first day we met I thought you were wonderful. I still remember how you saved me from that terrible man who tried to rob me. Later, when you introduced me to your family, you seemed so kind and warm, especially with your nephew, and you were so attentive to me. I even thought you looked splendid in your uniform. That was before I understood what the uniform meant!

When we made love that first time in your house with your parents gone, I found it incredi-bly exciting and thought I must certainly be in love. That is why it was so devastating to learn about the real you!

But learn I did, and when last night at the restaurant you accosted Richard and me, I saw how cruel and hurtful you can be. I can never forgive you for what you did later when I came to talk to you. I know that you think a man should treat a woman with force, that she wants to be controlled, but you are wrong.

Stay away from me, now and forever. You think Richard is weak and ineffectual, but it is not your place to make such judgments. Anyway, it does not matter. There is no more love between us, and never will be. Stay away from me!

Count Viroslav held the pieces of paper in his hand and smiled. He carefully replaced the letter and pictures.

"So, Rebecca," he whispered in the darkness, "your passion extends to all those you meet. Good. It will be useful if you are to become one of us."

Then he stepped to the window and leapt through it into the night.

Stryker finished his meal in the small dining room and returned upstairs to his bedroom, where he paced back and forth and waited for the hands on his watch to move. It had not gone the way he had planned out at the castle today. The servant had been rude and insulting, and the local constable had been of no help at all.

He glanced at his watch, saw that it was only just six o'clock, and pulled off his jacket. The car would not be here until seven-thirty, which would allow them to arrive at the castle by eight. Surely the owners of the estate would be there by then.

Strange people, he thought. But then, everything he had seen so far had been vaguely disturbing. The hairs on the back of his neck suddenly raised and he spun around, half expecting to find someone standing behind him. But the room was empty. Frowning, he went to the window and pulled it closed, then returned to the small table near the door and sat down.

There was a bottle of Glenlivet on the table, and he poured some into a small glass. He smiled slightly as he tossed it back. One should always travel in comfort, he thought. Then he looked around the room and scowled. Comfort was not to be found here, though, that was certain.

Stryker opened his briefcase and removed an envelope. He picked it up and opened it, then shook the contents out into his hand. He sorted through them until he came to two eight-by-ten glossy pictures, then laid them gently on the table. The pictures showed the old buildings of the university and students walking through falling leaves. In the center of the photograph, standing in the middle of a throng of their peers, stood Rebecca and Richard.

His gaze went between them for a few seconds, then settled on Rebecca. "Why did you choose him?"

He had had the pictures made, he told his supervisor, in case it became necessary to enlist local aid. That was a lie, of course, though possibly conceivable. Stryker hoped the colonel did not suspect that this trip was merely the pursuit of a lost love. If he did, there would be a ticket waiting for him when he returned that would take him to duty in a concentration camp. Stryker had worked very hard to convince everyone that it was important to capture Richard and Rebecca before they spread the word in America. He had worried slightly that his superior might ask what word they would spread, but his anxiety was unnecessary. Paranoia had already found a home in Berlin. He had been allowed to go after them with very little justification.

It was stupid, of course. In his most lucid moments Stryker could admit that to himself. At age thirty it was certainly stupid to be chasing after a woman almost ten years younger, an American woman at that. Stupid to have fallen for her in the first place, and even more stupid to have lost her.

And extremely stupid to have lost her to this young boy Richard.

He poured himself one more small glass of the whiskey. *Mustn't have any more*, he thought. But it helped him relax and think without distraction. He put the glass down again and closed his eyes.

As always when he shut his eyes, he saw her. She was there, a part of his thoughts whether in sleep or wakefulness. Just the way she had been the first day he had seen her. Her hair had danced on the unexpectedly warm early spring breeze that day, and her smile had been radiant. He had followed her halfway across the city, and then he had one of his hired thugs accost her at just the right moment. He smiled when he remembered how it had worked. It had not been the first time he had used that ploy, but this time it had backfired, and now he was caught in the web. He rubbed his eyebrows with the palm of one hand and tried to forget his own pain. Again she appeared to him as the innocent girl with whom he had fallen in love.

Naive did not describe her. She did not even recognize his uniform as being the Gestapo's. Barely seemed to know what the Gestapo was, but she was impressed by the way his boots gleamed and his uniform rustled with crispness. Her German was quite good, and her occasional mispronunciations and misinterpretations merely added to her charm. Her accent was impressive, and he had thought she was wonderful. Her beautiful face, filled with fear at Stryker's bulky villain and gratitude at his "heroic" act, affected him more than he thought possible. He had immediately put all his energy into seducing her.

She had crawled into bed with him, too. It had been thrilling, something all too rare for Stryker to know love with sex, to have sex with a young woman whom he had not paid. The love, so passionate that it could not exist without constant fighting, had been all consuming. He had hated her and loved her, and as he felt himself slipping out of control, out of being the dominant partner in the relationship, he sought desperately for a way to conquer her. What he settled for was a cheap and meaningless argument to assuage his own ego. When she called him cruel for the way he spoke to her, he told her that it was no more than she deserved. "German girls of the right class insist upon waiting until engagement at the very least, even marriage, before sex," he had said.

At that moment the pain and sense of betrayal in her eyes was worse than anything he had ever seen. That, he thought now, had been his downfall. He had told her that he had lost respect for her, but in truth it was she who had lost respect for him. Their relationship was never the same, though his attempts to salvage it became more and more frantic. Yet, in spite of himself, he did the wrong thing.

"Fine, Herr Stryker," he remembered her saying when he casually mentioned that he would be attending a function with one of the girls his mother had chosen. "She is probably a Nazi, like you."

He had looked at her in surprise. "Well, yes, of course."

It had been the tone in her voice that had caught him off guard. For the first time she had looked with disdain at his uniform.

"Why do you say it like that?"

He closed his eyes and saw the way she had looked when she crossed her arms and glared at him. "I have heard things about your organization, Eric. Things that are not good."

"What have you heard?"

He found out that she had heard a lot. Heard more than his mother, more than the girl he would be dating, more even than most of his friends. The look on her face had stunned him in its disgust and fury.

Stryker picked up the picture and held it in his hands. His eyes blurred slightly.

"But what we are doing is necessary, Rebecca," he had said.

"Ha. What you do is cruel. And you do it to defenseless people for no other reason than your own advantage."

After that it got worse. She refused to have anything to do with him, even to see him. And the more indifference she showed, the more wild he became to regain her love. He began ignoring his social commitments and chased after her, staying in the foyer at concerts he knew she would be attending or standing listlessly outside her apartment until the early morning, waiting like a dog for her to come home. It was disgraceful. His mother said so; even his sister berated him.

And still he could not stop himself.

He had begun to hate himself for his weakness, and in so doing he began to hate her. All summer he pursued her and got nothing but rejections. Finally she had come to him to plead that he leave her alone. Stryker remembered how he had hit her then and forced her onto the bed in his room, tearing at her clothes while she wept, and how afterward she had spit in his face and run out the door. Then she had left Berlin with this fool boy. Pain again racked his midsection as the emotion he fought so hard to control burned its way through his stomach.

He had pursued her all the way to this village; but now he was being recalled. The unfairness of it drove him to desperation. He had to find her and get her back, any way he could.

12

In the castle's music room, Rebecca and the countess had just finished a sonata for four hands.

"Wonderful," the countess exclaimed, speaking in English. She turned on the piano bench and faced Rebecca. "That was so much fun. You really play quite well, Rebecca. Especially for one who spends all her time with popular music."

"Thank you, Maria. I did enjoy that. Sometimes I miss the classical music I was brought up on. I was never good enough to perform professionally, and I guess I drifted into an area that guaranteed me an audience."

Maria smiled. "Well, you must return to it, if only for your own satisfaction. It is nice to have fun, but it is important to be serious sometimes, too, don't you agree?"

"Yes, I suppose so." Rebecca looked down thoughtfully at the keyboard. "It's just that it seems so much of my time has been spent being serious and depressed lately, that I take refuge in the trivial."

"Really?" The countess appeared surprised.

"Why ever should a pretty girl like you feel depressed?"

"It's about what has happened the last few months."

Maria raised her eyebrows knowingly. "Ah, a boyfriend then."

Rebecca sighed, then nodded.

"What a surprise," Maria said dryly.

This time Rebecca shot her a glance and said, "You don't know. You live in a beautiful castle with a handsome count for your husband. You are wealthy, married, and secure."

"Indeed. Well, it was not always this way."

"What do you mean? How long have you lived here, anyway, Maria? And how did you come to know the count?"

"*Ach!* So many questions." Maria slowly closed the lid to the piano keyboard, then stood up and walked over to a chair. "Come here, then, and I will tell you about my own little history, if you like."

Rebecca arose eagerly and went to sit in the chair next to the countess. "Please do. I am very interested."

Maria smiled at her, then touched the tips of her fingers together and looked pensively at the fire. "Well, I come from Russia. When I was a young girl no more than four years old, I was promised to a Russian prince. My parents were aristocrats, but the family fortune was long gone and we were living in genteel poverty. Except it was not very genteel. Many nights were cold in our Moscow suite, and many were the times I was forced to wear clothing that was ragged because my parents had almost no money at all.

"This Russian prince, Andrei Pashenka was his name, was already forty years old when I was born. By the time I was old enough to be brought out into society, he was in his mid-fifties, if you can imagine. Oh, in those days it was not thought improper at all, and many were the perverse old lechers who absconded with young girls and were thought none the worse for it."

"Goodness," Rebecca said, wide-eyed. "I know almost nothing of Russia, but I never imagined it is like that."

"Yes, well, it was," Maria countered, then quickly moved on lest she be questioned about time frames. "So I was married at age fifteen. It was not all bad, you understand. He was quite wealthy, and powerful as well. I moved into a large house in the center of Moscow and my life-style changed immediately. No longer did I have to wear second- or thirdhand clothes. Now I was dressed by the most fashionable seamstresses in the city.

"My meals were no longer meager, either. In fact, I was in danger of becoming quite fat the first year of my marriage, simply because of the abundance of food around me that I had never before seen.

"But also there was the endless round of parties and social events that my peers attended. Everywhere was dancing, laughter, and gaiety."

"This was before the revolution, obviously," Rebecca said frowning.

Maria shot her a glance, then looked back at the fire. "Yes," she said, then moved on quickly. "As I was saying, my life was quite pampered. There was only one thing amiss."

"Your old husband?" Rebecca giggled.

"Quite. I would go out to a ball or a party and dance with young men all evening long, then have to come home and crawl into bed with him. It was quite horrifying. Whenever he touched me I shivered, and when he made love to me, well, you can imagine what I went through.

"This went on for almost five years. I used to pray every night that I would wake to find him dead in the morning, but each new day he was as alive and healthy as the previous one.

"I am a woman who needs to be loved by one who knows how to love, Rebecca. I did not know this about myself when I was married, of course. Who would at such a tender young age? I was a bird in a cage until then." Maria snorted a cynical little laugh. "And of course my husband did not help me to realize my needs.

"Then one night, after an argument with my husband, I went off to a ball at the palace of the czar. It was a fabulous event, I tell you. Everyone was there. By rights I should have gone with old Andrei, of course. By the way, that is what I called him: old Andrei. But he refused, saying he did not feel up to it.

"I told everyone he was sick and got many a sympathetic glance from the ladies who were my friends. Angry and frustrated, I drank a wee bit too much. I was light, happy, and effusive. In fact, I dare say I must have generated enough attention toward myself to be nearly scandalous. After all, a young woman out without her husband was considered to be fair game among the rogues of the day.

"There was a certain rogue who charmed me,

too, I'm afraid. His name was Zivon Stasio, and he was visiting with his brother in Moscow. He was a magnificent dancer and dangerously good-looking, and I kept dancing with him until I raised more than a few eyebrows.

"The next day Andrei heard about it and was furious. He forbade me to leave the house, nearly locking me in my rooms. By now I was twenty-one and not willing to be treated like a child anymore. I made up my mind then and there to have an affair."

She looked at Rebecca again. "Oh, I can see that you think me horrible, Rebecca."

"No, not at all," Rebecca said. "You were in a horrible position is all. I can understand."

Maria nodded and stroked Rebecca's hand lightly once. "You are so good and kind. Anyway, a terrible blizzard hit, practically shutting down the whole city, and there was nothing for me to do for most of January that year, so I stayed home and sulked. Not until the first of March did I leave the house, and by then I was nearly wild to get out. I called on a good friend of mine, a young woman who like myself was married to an older man. We used to laugh at our husbands with each other over tea and tell the worst stories about them. She was the only one who kept me sane.

"Well, when I got to her house, who should be there but Zivon. She had set the whole thing up for me. As a dare, I often thought afterward, because she had gone out and sent the servants away, leaving the house empty for me. I went inside quite innocently and saw him standing by the fire.

"I was surprised to see him, though pleased. But I was frightened when I realized I was in the house alone with him. I did not know whether to be angry at my friend or to thank her.

"He came straight to me and kissed me, and I tell you, Rebecca, as soon as I felt his arms around me, I knew I was going to make love with him. It was that simple.

"In no time we were the subject of a great deal of sordid gossip. All of which, I am happy to say, was true. But once again word got back to Andrei, and this time he was apoplectic. He hit me, threatened to kill me, and promised he would kill Zivon.

"I hated him after he hit me," Maria said. She paused for the first time. "I decided to leave him. It was not easy, mind you, to run away from your husband. Especially since he was a very rich and powerful prince. I had to plan for a whole month and steal enough money from the house account to do it. But I was determined, and one night in early April I left the house with the expressed intent of going to a party. I never returned.

"Zivon was waiting for me with a buggy, and he took me immediately to the train station. We caught a midnight train from Moscow and headed west."

Rebecca sat back in her chair. "Goodness, Maria," she said. "What a story! But what happened to Zivon? And how did you end up here?"

Maria waved a hand in the air. "Zivon, unfortunately, was more in love with new love than current love. He left me in Kraków. It was there that I met Gregor. I was penniless and had to fend for myself, and Gregor came to my rescue."

"Oh, so you knew Gregor before you met Alexander. Was he your servant there as well?"

Maria smiled sadly and looked deep into Rebecca's eyes. She casually brushed back a lock of Rebecca's hair and said, "Rebecca, some things are very complicated, do you understand?"

Rebecca's eyes grew wide. "You mean, you and Gregor . . ."

Maria nodded. "He became my lover in Kraków. The terrible winter was not over yet, that year. A late snowstorm hit the city, and with no money I was forced out of the hotel where I had been staying. I was alone, walking the streets with my bundle of clothing in my hand and searching for shelter. Gregor found me after dark, huddled in a corner behind a store, and took me to his house. He fed me and put me to bed, never threatening or even behaving badly, if you know what I mean."

Rebecca nodded, her lips parted.

Maria sighed and leaned back in the chair. "I stayed with him there, and his love filled me with new hope. We were happy there. Perhaps we should never have left."

"But Maria, why did you? I mean, not that you and Alexander, that is, Alexander is so stunning I could see why . . ."

Maria smiled. "He thinks you're stunning, too."

"Oh. No. I didn't mean it like that." Rebecca blushed furiously.

But Maria could see that the girl was flattered nonetheless. She went on. "We were forced to leave Kraków when a series of small wars overtook the area."

"Small wars? I guess my European history is not as good as I thought. I cannot remember studying any small wars in Poland this century."

"We made our way quite by chance to Budapest. Not unlike you, I suppose." Maria watched Rebecca's face carefully to see what effect her statement and its implications might have. She was interested and amused to see a flash of worry cross Rebecca's face. She went on quickly. "And that is where I met Alexander. One look at him and I knew I was going no farther."

"Yes, I can see why," Rebecca muttered without thinking. "But what about Gregor? He stayed here with you and the count?"

Maria nodded. "He loves me," she said simply.

"Maria! How do they live here, both in love with you?"

Maria smiled again, pretending not to have heard. "So you see, I too have had at least a small amount of hardship. I am not completely unaware of what we women have to suffer from time to time."

"Oh, Maria, you are so right. I am sorry I was so presumptuous about your past. You have had a difficult time. But with a happy ending, at least. With two men in love with you, I envy you. I would that my ending were so happy."

"But it surely can be," Maria said, indulging in irony.

Rebecca missed the subtle tone in Maria's voice and shook her head, staring at the floor. "I'm not so sure. There is a man. A very bad man who is chasing me. I am afraid of him."

"He chased you this far? From Berlin?"

"Yes, Berlin."

"Is that where you met Richard, Rebecca?"

Rebecca nodded. "I came over to study at the university. I met Eric there, and we . . . well, we had an affair. Anyway, it did not last. Eric is cruel and heartless."

Maria listened carefully. "Sometimes the most fascinating men are," she murmured.

"Yes, it's true, isn't it? Perhaps that is why I was drawn to him. He was handsome and self-confident, but really with an incredible ego. When I got to know him well, I was appalled. Appalled and revolted. I left him."

"I understand."

"He came here this afternoon while you were out. I am afraid he will come back. He is threatening Richard and myself, and even you. I so regret bringing this upon you."

Maria smiled again and held Rebecca's hand. "Do not fear for us, Rebecca. We can take care of anyone who comes here. You are quite safe with us. We will not let anyone harm you."

Rebecca looked up at her with tears in her eyes. "Oh, Maria, that is so kind of you. But he is very bad, and he has a great deal of power. He is a Nazi, you see. He is obsessed with me, even to the point of threatening to kill Richard. That is why I made us flee."

"In Berlin he has power, perhaps. Here he does not. You must trust us to take care of you. He will not harm you, or Richard either. When Richard returns from the village," she added.

Rebecca wiped a tear from her cheek. "I am worried about Richard, though, Maria. Very worried. He would not be in this mess if it was not for me, and he is no match for Eric's ruthlessness. Richard is good, Maria, and I love him very much. I am very worried that he has not returned. Do you think he is all right?"

Maria stood and drew Rebecca to her feet.

"Yes, Rebecca, Richard is fine. Do not worry about him. We will look after both of you."

"But where is he, Maria? Why doesn't he come back to me?"

"He is probably having a little difficulty sending a message to his family in America. You must remember we are rather isolated here. Now you must relax and know this Eric will harm neither you nor Richard, now or ever. And it will be you, not him, who controls the outcome of this contest."

Rebecca looked at her hopefully. "Really?"

"Yes, dear. Now relax. Nothing can harm you here. Tonight we will play. We shall have a masquerade. Go now to your room and have a bath. I have asked Gregor to lay out a costume for you."

Rebecca nodded. "Yes, that will be fun. But you are certain Richard will be all right?"

"Richard will be as safe as if he were here in the castle. As safe as you are."

Rebecca threw her arms around Maria and hugged her. "Thank you. I feel better already. And as soon as Richard returns I will be completely happy."

Maria smiled. "Go get ready for dinner, Rebecca. You must be happy now, and we will do our best to make this evening very special for you."

"Thank you, Maria," Rebecca said, and walked out of the room.

Maria watched Rebecca go, her mouth parted slightly while she rubbed the sharp point of her teeth over her lower lip.

✳

13

Maria slipped into the room quietly and closed the door behind her. Alexander was already at the wall, peering through the small hole into Rebecca's bedroom.

"Is Rebecca in there?" she asked. "I sent her up for a bath and told her to change for dinner. I made her think we occasionally dress up for dinner in masquerade. She agreed; I think she liked the idea. Her costume is laid out on the bed."

"Yes, she came in a minute ago. She liked the dress you put out, but she has not tried it on yet."

The countess smirked a little. "You mean she is not in front of the mirror?"

"She moves back and forth. Would you like to see?"

"Is it more exciting to spy on her than to have her?"

"One does not exclude the other. Sometimes I think you enjoy the conspiracy as much as I, my dear."

Now the countess wore a very tiny smile. "Perhaps more so."

The count looked at her without moving his head. Then he jerked his eyes back as Rebecca walked through the circle of view afforded by the small hole in the wall. She was wrapped in a towel and brushing her hair. When she got to the mirror she stopped and looked into it, then dropped the towel around her ankles. She looked at her own reflection in fascination for several seconds, then walked out of view again.

"You enjoy it all, my dear. But why do you allow all the young men to die?" he asked as Rebecca disappeared. He turned to his wife.

She shrugged her shoulders. "They want me too much. And anyway, if they cannot become one of us, they might as well die."

"Except for Gregor."

Her eyes flashed angrily for just a moment. "Gregor is my responsibility. I will take care of him, and he will live as long as I do."

"Have you decided how long that is?"

"No." She forced a smile. "Let us not talk of such things now. It is exciting, don't you think, that we are this close to having her join us?"

"Yes, I do."

"She will make a good vampire, Alexander. I'm certain of it."

He considered that while he glanced through the hole. Rebecca was still out of the line of his vision.

"She did not want her wine," the countess said after a minute.

"Really?"

"I shamed her into taking a little, but when she

thought I was not looking, she poured it into a plant." She watched her husband carefully.

"There was a Nazi officer here today," he said.

"Yes, she told me downstairs. It was her ex-lover."

"I suspected as much. I went to the village." He told her about the photographs and the letter he had found.

"She told me his name is Eric," Maria said. "It would appear this Eric is quite obsessed with our Rebecca."

"What does she feel for him?"

"Nothing."

"Nothing?"

"I am quite sure of it."

"Perhaps she can do away with him, then. He could be her first kill once she has come out of the cocoon."

Maria considered that. "It could be dangerous."

Alexander shrugged. "He asked to speak with us," he said, going on.

"Will he return this evening?"

"I sent Gregor off to destroy the bridge. The wolves will keep them from trying to repair it in the middle of the night."

She approved. "Good. That will give us at least until tomorrow night."

"Gregor told me she was very heavy this morning. He heard her get out of bed; she could barely move. That means she almost turned last night. Most exceptional."

"Yet she is walking tonight," his wife said.

"Yes. Like Denyse, Rebecca is very strong."

"Denyse graced our hallway quite nicely," the countess said, staring at him. "Rebecca will as well."

"Yes, she will."

"Like all the others."

"Yes, like all the others we have had and will always have."

"Forever?"

The count sighed. "Legend has it otherwise. Nothing's forever. Not even the life of a vampire. The Black Prince warned of betrayal."

"This one will not be the one to betray you, my darling. And you'll see, she will also grace our hallway, of her own choosing."

He smiled. "She will look good there, don't you think?"

"Yes, I do. Sometimes I think a male would as well."

The count frowned but said nothing, and for a minute they stood in silence. He stared down at his wife, suddenly wanting her. It was of course mad to have made her a vampire, he thought for the thousandth time.

The countess suddenly looked up at him, her mood changed. "You must do it to her again tonight, of course."

He looked into her beautiful face, her brilliant eyes. He nodded slowly. "But the wine . . ."

"Why, count," she said teasingly. "Do you think it is only wine that sends these girls to you? How modest you are."

Rebecca walked back past the spy hole, and the count turned to look at her. To his delight he saw that she was nude. She picked up the dress Maria had laid out for her and tried it on. She looked in the mirror with it on, then slipped out of it and went into the adjoining art deco bathroom and shut the door behind her.

The countess spoke over his shoulder. "Do you have a plan?"

"I do not. However, you . . ."

"I cannot do it, Alexander."

His mood lightened. "I want you to go in there," he said. "There's something I want you to tell her."

Rebecca sat in the hot water, luxuriating. The bathroom was very warm and humid, and steam rose heavily from the bathtub-on-legs. That's what it was to Rebecca. She even called it that.

She liked to sit in the hot water until it was almost more than she could stand, and then rise slowly, watching her body in the mirror, exuding steam and covered with bubbles. Then she would sigh and slip back into the warmth, allowing one leg to stay above the waterline.

She thought about Richard and what the countess had told her, and she frowned. It was really very inconsiderate for him to have gone into the village and not at least to have tried to wake her. When they got back to America, she was going to have to rethink this entire relationship.

The count loomed up from somewhere in her mind and Rebecca remembered her dream. It did not trouble her as much as it had earlier. She considered it for a moment and laughed at herself for worrying.

Then she sighed and thought about the costume dress in the bedroom. It really was a beautiful dress. For a moment she regretted being born in the twentieth century. Things were really much more romantic in the previous one.

It's amazing how the water does not seem to cool off. Rebecca put her arms on the sides and pulled herself up to her knees. As she got to her feet, the door opened and the countess walked in, smiling.

"Hello, is everything all right?"

"Oh! Yes, Countess Maria," Rebecca said, suddenly shy. "Thank you."

The countess closed the door behind her. "You look like a goddess dressed in foam," she said, and laughed.

Rebecca laughed also. "I don't feel like one," she said, and immediately wondered why she had said that.

"No. You are as beautiful as a goddess. But you are getting out? Let me get you a towel." The countess pulled a heavy red Turkish towel from a rack and held the corners open. Self-consciously, Rebecca stepped into it as the countess wrapped it around her.

Rebecca took the corners, and the countess backed away from her.

"Did you like the Victorian dress, Rebecca?"

"Oh, yes, thank you very much," Rebecca said. She began to dry herself with the towel, reveling in the sensuous feeling of the rough material on her skin.

The countess leaned against the wall and watched her. "I'm very glad. It is an old dress, really. Authentic. It belonged to . . . my grandmother."

Rebecca stopped drying herself and looked at the countess wide-eyed. "Really? I'm afraid to try it on!"

The countess stared at her for the briefest of moments, knowing that Rebecca had, in fact, already tried it on. Then her expression became happy.

"Nonsense," she said. "It will look wonderful

on you, and the old dear had hundreds of gowns. The count is already getting into his clothes, and I am about to go up and do the same. I just wanted to make certain everything was all right here."

Maria's eyes looked downward for a second, and Rebecca suddenly realized that she had allowed the towel to fall open. She blushed and quickly began drying herself again.

"There's something you must know, Rebecca," Maria said.

Rebecca stopped rubbing the towel across her pink skin and looked at Maria. "Yes?"

"Alexander has told me some news about Richard."

"Oh, what is it? Is Richard all right?"

"Richard has had to go on without you, my dear. Only for a little while. He promised to return as soon as possible."

"But that's impossible! He would never leave me here!" Rebecca's lips began to tremble.

"I'm afraid it is true. Your other . . . admirer, Eric, apparently nearly caught up with him in the village today, and he was forced to leave in a hurry. I wanted you to know."

"Oh, Maria! What am I to do?" Rebecca wailed.

"Do not be afraid, Rebecca. It will be all right. You must stay with us until the danger has passed. Until Eric has returned to Germany. He will not be able to stay away long, will he?"

Rebecca frowned. "No, I suppose not," she said slowly.

"Then stay with us for the next day or two, and we will help you get home. You will be safest with us here, and then you can return. In a day or so," Maria said again, watching Rebecca's face for her acquiescence.

"But Richard . . ." Rebecca said again. She sat down on a stool and shook her head. "I would never have believed that he would just leave me here."

"Do not blame him too much, Rebecca. He was under great pressure."

"But he left me!"

"I know. But you are among friends, and you can return home soon. You will see him again, I promise."

"You seem to know so much, Maria. You speak with such confidence that sometimes I almost think you can foretell the future."

Maria saw that Rebecca wanted to believe. She smiled. "Perhaps I can, at least sometimes. Like now."

Rebecca stared into Maria's eyes and felt a rush of warmth and serenity flow into her from those dark pools. She felt comforted. "Yes, I think maybe you can," she said.

"Meet us in the drawing room, dear," Maria said as she backed through the door. "It is to your right when you reach the great hall."

"All right," Rebecca responded. "That is what I will do. I'll meet you in the drawing room. To my right."

"She'll be finding the photographs now," the countess said.

Her husband was pulling his tie tight. "What do you think she'll do?"

Maria laced up her gown and pretended to think for a moment. "She'll be alone in the room. Her eyes will get very wide when she realizes what she sees on the wall. I would guess she might even blush."

"Really? She's a little tiger, you know."

"She maintains the illusion of modesty to herself."

"You know her quite well."

Maria smiled, lost in thought. "It will be number four that gets her."

Gregor had handed Rebecca a glass of wine as soon as she entered the room. She had thanked him, then turned away from him. After a minute she heard the door close, and when she looked he was gone.

She sniffed at the wine. Her headache was gone, and it did smell delicious. She took a small sip. It made her feel so comforted! Rebecca spun gracefully in a full circle, enjoying the way the crinoline petticoats felt under the gown, remembering how the low-cut bodice had looked in the mirror. She had been very pleased with the way her breasts fit into it.

She took another tiny sip. Then she put down the glass and looked around the empty room. For a moment she thought about the Victorians. She decided they were a perverse lot. Perverse but somehow very exciting.

The count knew what to do without having to be told.

Where did that come from? Rebecca spun around, found her wine glass, and drank from it.

She reminded herself solemnly, *I am not going to get drunk tonight.* She took one more sip, then very deliberately placed the goblet on a table and walked away from it. Her heart was pounding in her chest. She tried taking a deep breath, but even that was difficult in the tight dress. To calm herself, she decided to examine the room.

Like the others, it was fabulous. The rich mahogany paneling rose fifteen feet to the ceiling. The four walls were covered with beautiful fresco paintings of hunting. Below were at least two hundred photographs, handsomely mounted and hung all around. Rebecca stepped to the right of the door and looked at the first of them.

It was a picture of the countess. Except it was not the countess. It was a young girl who looked like the countess, Rebecca realized. The girl was smiling, the look on her face very suggestive. She was wearing a peasant blouse that fell forward to expose most of her cleavage, and a wide skirt that she held above her knees. Rebecca studied it for a minute, then stepped to her right and looked at the next picture.

This time the same girl was standing in front of a stone wall. Her clothes were torn and she was almost completely exposed, but she stood staring defiantly at the camera. The look was intriguing, and Rebecca stood still for another minute or two, studying it.

The third picture along the wall was undeniably of the count and countess. They stood in front of the castle entrance, obviously posing for the camera. It seemed very amateurish, and Rebecca moved on.

The fourth picture made her catch her breath. This time it was a picture of a woman, stripped and hanging by her arms. A man stood in front of her with a whip. He was naked from the waist up, wearing only a pair of tight black trousers. Rebecca looked at him, caught the play of the light on his broad shoulders, his heavy biceps. Her eyes moved to the woman, beheld the way the woman's nakedness was captured on film in

perfect form, the shadows accentuating her voluptuousness.

Rebecca reached for the glass of wine without
thinking and took a deep swallow. For a moment
she had imagined herself hanging naked in front
of a man.

No. The pedestal for me.

She took another sip of the wine. Then she put
it down. She wasn't drunk now. Relaxed, yes.
Happy. Not drunk. Rebecca looked back at the
photograph.

Behind her the door swung open. "Here you
are!" the countess said.

Rebecca turned and watched her come into the
room. The countess looked stunning in her full-
length Russian gown. Her figure showed well in
the tight, low-cut dress. Rebecca bowed playfully
but found that she had a bit of trouble standing
up again.

Gregor appeared with a silver tray, two goblets,
and pâté. The countess took a glass from him and
he presented the tray to Rebecca. Rebecca took an
hors d'óeuvre and sampled it.

The countess did not have any, saying, "I must
watch my figure or I shall never get into this gown
again."

Rebecca looked at her. Her long neck was
presented exquisitely, tapering into the small
chest that was almost completely bare. The gown
she wore was so deep that almost all of her
breasts were exposed, and Rebecca could not help
but wonder if her nipples might pop out from
under the laced top at any moment. The light
made her seem almost aglow.

"Do you like it, Rebecca?" the countess said.

Rebecca nodded. "Yes, your gown is lovely."

Maria smiled. "Thank you," she said.

She looked at the wall next to where Rebecca was standing. "Did you enjoy our photographs, Rebecca?"

Rebecca was determined to be sophisticated. "Yes, Maria, but really, who posed for these shots? They're quite risqué."

The countess looked at her. She put her hand on Rebecca's cheek and bent forward slightly. Rebecca swallowed nervously as the countess kissed her lightly on the lips. "You do look so lovely in that dress. Are you certain you were not the grand duchess of Russia, perhaps? In your last life."

Rebecca bowed. "Actually, I was Catherine the Great."

"Really? She was very risqué, you know."

Rebecca's face burned. "Actually, I just meant that I was royalty. It was only a joke."

The countess smiled.

Rebecca felt silly, stupid, naive. She took another sip from her goblet, forgetting that she had promised herself not to drink too much that evening.

14

The count was upstairs, dressing slowly. As a rule he did not much enjoy masquerades, but he respected his wife's unfailing intuition in these matters. Anyway, the girl looked stunning in the gown. She had been pretty to start with and was rapidly becoming a real beauty. Maria could recognize potential; there was no doubt about that.

He considered the evening ahead and found himself bemused at what would happen if they were successful. Of course, if they were not successful it would be tantamount to rape, but he hoped it would not come to that. He frowned and shook his head. It had only happened like that once. Terrible it had been. When the girl found out what it all meant, she had been so shocked that she had killed herself, breaking a goblet and jabbing a shard of broken glass into her neck.

Maria was right; this girl would not be allowed to leave here, but it should not have to be that way, no matter how necessary. It occurred to him that from what they had learned of her character so far, the journey from mortal to vampire might not be a long one for her. He remembered last night. She certainly was a lusty young wench. He smiled at his own description. Wench, or whatever it was they called such girls these days.

He thought again of the German officer who had come to the castle, and he shook his head. This century was certainly different from what he had been used to. No commoner would have dared come to the castle of a count with such arrogance in times past, and certainly not one from another country. He had always been able to do whatever he wanted, whenever he wanted, and to whomever he wanted.

His fingers found the last button on his shirt, and then he picked up the white bow tie and began to weave it under his collar.

His thoughts turned backward to the other girls. At first Maria had been wildly jealous. Angry and insecure enough to allow them to die. They had many a row about it! She, refusing at first to believe the necessity, chose rather to believe that it was his own personal fantasy.

He stopped and looked out the window at the moon.

Perhaps it is just a fantasy.

Fantasy or not, it was the only way their kind could reproduce, such as it was.

Carrying on the species is the unequivocal push of all things. Even for vampires.

His eyes fell from the moon to the garden, where Denyse stood silently on her pedestal. He had feigned indifference earlier to his wife (who of course was not fooled—the entire dreamscape had proved that!) when he had pretended not even to recall the girl's name. For whom had he done that? Was it because he had seen Maria earlier in the garden staring up at Denyse, a tear on her cheek?

The count knew that Maria grew tired of the game. It worried him and also made him sad. Charlotte had helped him make Maria more than two hundred years ago, giving herself over after it was done. The strain of being a vampire was too much for some women, he thought. Charlotte had been his second countess, Maria his third. Elizabeth had been the first, so long ago that he could no longer recall her face, even with his acute vampire mind. More than five hundred years of it in all, and still he did not want it to stop. His pleasure in it was the ability to enforce his will. And yet there were times when even he could not avoid the questions of limitless age.

With the life of a normal human, the questions of life become more layered, more complex with age. With a vampire, those questions continued to increase in paradox and in hypothesis.

"If depth comes with age and the repetition of the same questions, and of course it does," he muttered out loud, "then with centuries of life experience comes a depth beyond imagination. Terrifying depth of the self. Perhaps a character so developed that cynicism and hope are not even relevant. Or perhaps I am just growing morbid.

"Still, how can I exist so long while no one else can?"

The thought challenged him, even threatened him. He relegated it to the darkest corner of his mind from which it had come and turned deliberately to the safety of lust. It was lust that kept him free of the madness that stalked all vampires. So he put philosophy out of his mind and thought again of the pretty young girl, Denyse.

She had been so full of life and energy, eager to take both of them on. Many a night they had played together, carefully at first, because in spite of themselves they had both loved her and did not want to take advantage of her.

Amazingly, it was Denyse who had gradually taken the lead and encouraged them onward, even when they tried to back away. Finally the count had not been able to stand it anymore. He and Maria had gone to her nervously to explain the secret, but to their surprise Denyse had winked and insisted they try, without a moment's hesitation. They had really hoped the transformation to vampire from human would work with her.

But that had been almost ten years ago, and Denyse had never come out of it. The count thought again of Maria, standing in the garden staring up at Denyse, and wondered what she had been thinking. Curious how after two hundred years a husband still could not always tell what was going through his wife's mind.

He finished tying the bow tie and thought of the other girls whom they had tried to make into vampires. Only one had actually survived the ordeal, a pretty young thing named Clarisse. They had found her in a girl's school in Prague and lured her away, promising her all sorts of things. She had gone for it, too, and made it through to the other side. It had given them both a strange sort of joy, having her there, their daughter of sorts.

Daughter and other.

She was willful. Went out on her own and was

caught by a band of gypsies, who bound her in chains so heavy even her vampire's strength could not free her. He could still hear the terrible screams when the sun had come up and scorched her to death.

They had not tried again after that for nearly half a century, content to let their playmates die the peaceful death. It took a strong will to survive the cocoon. A strong will and luck.

His thought returned to Denyse. It had been tragic when Denyse's cocoon had cracked. If the cocoon cracked before it was time, the result was an agonizing death. He had not told Maria, but he watched it happen by himself, gauging the progress of the spreading crack day by day.

You're becoming maudlin.

Whenever he became depressed it was usually Maria who brought him out of it. His need for her had been paramount since the night he first met her. She had entered his existence at a time when he had begun to question it. Charlotte had seen it in him and encouraged him to find another woman whom he could "turn."

Charlotte had been understanding. Understanding and ready to die herself. Perhaps it was the only salvation for a vampire, he thought, the wish to die.

In which case there is no salvation for me.

Again he turned his thoughts away from such inwardly spiraling depression. He remembered how he had first met Maria, and how when he seduced her and explained everything, she had agreed.

"With one condition," she had said, staring up at him with her beautiful eyes and presenting that incredible body (incredible even before it became that of a vampire) to him.

He remembered how he had stared at her warily. "What is your condition?"

"That Gregor is not left alone."

He had agreed, convincing himself that a non-vampire who could be trusted would be an asset. And Gregor had performed as required. But part of Maria's love was reserved for the man, Alexander knew, even though he often tried to deny it. There were times when he had seriously considered killing Gregor just so he would not have to stare into those judgmental eyes. But Maria would have left him instantly, of that he was certain, even if it meant her own death. So he had never carried out his desire to be rid of Gregor, though it had been a thorn in his side for two hundred years. The only good that came out of sharing his castle and wife with Gregor had been that he knew how much it pained Gregor to watch Maria with himself.

Alexander chuckled.

He remembered Maria in the cocoon. She had gone through it fairly easily, all things considered. It had frightened her, knowing what was coming and then waiting to be rid of the shell, but he had explained to her that there was no other way. She had demanded to know everything before she started, no matter how unpleasant. And insisted and argued and forced him to tell her every minute detail of how he had become a vampire. Explaining to her had been painful, especially because he had to explain his ultimate humiliation from his vampire father, the Black Prince.

He thought of the Black Prince. How little he

knew of him, except what he had been told. That his father's time stretched back five centuries before his own began. A prince by birth, he had carved out a small empire in eastern Europe at a time when even the church hid in fear of such evil. The Black Prince, as he was called, had lived in this very castle. Alexander had been brought to him as a teenager, an orphan when his father had been killed by the Black Prince.

He looked out the front window now, letting his mind drift back to that day.

Alexander had walked into the great hall of the castle, which had belonged to his very own real father, and his legs trembled as he beheld its new owner. The Black Prince had stared down at him, regarding the boy with a curious expression.

"Your name, boy," the large man had said. The hangers-on who lined the hall became silent, waiting to see how the conquered dead man's son would answer.

"I am"—he swallowed hard—"Count Viroslav."

"Count Viroslav is dead." The eyes, full of power and mystery, had probed him like flashes of lightning.

"My father was killed by you. I retain his title. And"—he took a huge chance—"rightful claim to these lands and this castle."

The men and women in the hall had gasped collectively, but a smile had played on the lips of the Black Prince. He nodded thoughtfully.

"In that case, Count Viroslav," he had said, "we appreciate your allowing us the use of it."

There was an explosion of laughter all around him. Alexander felt his ears burn, but he looked bravely into the eyes of the Black Prince and the babble around him faded away. The conqueror held him with his eyes, and surprisingly Alexander's fear dropped away.

For several seconds he stayed, now entranced with this personification of power, and then the Black Prince dropped the gaze and turned to his left. Alexander blinked heavily, turned his eyes also, and saw the prince's consort for the first time.

The impression was lasting. She was not as beautiful as he had imagined she would be, though she certainly was not ugly. She was tall, well built, and strong, a woman who would be able to swing a broadsword if necessary and, by appearances, would not hesitate to do so.

Her presence was at once sensual and maternal, erotic yet nurturing. Alexander had never imagined a woman like her. Realizing his jaw hung open, he quickly shut it.

"Perhaps, young count," the Black Prince had said, studying the look on Alexander's face, "you might take dinner with us? There is much to discuss." With that he had taken the woman's arm and gone into the dining hall. The wave of people surrounding him parted, and Alexander followed on their heels.

The room filled quickly with people, and a musician standing in the corner began to play a guitar and sing. A jester jumped out of the back and began doing handstands across the floor. Laughter and talk filled the room, and servants, his father's servants, stepped forward with candles to light up every corner, making the room festive. Alexander stood still for a moment, amazed at the transformation and disturbed at how quickly the place had ceased to become the home he had known. It had been the consort who stepped in at that moment. She took his arm and led him around to the head of the table. She sat down next to the prince and indicated that he should sit on her left.

"Count," the Black Prince said, "this lovely woman is the lady Alicia. What do you think of her?"

Alexander smiled nervously at her. Her dark hair framed her face, showing off the whiteness of her skin. "She is very nice," he said.

She regarded him with large dark eyes. A suckling pig was brought into the hall and placed in the center of the table. Wine flowed and the mood heightened.

Again Alexander was overwhelmed, but the Black Prince and Lady Alicia were kind, even deferential, and he accepted their solicitude with confused relief.

"Your father was a great warrior, lad," the prince said. "He did himself and your family proud. I myself had great respect for him. It is sad that this world demands sacrifice, but when one gives it with such magnificent style, it is a great honor, and somehow justified."

The Black Prince had then done the unheard-of gesture of raising his goblet and toasting Alexander's father, whom he had just slain!

Alexander had raised his own goblet and drunk his first ever glass of wine. Lady Alicia had smiled at him, and all the court cheered the "fallen hero." They filled and refilled Alexander's glass. She had ensnared him that very first night, coaxing, teasing, flattering him, until flushed with the wine and lost in his innocence and grief, he looked upon her as an angel sent to love and protect him in place of his lost mother.

But of course, even then I knew there was more to my attraction for her than the honest and simple love of a boy for his mother. Seduction is at the heart of this game. It always has been.

He thought backward again, this time deeper.

She had planned it all from the beginning. They had both wanted him to become one of them, and they had made him want it, too. He had stayed in the castle, a ward of the Black Prince, favored among all, privileged, and, in spite of himself, grateful.

Lady Alicia had always found time for him in the evenings, and their friendship became very deep, very quickly. He looked forward all day to the time when he would be able to see her. Night after night he found himself alone with her, and she pulled his secrets, hopes, fears, and wants from him as though they were fishes on strings, and he soon needed her companionship almost desperately.

When had that first illicit kiss come? When had his lips found hers for the very first time, awkwardly, desperately? She had feigned surprise, even shock, but brought him forward all the same, playing him as though he were a musical instrument, allowing the caresses, showing him the way without him even realizing it.

He had thought the prince unaware of his love for Alicia, for the prince was never around in the early evenings. Night after night they were left alone, the prince not returning except for late supper, always smiling, always generous. Alexander had felt guilty and afraid, but he could not stop what was happening.

The count now remembered the first time and almost laughed out loud.

It had been so easy for them. Full of adolescence and youthful exuberance, he had clumsily but with great determination pursued the path to heavenly pleasure, not realizing it would twist and turn and bring him crashing downward to hell.

They had stayed up late, night after night, talking of poetry, love, heroism, and matters of consequence. They took walks in the garden under a full moon, or sat in the windowsill staring down at the shadows on the lawn, or climbed the high turrets.

He had never seen either of them during the daylight hours, and now shook his head, wondering at his own incredible naïveté.

What stupidity. Or perhaps it was just the last innocence I knew.

She had taken him on long flights of fancy and spoken of romance, making it sound real, and seduced him over his fears and awkwardness, making it seem natural and at the same time completely his own doing.

Or undoing.

The clothes she wore over time had changed subtly; so cleverly did she do it that he did not realize that more and more of her wondrous skin was becoming visible to him on those long evenings. Slowly, expertly, she made him desire her beyond caution. She drove him to a fine madness.

Then finally, one night when they were alone in the highest turret, and the moon was full, and the gown she wore seemed to have been painted to her narrow waist, yet cut so low that he could see so much but not quite enough. No, never enough of her. Then he had put his hands on her shoulders and pulled her to him. And she had let him, opening her lips to him and yielding her soft, full mouth.

Their tongues had met, and he had pursued her across her teeth, teeth that were very sharp, and a voice in his mind had tried to warn him, but he had ignored it.

He had wanted her desperately for nearly a full year, lying awake into the dawn night after night, his body on fire, his soul alight. Now at last she was his, and as he kissed her the dress she wore fell away from her body. He tasted her, felt her skin, and smelled her; and wild with passion and far beyond the last semblance of rationality, he slid his hands down the curve of her back as she pressed against him, realizing with surprise that she had worn nothing beneath the dress.

Why would she be naked beneath the dress? Ready for him, even though she had professed surprise at his attentions?

His youthful vanity and raging lust stepped in and shouted down the question, wild with its concept of victory.

She had melted against him and become slack, pulling him down on top of her. She helped him tear his own clothes free, and then spread her legs wide for him. Trembling, he had crawled forward and she had put her arms around his neck and pulled him down into her.

She had controlled him with her eyes, kept him suspended in the rhythm of passion until he could not bear any more, and then she had bitten him on the neck. She sucked his blood viciously, and he had felt himself weaken. Her saliva had felt like fire mixing with his blood, and he had screamed and exploded into her and felt her match him and come with him into the dream world of unimaginable pleasure.

There was more, of course. The count stared at his hands, imagining Maria downstairs with the girl, preparing her. He had never tried to have a "son." Only daughters. A son was too much. He had not wanted to do it, and Maria had never insisted. His own "birth," his own "conception," had been too terrible, too shameful. He frowned, tried to put it from his mind, and found he could not.

He remembered the Black Prince suddenly standing behind him, towering over the youth and his consort.

"Come, my love," Lady Alicia had said. "Let us bring this youth forward, make him one of us!"

In great terror Alexander had felt the presence of the Prince of Darkness and was certain that he would be killed. Slowed by his passionate release, he tried in vain to swim upward, to climb out of his stupor and free himself from her grasp. But she held him to her and her strength was too great.

"No!" he had cried out, feeling the hands on his naked buttocks, pressing, probing.

"No! Please, I beg of you!" he cried out as he felt those hands spreading his buttocks apart.

"Stop! Please!" He shouted and struggled to break free but could not. Tears poured down his cheeks as he realized the Black Prince was kneeling between his legs. He felt the masculine hands groping his own sexual organs.

"No! Never!" He screamed as he felt a finger penetrate his anus. A finger, and then . . . and then the weight coming down on him, the hot, steamy breath on his shoulders, his neck.

The pain had been terrible, but the humiliation worse. Throughout it all he had maintained a denial of the sensation, both the obscene pleasure and then the bite, again the bite on his neck. He had felt his blood being drained and the last of his strength being taken from him.

Count Viroslav stood up, shaking violently with the memory. He bit his own lip with a sharp canine tooth until he felt a cold sweat on his forehead.

The prince had left him soon after, explaining to Alexander that he would become a vampire and telling him he was free to reign in terror of his own choosing.

And he had. Angrily, and for the most part without mercy or regret. As, he told himself, he would continue to do so.

Breathing hard, his hands shaking, he walked out of the room and down the hall toward the stairs, toward the great hall and his wife . . . and toward Rebecca.

15

Maria stepped out into the hallway, momentarily leaving Rebecca alone among the photographs. Her long, flowing gown drifted on the marble floor, and she raised her left arm, letting her fingertips slide along the stone wall as she walked. Gregor, watching her from the shadows, saw her tiny feet barely touch down as she moved, and as always his heart beat quicker upon her approach. When she saw him she stopped and motioned for him to come to her.

"Gregor," she said, "is everything ready for tonight?"

He nodded sullenly.

She frowned. "What is it, Gregor? Why are you morose?"

"Maria, do you know what you are doing?"

"Why, Gregor, of course I know what I am doing," she answered. "Our lovely guest is going to try and make the transition this evening. With luck and our help she will succeed."

"But she does not know what you are planning for her."

"That is unimportant."

"Really? Everyone else had always been told beforehand. You knew before you got into it."

Maria sighed. "We cannot risk it. She cannot be given the choice. It is a different era now. People do not readily accept the supernatural any longer. Even though I think she will be satisfied with what we give her, she is terribly naive and the shock of it might turn her against the experiment. That and the fear of failure. She does not have the sophistication that the rest of us have all had."

"And if you do succeed? What then?" he demanded.

She stroked his chin with the long index finger of her right hand. "Why then, Gregor, Alexander will have a new bride. Do you not realize what that means? It means that I can leave him and go with you at last."

"He will never allow it."

She smiled and shook her head. "You worry over nothing, my love. He wants a new lover, and this one is beautiful, is she not?"

"What if she is? He will still want you. He'll want both of you."

Her face grew serious. "He cannot have both of us. I have told him how I feel."

"What did you say to him, Maria? That you want to leave him and go with me somewhere?"

She withdrew her hand from his cheek. "Not exactly . . ."

"And where will we go? We have lived in this castle for two hundred years," Gregor said, repeating the thoughts that had been fermenting in his mind since he had spoken to Richard in the dungeon.

She shrugged her shoulders. "Where will we go? What a funny question. I do not know where we will go, Gregor." Narrowing her eyes, she peered at him and said, "Do you not *want* to leave here and be with me? Do you not want to have me to yourself?"

He put his arms on her narrow shoulders, luxuriating in the soft, apparent frailty of her body even while knowing that she had twice his strength. "Of course I do, Maria! Have I not waited for a dozen lifetimes for you? I love you more than anything in this world. You know that. Why else would I sit here in this hell, playing servant to *him*, watching you be with *him*, for all these years?"

But Maria did not respond to his impassioned speech. "Well then, Gregor," she said with a trace of irritation. "What is the problem? Tonight Rebecca will be raised to a level of lust and desire she has never known before, the level that is necessary for her to become a vampire. She will go through the cocooning stage, and if all goes well she will come out the other side a full-fledged vampire. When that happens you and I can slip away. It's been done before. My own predecessor—"

Gregor cut her off. "That was a long time ago, Maria. Things have changed. He has changed, and you and I have changed. None of us is human any more, yet the world outside this castle is as human as it ever was! He is a monster, Maria. He wants it all to himself, including you. He has always been that way. He will track us down. And even if we do escape from him, how will we live in this new world?"

"Don't be a coward, Gregor," she said, pushing

him away. "I am not afraid of the world; why should you be?"

"You live as a vampire in a world of fantasy. You do not pay attention to the changes taking place in Europe. Maria, the world out there is shrinking. People cannot just move anywhere they want anymore! There are newspapers that speak of trends, and telephones, and the police are becoming better at hunting down those they want to destroy. How will we deal with this strange new world? It may still be safe to live as a vampire in the crumbling, deserted ruins of eastern Europe, but where else? If we leave here to run from him, where will we go?"

Maria pursed her lips and frowned. "Would you rather stay here with Alexander, then?" she said.

Gregor shook his head. "No, of course not."

Her face softened and she straightened his lapels with her fingers. "Then do not fear, Gregor; we will succeed. Rebecca is young and beautiful and quite capable of sustaining lust, I believe. And when she has made the transition, we will leave. We almost left before, Gregor. Next time we will succeed. Meeting her coming off the train was an omen."

He sighed. "You really believe so, Maria?"

"Yes! It will be as we had planned. Soon, my love, I will be yours entirely, and you mine alone. We will live forever, as we had always planned from the first."

"You mean when he was supposed to make both of us vampires and not just you. That was the agreement originally, in case you have forgotten."

She studied him, and when she spoke it was as

if to a slightly slow child. "Alexander has survived these centuries by strength, Gregor. It is his most endearing quality. He did not believe you could make the transition."

Her condescending manner infuriated him. "That's a lie, Maria! You know it is. I could have made the transition, but he did not want me to make it."

"Perhaps, but it cannot be helped now. We can still live throughout eternity together, Gregor. And it is better that one of us not be a vampire. It is safer that way."

She raised a hand dismissively, not realizing the effect her gesture would have on him. "Now I must be off. I need to study her before Alexander comes down. I will have to travel into her subconscious to see what her secret sexual fantasies are if we are to use them this evening."

"Maria, you mustn't! It is too dangerous. You promised you would never do that again!"

"I must do it. For us to succeed we must know what it is that excites this young woman. Her secret fantasies, desires, things that she would never tell anyone, those we must know and use on her. Alexander cannot do it. Only a woman can, as you very well know. And we must not fail this evening."

"But if you get lost inside her mind, you will cease to be!"

She frowned at him. "Stop it, Gregor. I will do what I will do. Now prepare things for this evening." With that she turned from him and moved away.

Gregor stepped back and watched her walk down the hall. His face was a mask of swirling emotions and fears as he muttered to her retreating form, "You are a perfect vampire, aren't you, Maria? And you will make her one, too." He glanced at the entrance to the dungeon on his right, where Richard still lay bound and helpless. "And then he will become one like me."

Rebecca had moved to the window and was staring out through the large, arched pane into the garden. The full moon was rising, and Rebecca looked at the statue facing the window. A bare arm and shoulder were exposed in the soft light, but the rest of the figure was wrapped in black shadows. The view seemed familiar, but only just. Like seeing an acquaintance from long ago, someone you almost recognized but were unable to place.

Déjà vu, she thought.

For some reason Rebecca wondered whether the statue was a nude.

She shook her head. The truth, she admitted to herself, was that she had been thinking about almost nothing but sex all day long. It must be the dreams she had had last night. They had been so real, so graphic, and they had taken up a very proprietory residence in her mind. She had awakened with her whole body tingling and it had stayed that way. And then there was the dream this afternoon.

The garden! Of course, the garden was in my dream.

Rebecca stared out at it, trying to put the pieces together. It had been extremely erotic. What that meant was unclear, but ever since she had arrived here her mind had been in the gutter. She looked around the room.

Perhaps it is just the romance of this old castle.

But the tingling had become much more than a

pleasant sensation. It had grown into a desperate need. By late afternoon she craved physical attention as never before. Since she had awakened on the steps outside, even being in the same room as another human sent her heart racing and made her skin supersensitive. And the wonderful aches and nearly painful throbbing that continually passed through her breasts and loins made it difficult to concentrate. Earlier, coming out of the bathtub, she had almost been caught touching herself by the countess. And worse, Rebecca thought with a blush, at that very moment she had been tempted to display her own eroticism.

She wanted Richard badly. To make matters worse, she felt abandoned by him.

She picked up a piece of paper and fanned herself with it.

Where was Richard, anyway? Rebecca was becoming cross with him.

And the costume dress did not help much. The bodice cupped her breasts like two hands, and the stiff front went all the way down between her legs, pushing against her lasciviously, keeping her constantly aroused. She took a deep breath and let it out slowly.

Again she saw the photographs in her mind and wondered what it would have been like to be the model. Had they been real? Had it been exciting for the woman to be stripped and bound, naked and helpless in front of the photographer? He must have been her lover, and . . .

What is happening to me! she wondered abruptly.

The countess walked in quietly and stood behind Rebecca, watching her and knowing exactly what was happening. She had not missed the slight awkwardness in the way Rebecca walked, nor the constant flaring of her nostrils and the overly bright eyes. She smiled as she remembered her own change and the cocooning that she herself had gone through.

And of course it had been the same with the others. It was always exciting to watch it happen. But especially to one as beautiful as Rebecca. It was inspiring, the way the change gave such wondrous beauty.

Maria briefly thought of what Gregor had said and frowned again. He doubted her word, and secretly she could not blame him; still it irritated her. It was true that she had not left when any of the other young women had changed, but those times were different. He could not be expected to understand. This time she would leave. Maria put it out of her mind and considered the evening's events.

She had discussed the plan in detail with Alexander as soon as he had returned. According to their plan, he would give them another fifteen or twenty minutes before he came down.

Maria, too, thought of the photographs. They had worked very well indeed. One never knew completely what one person's idea of the erotic might be, but after the dreamscape she was sure Rebecca would be interested in such things. With the right encouragement Rebecca might even be as wild as Denyse. It was always interesting to play the game. In fact, she thought with a momentary sense of ruefulness, it was the only really interesting thing about being a vampire.

Maria brushed a lock of her long black hair back from her face and regarded Rebecca again. The time to peek into Rebecca's unconscious was now. Though she had learned much in the dreamscape earlier, there were certain things that could only be learned when the subject was awake. It was important to know everything before tonight. There must be no chance of failure.

Again she remembered what she had told Gregor, that he should not worry. But though she had acted fearless to him, in truth she knew it was as dangerous as Gregor had said, and the thought of being imprisoned in another's consciousness was very frightening. But there was no choice. Rebecca's total sexuality must be revealed, and then they would be able to drag her into the change, whether she agreed or not. Maria braced herself.

This time I will give Alexander a success that will be total!

With a flick of her tongue she felt the edges of her teeth. The ultrasharp canines were expanding a little as her blood grew warmer.

Maria slowly stopped her breathing. She stood perfectly still and began to concentrate, not moving so much as an eyelash. Soon she became aware of the sound of her own blood rushing through her veins. She blocked it out and immediately became aware of valves opening and closing in her heart. She brought her heartbeat down and listened harder. Gradually her mind cleared and she became aware of other things in the room. After a minute she gathered her forces and began to push herself up and out of her body. She knew she would not be able to sustain it long.

I must hurry.

There was a cockroach under the wallpaper to her right, scratching. She blocked it. Blocked the noise of the wood fibers on the floor settling, blocked the sound of air molecules colliding. The room began to grow dark.

Will pass out soon.

She could hear Rebecca's hair growing. She pushed harder, stretched herself outward across the room. Sudden pain hit her chest. She forced herself to ignore it and continue her search for an entryway into Rebecca's mind. Her sight began to fade as the effort of will robbed energy and strength from every cell in her body.

It had to be there, but she had so very little time. Drawing deeper on her reserves of strength, Maria peered into the metaphysical world surrounding the two of them. Where was Rebecca's secret?

Suddenly there it was, the long narrow pipeline that would take her into Rebecca's mind. It opened up in front of her and she dived quickly into it.

With ease she slid through it. Losing herself, almost forgetting her own identity, becoming . . . Rebecca! Just the tiniest bit of Countess Maria Viroslav remained in her consciousness.

Only two or three more seconds.

She raced through Rebecca's thoughts like a vandal in a library, turning things over and tossing them aside. All at once she saw Richard, then three or four Richards together. A warmth hit her that quickly turned into an intense heat. There was a strong Richard, certain of his righteousness, followed by a nude Richard, then a Richard in knight garb on a white horse and finally a weak, confused Richard.

Something lurked behind the weak Richard.

Though Maria was aware of the danger of staying too long inside the consciousness of another, she also knew that she had not yet found what she had come for. She had to know what it was that Rebecca kept hidden from all others. It was that which would drive Rebecca to the heights necessary for the change to occur. She looked closely, saw it was another figure . . . the count!

Time to go!

It was adultery, then, Maria thought. She saw her husband lurking in the shadowy netherworld of Rebecca's subconscious. The count, seminaked, watched Maria, and then with a smirk he turned and gestured behind himself, and as Maria peered into the swirling light and shadows that glowed with raw excitement, she became aware of shame tinged with curiosity and unbridled passion. A figure danced in those mysterious lights, and when it stepped forward for a moment Maria saw with a jolt that it was herself. She felt the aura of eroticism and reached forward and touched her other thought-self and . . .

Go!

. . . let go, sliding, flying backward across the room, slamming into her body so violently that it knocked her backward, and she collapsed into a chair.

Rebecca opened her eyes wide. She remembered thinking about Richard, wondering why he did not come back. Musing about men, about the count, about the dreams. Strange thoughts, frightening yet uncontrollable and still very exciting.

She realized she had been very aware of the countess. This time it had not been a passing thought. It had been so real and strong that she had shuddered. With a start, she wondered if she was losing the ability to reason.

And then she had known without a doubt that the countess was going to fall backward. Rebecca had turned just in time to see it actually happen, and she put her hand to her mouth in astonishment, fear, and wonder.

"Countess! Maria!" she had said, and raced across the room.

The countess immediately held up her hand, palm out. It was time to begin the next act, to bring Rebecca along. "It's all right, my dear, I'm fine," she said, and displayed a brave smile.

Rebecca knelt beside her, feeling the stiff, wiry fabric of the costume pressing against her. She put a hand to Maria's cheek and looked rapidly from eye to eye. "What happened?" she said.

"I don't know. I was just standing there, thinking how wonderful you looked in that dress, and suddenly I got this strange feeling."

Maria lightly stroked the back of Rebecca's hand, and Rebecca blushed.

The countess lowered her eyes, her face showing her embarrassment. "I felt," she said, and hesitated slightly. "Oh, I don't know. I just felt very happy that you are here tonight."

Rebecca swallowed again. Her body tingled and once again her need grew, and she drifted in the sensuality that swirled between them like the silk petticoats and flowing dresses that they wore.

The countess took a couple of deep breaths. "Oh, that's better," she said. "But these gowns, they are tight, aren't they?"

Rebecca sighed dramatically and rolled her eyes, laughing with her. "Yes, the women in those days really suffered."

"They certainly did. Still," the countess said, looking down at Rebecca's dress, "you must admit they were quite elegant, and if you had the figure for it, you could make quite an entrance at the ball. You could have stopped the orchestra, Rebecca."

Rebecca stared at her. "It's almost as if you had been there," she said.

Maria smiled. "Yes, almost."

For a minute Rebecca could think of nothing to say.

"But tell me," Maria said, breaking the strangely awkward silence and pulling herself to her feet, "what sort of social functions do you have in America?"

Rebecca stood up also. "We have dances, with a band that plays jazz music. Everyone goes and we dance all night long sometimes."

"You must have tired feet at the end. I doubt the young men let you alone, as pretty as you are."

Rebecca smiled.

"Do you have many boyfriends back home contemplating suicide over your self-imposed banishment?"

"Oh no, not really. There's just Richard, right now at least. I came to Europe mostly to get away from a love affair that turned bad."

"Richard is a very lucky boy to have such a beauty as yourself. Believe me, I am an expert in the art of beauty. I know whereof I speak."

Rebecca studied the countess' mannerism. When she had uttered the phrase, she had nodded her head as a very old woman might have. And yet, as Rebecca's eyes consciously followed the graceful neck, delicate chest, and firm young breasts, she could see no signs of age at all. Certainly her face was free of lines and her eyes were smooth and clear. It must be just a cultural oddity, she decided.

"You are very kind, Maria."

The countess heard her husband's footsteps on the stairs but knew that Rebecca had not. "Tell me about Richard," she said suddenly. Her eyes narrowed in comic conspiracy. "Is he good? In bed, I mean?"

Rebecca laughed out loud. Maria was so unpredictable. "He's good," she said. "He gives me pleasure."

"I thought so; in fact, I told the count that!"

Rebecca was shocked. "You did?"

But the countess merely looked surprised by the question. "Why, yes of course, dear. You don't mind that I said that, do you? I certainly would not have mentioned it if I knew that sort of thing bothered you."

Rebecca shook her head quickly, not wishing to appear unsophisticated. "Oh, no. No, not at all."

Now the countess smiled. "Good, darling, because really, sex is a wonderful thing and not to be kept locked up and hidden. Don't you think?"

Rebecca nodded. *If the countess only knew,* she thought, *that sex seems to be all I am capable of thinking about!*

The countess bent her head slightly, hearing the footsteps. "I'll let you in on a secret," she whispered.

Rebecca leaned forward eagerly, enjoying her part in a feminine conspiracy.

"The count sometimes exhausts me."

Rebecca smiled. "Really?"

Maria nodded with comic exaggeration. "Yes. He is magnificent, though. Did you begin young, Rebecca?"

Rebecca bit her lower lip shyly. "I lost my virginity when I was eighteen. Gave it up quite readily to my professor at college."

The countess held Rebecca's hand as though for support, then leaned forward and spoke softly. "Did you have other lovers before that?"

Rebecca blushed and looked at the floor. "What do you mean?" she said.

"Special lovers. Best friend lovers."

"No." Rebecca tried to pull her hand free.

"Really? Not a friend at school?"

Rebecca bit her lip and shook her head, and the countess let go of her hand.

"Most girls do at first." Her face became an expression of curiosity. "I didn't shock you, did I, Rebecca?"

Rebecca took a deep breath. The gown was so tight! It was enclosing her, ensnaring her! Rebecca was suddenly aware of just how much of her breasts were visible above the top of the gown. She was breathing deeply and she felt as though she might fall out of the gown. She shook her head again and answered a little too loudly, "No."

The countess backed away a step and raised an eyebrow.

"I mean, I'm sorry, it's just that we don't usually talk about such things in America. I'm still not used to how things are done in Europe." She put her hand to her chest. Her face felt warm, and it was becoming increasingly difficult to breathe.

"I'm sorry, my dear." The countess shrugged

her shoulders. She heard the count right outside the door. She smiled warmly at Rebecca. "But you and I, we should compare tales of what went on in our girls' schools sometime," she said, and winked merrily. "After the lights went out."

Maria turned toward the door. "Ah, here is the count."

16

The count looked dazzlingly handsome. It was the only way Rebecca could describe him. Tall and debonair in his costume, a mid-century formal suit, he seemed to have stepped out of another more romantic era. She thought of what the countess had told her, that he was a tiger in bed, and sighed. She was vaguely aware that the action caused her breasts to push up to the top of the gown. As he came toward her she imagined what he looked like without any clothes and was at once aware of the center strip of the gown pressing against her.

He reached down to her side and took her hand in his, then lifted it slowly to his lips and kissed it.

"Maria, she looks marvelous in that gown," he said, staring at her. He kept hold of her hand for several seconds, finally lowering it when his wife spoke.

"She is very beautiful. She looks as though it were made for her." Maria smiled mischievously.

"Actually, Rebecca, it is something of a collector's piece. It was made for Catherine the Great," Alexander said.

Rebecca was astonished. "Really? But I thought it was your grandmother's."

"Oh well, I'm afraid Alexander has told my secret. Yes, it was made for that magnificent lover of pleasure. I won't even tell you what we went through to get it here."

"She was quite the one," the count said, and winked at Rebecca behind the back of the countess. "Catherine, I mean."

Rebecca smiled and looked from the count to his wife and back to him.

"She's worried about Richard, Alexander," the countess said, stepping around Rebecca.

"Oh, nothing to worry about, my dear," he said, and shook his head as if it could not be anything but alright. "He's gone to look for a way for the two of you to get out of the country and home. I spoke with him earlier. He wanted to talk to you but was in a hurry, and he asked me to tell you he would be back as soon as he could. He's certainly not in any danger. He'll probably be back tomorrow."

The countess smiled. "There, you see? Nothing to worry about."

"But . . ." Rebecca said. *But what? What can I do but trust them and wait?*

They both looked at her expectantly for a second, and Gregor appeared with glasses.

Maria took one and Alexander did also, but Rebecca shook her head.

"The wine bothered Rebecca last night," Maria said.

"Oh?" The count raised an eyebrow. "Not feeling bad, I hope?"

Rebecca shook her head. "No, I'm fine. It's just

that I think I drank too much last night, and I'm not used to it. I . . . I feel I may have embarrassed myself by getting tipsy."

Alexander and Maria shook their heads in unison and frowned unhappily. "No, of course not," the count said. "We all were having such a nice time. I hope you didn't really think that."

"Well . . ."

"It was one of the most marvelous evenings we've had in a very long time," Maria said. "Really. We feast too extravagantly, Alexander. Poor Rebecca must think we are very wasteful people."

"No, that's not it at all. . . ."

"You see, Rebecca," Alexander said, "the truth is we really do not feast very often at all. Having you here has given us the excuse to celebrate. Soon you will be gone, back to far-off America, and we will return to our quiet ways."

Maria sighed. "Yes, this is probably your last night with us, Rebecca. We just wanted to have a little party and be festive."

They all looked at one another. Rebecca gave in. "Well, of course. I mean, I would not want to be the spoiler. I'd be happy to have some wine," she said, and took the glass from Gregor.

"Marvelous," said the count. "A toast then. To another pleasant evening among friends."

They touched glasses around and they all sipped from their glasses.

Instantly the wine coursed through Rebecca. How wonderful it felt! Its taste was light and fruity, yet very full-bodied. It seemed to spread through her, filling her with warmth and happiness. Rebecca felt as though she glowed. All apprehension flowed out of her, replaced by a feeling of complete and utter well-being.

Rebecca became aware of the sounds of a string quartet. "What is that?" she said.

The count smiled. "Being that we are pretending to be in the nineteenth century, I've hired a small local group to provide some music. They're in the dining room."

"Oh, how nice; I love a string quartet!" Rebecca said.

"Wonderful," said the count. "Shall we, then?"

The three of them joined arms and walked through to the dining room. The table was furnished magnificently. They approached the door and Rebecca turned slightly, pressing against the count as she did so, then walked through the entrance.

The fire was blazing, and there was a candelabra in the center of the table, but otherwise the room was completely dark.

"No electricity one hundred years ago," the count said.

Rebecca's eyes opened wide. "It's very romantic."

They deposited her in her chair. She barely noticed that there were only three places tonight. Rebecca took another sip of wine and looked around the room. She could not see the musicians, but she assumed they were sitting in a dark corner behind her. "It's very mysterious," she said.

The count looked at his wife, then at Rebecca. "Mysterious?"

"Yes." Rebecca nodded. "This castle, the shadows in the room. Are there any ghosts in this castle?"

"Actually, yes," the count said, looking very solemn. "But only one."

"Really?"

"Oh, yes, she was a young girl. Italian. Very beautiful."

"What happened?" Rebecca turned from one to the other.

The count took a sip from his glass and shrugged his shoulders. "Ah, it is sad. She came to the castle on a bitter cold evening."

"When? I mean, what year?"

He was evasive. "A long time ago. Very long. I'm not even quite certain what year it was. But anyway, she had been fleeing a crime. The current lord took her in, but he was very perverse."

"What happened?" Rebecca stared at him.

Alexander smiled and raised his eyebrows, then bent his head toward her as if speaking confidentially. "That count never let her go. He made her his captive, made her submit to him completely."

"No."

"Oh, yes. She had to do all sorts of things. She was not allowed to wear clothes at all except on Wednesdays. Then she had to dress formally and wear so many clothes that she almost suffocated."

"What a strange sense of humor," Rebecca said. "But how did she become a ghost?"

He sat back in his chair and smiled at his wife, then turned back to Rebecca. "Well, as I said, she was nude almost all of the time, and dressed only once a week, most unpleasantly. The count was training her, you see."

"Training her? What a cad!"

"I agree. But it worked, apparently. After awhile she went to him and begged to be allowed to be naked all the time."

"She did?" Rebecca took another sip of wine. The warmth within her grew, but it was not an unpleasant heat. Rather it increased her feeling of eagerness and her enjoyment of the evening. She forgot everything that was happening outside the castle and sat up straight as an unexpected rush of erotic longing passed through her loins.

"The count agreed," Alexander went on, pretending not to notice the flushed cheeks and brightening eyes in Rebecca's face, "but made the stipulation that she would have to receive guests."

"At first it embarrassed her terribly, of course," Maria interjected.

"I should think so!" Rebecca blurted out.

Alexander smiled. "But she came to enjoy it. After that, whenever anyone came to visit, she would have to receive them formally, yet completely naked. Afternoon tea, evening dinner, social events, everything. People began to come from miles around to see the count's beautiful nude."

"Oh, my. Imagine that," Rebecca said, and took another sip. Now it seemed to her that the effect of the wine was changing. Each sip made her skin tingle.

"Then one day a young man came to the castle. The girl fell in love with him as soon as she saw him coming up the drive, and for the first time her modesty overcame her. Before going down to greet him, she put on her clothes again."

Alexander leaned across the table toward Rebecca until his face was only inches from hers. His voice raised slightly as he continued the story. "The count, of course, realized right away that she was being unfaithful to him, if not in body then certainly in her heart, and he was furious. He ordered her stripped in front of the young man. The servants grabbed her arms, and the head butler performed the task, tearing the clothes from her!''

Rebecca swallowed hard and shook her head. In her mind she saw the young girl being held in the strong arms of handsome young men, clothes being torn to shreds.

''When the young man saw what was happening, he ran from the castle. She was heartbroken and climbed to the highest turret, the west one, and jumped from it. Now it's said that she still roams the castle, completely naked, and comforts lonely guests.''

Rebecca was breathing hard. ''Is that really the legend?'' she said.

''Yes, but only a legend,'' the countess said with a smile. ''I have never seen her, and personally I don't think she exists.''

''There are other legends about these walls,'' the count volunteered.

''Oh, but they're all just stories that young counts tell themselves.''

Rebecca looked at Maria and caught her wink. She laughed. ''Like what?''

''Well, this has to do with your gown,'' the countess said. ''According to one legend, Catherine the Great came to this hall to hold a secret meeting with the king of France. Here in this room they discussed the foreign policies of their respective nations. Anyway, they talked long into the night and apparently got along quite well. When they had eaten and drunk a great deal, she dismissed all the ministers, aides, and servants and shut the door.''

The countess stood up and walked dramatically to the fireplace. ''She came here and turned toward the king and said, 'Much can be done when two leaders know each other well.' "

Maria frowned majestically, then clowning, bobbed her eyebrows up and down lasciviously. "The king," she said, "being somewhat lecherous and quite taken with Catherine, answered that he would like to know her very well. Well, she crawled up onto the table and lifted the bottom of that dress you're wearing and told him to show her how much."

Rebecca's mouth was open, and now she saw the queen of Russia baring herself to another person of royalty. A maddening heat gathered between her legs.

The count was laughing, and finally realizing she was being teased, Rebecca laughed along with him.

"Go on, Rebecca," he said. "Ask her how much."

Rebecca looked from him to Maria. "How much?"

"About twelve inches, as the story goes. But, of course, that may have been embellished a bit. Nonetheless, there was no war between Russia and France for quite some time."

Rebecca laughed politely and took another sip of the wine. Her head was spinning. She felt slightly dizzy and closed her eyes, but as soon as she did she saw nude figures cavorting. She put a hand to her head.

I cannot stop thinking about nudity and sex.

With an effort she raised a hand to her chest and took a deep breath. The gown was making it nearly impossible to breathe.

"How could she wear this gown?" Rebecca said, gasping.

Then all at once Rebecca was dreaming furiously, except that she knew it wasn't a dream. They were standing over her, looking worried. She could see them, but she could not speak.

"It's that gown," Maria was saying. "I really should never have given it to her to wear. It's much too small, a torture chamber, really."

"A delightful one, though," said the count.

Rebecca opened her mouth, but she could not make any words come out.

"Quick, help me loosen it. She can't breathe!"

The count then bent down and scooped her up as though she weighed nothing. Maria pushed aside the plates and dishes on the table, making a wide empty space at the side nearest the fire. Rebecca felt herself flying on the strong, hard arms of the count. Black motes appeared before her eyes, and she fought desperately to keep herself from fainting.

Alexander laid her down on top of the table, where Maria had cleared. Maria helped prop her up so that she was half sitting, and her legs hung over the edge. Alexander stepped between them.

The black motes grew larger. Her arms lay useless at her sides. Rebecca watched him undo the stays of the corset, certain she would soon pass out. She could barely breathe as his fingers raced across the garment. Like a spectator watching it happen to someone else, she let him take control of her clothing.

The front of the gown burst open, and just as she began to lose consciousness, she felt the release of tension, and air rushed into her lungs. The countess grabbed the material and tugged the bodice wide open and then off Rebecca's shoulders.

Rebecca took a deep breath and choked.

"Quick, help her lie down!" the count said. "We must remove the rest of this gown!"

Rebecca could not move. She choked, cried out softly, and gasped and choked again. She was vaguely aware that her breasts were bare and free to Alexander's view.

Together they pulled her down on her back. Rebecca felt his hands on her stomach. She turned her head back and forth, beginning to breathe again. Again she tried to speak, tried to tell them they had done enough, but she could not form the words and, to her embarrassment, they continued removing more of her clothing.

The buttons of the heavy skirt came undone. She was still gasping for breath when the last button came free, and then the count grasped the top of the skirt.

"N-no," Rebecca sputtered, but he did not seem to hear her.

Instead he tugged it downward. Rebecca tried to tell them that she was feeling better and could breathe alright. But she could not stop them. Their hands were everywhere. The light from the fire danced across her body as more and more of it became bared. Shadows flickered on the forms bent over her. She became aware that her legs were spread and that Alexander was standing between her knees.

Never had Rebecca felt so helpless and yet at the same time so erotically charged. The hands that moved over her body sent thrill after thrill into her. Alexander's incredibly strong hands slid under her bottom and lifted her off the table, and she let out a small gasp as the skirt slid across her knees and down her ankles.

Rebecca lay on the table, still unable to move. She was aware of the material of Alexander's clothing against the inside of her left leg. Her mind swirled. Strange figures flowed in and out of her consciousness, people she had never seen before, peering over her. She thought she saw Catherine the Great, and the king of France, and countless well-dressed noblemen and bejeweled women in all manner of gowns. But they all vanished as soon as she focused on them.

Gradually the figures stopped coming until it was just the three of them alone in the room again. Even the musicians had left, apparently. Rebecca sighed, and then she realized that she had on only the black lace tap pants that she had worn under the gown.

She thought they would stop now, as she could breathe normally again, and they would not remove this last article of clothing unnecessarily. But suddenly she felt fingers slip beneath the elastic of the pants, and before she knew anything the pants were tugged down her legs and off her ankles, then thrown away into the darkness.

She lay on the table, feeling self-conscious about her nudity even though her nipples stood erect, demanding attention, and the heat between her legs had turned moist. She crossed her arms over her breasts and tried to turn away from them. "I'm okay now," she said, her voice hoarse. She coughed once and repeated herself.

"I'm so glad, my dear," Maria said.

"Yes, that was a close one. Damnable things, those old gowns," the count said. He had not moved from between her knees, and the sense of being wide-open to their view affected Rebecca in a way she would never have imagined, surprisingly heightening her sexual longing rather than repressing it.

"That dress should never be worn again. The women were smaller then; that's why the gown was so small. I'm getting rid of it right now."

As Rebecca watched in amazement, the countess bundled up the clothes and threw them all into the fireplace. There was a burst of sparks and a thunderous roar up the chimney as the dress caught fire, and then suddenly there was nothing left. Alexander moved away and Rebecca sat upright, still keeping her arms across her chest, and put one leg over the other, swinging them over the side of the table.

"But . . . that was a beautiful dress," Rebecca said. "And a collector's item. And . . . now I have nothing to wear."

The count came over and held up his glass in a toast. When he spoke his voice was low and solemn. "Rebecca, when one is as comely as you, clothing is merely an accessory. Your body is a tribute to womanhood, and though you display unrequired modesty by your posture, still it is apparent that you should not hide such resplendent beauty too often. Here, tonight, you need not dress at all." With that he bowed to her and sipped his wine.

"Well, thank you, but . . ."

Maria stepped in. "Rebecca," she said quickly, "you need not, really. Not only are we not offended by the human body, we admire and respect it. Please, do not feel that because we are living in this lonely outpost of humanity that we are rural in our thinking."

"No, I didn't mean that, it's just . . ."

The count stepped to her right and studied her

profile. "Hold your chin up just a bit, dear," he said.

Rebecca closed her mouth and swallowed hard. She glanced wide-eyed at Maria, then lifted her chin.

"Yes! I thought so. Maria, look at this profile."

The countess stepped next to him and she, too, studied Rebecca, who remained motionless. "Yes, it's the Hapsburg cheek line. Rebecca, are you sure you are not from aristocracy?"

Rebecca slowly lowered her arms, barely aware and not caring that her breasts were now uncovered. She sat upright, straightening her back, looking at the fire.

"No, I don't think so," she said.

"How beautiful you are, dear," Maria said. "Have you ever posed?"

"No, nobody has ever asked me before. Although I probably would have been too shy to do it."

The count nodded. "Sad that you would say that."

"Enough of that," Maria said. "Come here, Rebecca, by the fire. It is a bit chilly over there, certainly *au naturel*." She motioned for Rebecca to follow her, and Rebecca slid off the table. She walked over to the fire and stood next to Maria.

Gregor appeared silently from the shadows with goblets on top of a tray. Rebecca gasped as she saw him and turned her face toward the fire. He walked slowly around the room, exchanging empty glasses for full ones while they discussed her body in the most complimentary terms.

"Miss?" He was standing right behind Rebecca.

She bit her lip and turned around, then quickly took the proffered goblet. His gray eyes stared into hers the whole time, and when she had hold of the glass, he nodded slightly and walked away. Rebecca wondered if he had even realized she was nude.

She drank deeply from the glass and immediately relaxed. The count came over and stood by her side.

"I am," he said, "a great believer in sensual love. I see in you quite possibly a woman capable of great sensual love. Is that true?"

"Yes," Rebecca answered, aware of her body's growing need to be touched.

"But I think that potential must be developed."

"What do you mean? I am a very good lover."

"Really?" He seemed to doubt it.

"I've never had any complaints."

"No, no, I'm sure you haven't. But I'm not talking about schoolboy flings."

Rebecca's face burned. "I . . ." She began to say something, then shut her mouth.

"Maria is a magnificent lover. She can become love personified as easily as you could say hello to your neighbor."

The countess stepped forward. "Now, now," she said, putting her arm on Rebecca's shoulder. "You must not try to compare me. I have been taught in the arts of love. It is not in Rebecca's culture."

Rebecca stuck her chin out. "What do you want me to do?"

"Could you kiss and achieve satisfaction by no other touch?"

Rebecca thought for a moment. If it was a challenge, and of course it was, then she was not one to ignore it. She had wondered what it would be like to kiss the count even yesterday when they had first met. Rebecca sneaked a peak at Maria to appraise her reaction to this, but Maria merely looked interested in the answer, as though they were discussing garden flowers or architecture. It was very risqué, and so sophisticated, what the three of them were doing.

"I could try."

The count stepped in front of her and looked down into her eyes. She was aware of Maria looking on, aware of being on stage. But when he looked at her, Rebecca felt weak, even before their lips touched.

She swallowed. Gulped air even as he bent down slowly, his lips coming toward hers. She felt like a mouse in front of a cobra, a goddess in front of a devotee, and she was not sure who was what until their lips met in a burst of electricity and her knees began to bend.

The pent-up desire that had lurked within her all day suddenly burst free. Her breasts ached wonderfully and the heat within her burned. She trembled almost desperately and moaned as his kiss became deeper and more passionate. One moment she was being taken away by the intensity of his kiss, and then suddenly Rebecca felt herself spasming. He broke the kiss, and she took a deep breath.

"Oh, my," she said in wonderment.

"Wonderful," the count said. "You might just rival the goddess of love in the garden."

17

Captain Eric Stryker was angry.

After dinner, which had been tasteless and poorly cooked, he had gone to find the constable, only to learn that the car would be late due to mechanical problems. He had been forced to sit in a drab office while he waited for the driver so he could return to the castle and interrogate the count.

He was fed up with listening to the stupid village policeman babble incessantly about local gossip. There was not even a decent beer hall or café in the village where he could go to escape. To make matters worse, he had been forced to accept the hospitality of the constable's fat wife even to get dinner. There were no other trains tonight, so he would not get out of this provincial dump of a village before tomorrow. That, of course, was assuming that everything went well tonight once they got back to the castle. Even that was beginning to seem less and less likely.

Finally the car arrived. The driver, a young boy barely out of school, had maneuvered the long

Mercedes through the narrow streets carefully and pulled up in front of the jail at six-thirty, nearly a half hour late. Stryker stomped out of the office with Hans and the constable behind him, then he climbed into the back seat, imperiously slamming the door behind him. The driver noted his expression and got the car going as soon as everyone was inside. As they turned north past the last building, heading into the woods along the only road that led to the castle, Stryker stared out the window and considered his prey.

They were there, all right. He did not doubt it for a minute. He had traced them this far, and the trail now pointed in only one direction. They had gotten off the train at this station; that much he had confirmed earlier through a series of demanding telegraphs up and down the line. Also, one of the locals had mentioned seeing the young couple earlier. A quick search had made certain they were not in the village, or that they had gone anywhere else in this mountainous country.

Stryker ground his teeth angrily. Waiting all afternoon, cooling his heels for this unimportant Count Viroslav, had hurt his pride. Who did this Romanian nobody think he was, anyway? Count or not, he should have come into town immediately, dragging Rebecca and her boyfriend by the hair. Stryker imagined them laughing at him and cursed under his breath. He would have stormed the castle right then and there if he had been given enough manpower.

Instead he was caught in the bureaucratic vise, twisted so skillfully by his superior. He realized that his case had been weak from the start. There was very little reason, even for the Nazi party, to go after Richard. Only Stryker's good record at capturing anti-party collaborators had allowed him to be given this much leeway in hunting down the two of them. It had degenerated into a political battle in the end, with Eric pulling in all his favors to force his superior to allow him to undertake the hunt off German soil. It had cost him a lot, and his position in Berlin had been weakened because of it. The people who came to his aid in payment for past favors abandoned him once the obligation had been met. He had gone over the head of his colonel, and his victory in being allowed to pursue Rebecca had made an enemy of him.

The man had signed the authorization papers reluctantly and with great theatrics that left no doubt he was doing it under duress, and that he would make Stryker remember it.

It was a small task, the balding man had said, pursing his fat lips and staring curtly at Stryker. "Anybody can see that capturing these schoolchildren is no challenge. Any competent SS captain looking for opportunities for advancement should have no trouble picking them up."

It had been madness, of course. To risk his career to pursue this girl who did not even love him was the most foolish thing he had ever done. Now here he was, provided with only this constable and a boy barely out of school by the local Nazi party. At least he had been given Hans. Stryker looked up at the thick back of the blond German's head in front of him, reassuring himself, then sat back and continued to fume.

He was contemplating seeing Rebecca again, when suddenly the car swerved severely to the right, throwing him against the door.

"Damn it! Watch where you're going!"

"Sorry, sir, it's this road," said the boy, and Stryker noted how clumsy his German was. "It's full of mud holes, and it is very dark through this part of the forest. Something just jumped in front of the headlights, and I had to turn hard to miss hitting it."

"Well, drive more carefully."

"Yes, sir."

Stryker turned to Hans. "What did you see, Hans?" he asked.

"It looked like a wolf, sir."

At least he had been allowed to bring Hans, Eric thought again with relief. Eric liked having Hans around. Hans was big and incredibly strong. Hans was also stupid, obeyed orders, and had no compunction about getting his hands dirty. Liked it, in fact. If there was trouble, it was good for him to have Hans there.

"It might have been one," the constable said from Eric's left. "The woods are full of them."

A wolf. Marvelous. What would it be next? Damn this count and his country life. Stryker thought of Berlin. That's where he should be now. By a warm fire back in Berlin with Rebecca. Not in this godforsaken country. He scowled and glanced to his left at the constable.

Something hit the car full on, and it swerved unsteadily on the road.

"What the hell? Another wolf, Hans?"

"Yes."

"A huge one," the driver said. His nervousness was evident.

Eric looked at him closely, thinking that he certainly would not be much use in a conflict. A teenager, probably out of work until the advance

Nazi political arm swept him up with tales of glory and gave him a job.

The road began to climb and as it did it became worse. The limousine bounced and rocked back and forth for several minutes, throwing all of them around uncomfortably. Then, just as the road began to level out, without warning the driver slammed on the brakes and the automobile began to slide forward on the muddy road toward an embankment. For a few heart-stopping seconds the front of the car went one way while the back went another, and Eric had to bite his lip hard to keep from shouting. He felt a sickening sensation of fear deep within him and he was afraid that he would embarrass himself. Then to his infinite relief the tires caught dry ground and with a lurch the car came to a halt only a few inches from the edge of the river embankment.

The constable was the first to speak. "What is it, Michael?"

"The bridge is out, sir. I couldn't see it until we were almost on top of it."

Eric looked out the side window at the smashed timber of the bridge that he had ridden across earlier in the afternoon. The moon furnished enough light to show that the spot was vacant. He began to open the door, remembered the wolf, and quickly looked through all the windows. When he was certain there was no threat from wild animals, he opened the door and stepped out. Hans climbed out at the same time, and together they walked over to the river's edge.

"Blasted through, Captain Eric," Hans said.

"Yes. It would appear we are not welcome at the count's."

The constable caught up with them. He followed their gaze, then spoke slowly in his accented German. "Oh dear. This appears to be deliberate."

Eric ignored him. "Is there another way?" he said to the driver.

"Yes, sir, but it's about twenty kilometers extra, and the road is no better than the one we have just come up."

Eric put a polished leather boot down on the top of a charred pole and gently rolled it over. Finally he turned to the local police chief. Scratching his chin, he said, "Who would have done this, Constable?"

The constable shrugged his round shoulders. "I'm not sure." Then he added uncomfortably, "Sir."

Eric looked up at him. He had heard something in the man's voice. "Surely not the count?"

"The count . . . has been here a long time. In this country, I mean. His family, of course." He took out a handkerchief and wiped his forehead. "He is sort of the local authority figure, if you understand what I mean. That is, the locals all . . . respect him greatly. Some confused person might have thought he was protecting the count. If you see what I mean."

Eric regarded him in silence for a full minute and the policeman visibly wilted under his stare. "Yes, Constable," he said finally. "I do believe I see what you mean."

"So perhaps"—the constable shrugged his shoulders hopefully—"perhaps we should try again in the morning?"

"The count does not seem to be available except in the evenings. I am looking for two escaped criminals, Constable. I cannot wait for them to make themselves available. I believe the count knows where these criminals might be. I will not wait any longer." He turned on his hard inch-and-a-half heel and walked back to the car. "Come. We will take the alternate route."

At that same instant, a huge gray timber wolf sprang from behind a bush not twenty feet away from the car. Its eyes red and its teeth bared, it raced across the small opening toward Eric.

"Look out!" Hans cried to his leader, then ran back toward the car to protect him.

Eric, who had already turned to climb inside, spun around and saw the wolf coming at him. He recognized the wild fury of the beast by its movement, because all he could see was the mottled and mangy silver fur in the moonlight. Instinctive self-preservation was the only thing that saved him. He ducked behind the car door just as the beast leapt through the air at him.

The wolf hit the door with enough force to leave a dent in the metal. Eric was thrown inward, landing painfully on the floor but otherwise safe. He climbed up on the seat and pulled the door shut as quickly as he could.

As Eric stared out the window, Hans jumped on the back of the wolf. Eric saw the constable hesitate, unsure whether he should seek the safety of the automobile or help Hans. Then Eric saw Michael, in a burst of unexpected courage and coolheaded thinking, pull the pistol from the holster at his side and point it at the wolf.

Eric looked back at Hans, who meanwhile was using his own weight to wrestle the animal to the ground. They went down together on the soft pine needles that covered the earth and he wrapped two beefy arms around its neck. Hans pinioned it with his knees and began to pull backward on its head with all his strength. Michael ran forward, stopping just out of range of the snapping jaws, and tried to get a clear shot at the animal.

"Stop," the constable said, suddenly running forward. "You'll miss the wolf and shoot the man!"

Michael hesitated, then saw what was happening and, awestruck, slowly lowered his gun. Hans was continuing to pull backward on the wolf's neck. His arms bulged with the exertion, but it was clear the wolf was losing the battle. As they all watched, the wolf's head was forced back at an impossible angle. Then Michael looked up at Hans and gasped.

Hans' eyes were wide open. To Michael's surprise and revulsion, the look on Hans' face was lustful as he pulled back on the wolf's neck. The animal, now realizing its own death, let out a long, mournful cry that echoed through the mountains and sent chills through the men. There was a brief pause, and then Hans gave a sudden jerk with his hands. With a loud, sickening crack, the animal's neck broke and Hans dropped it on the ground. Then he stood back from the carcass, grinning. While the rest of them stared at the wolf's carcass, Eric took the opportunity to climb out of the car.

"Well done, Hans," he said. He stepped forward and examined the dead animal. "I do think it meant to kill me specifically," he said, keeping his voice deliberately calm. He kicked it with his boot, then turned toward the car again. "Come on, let us go. We still have twenty kilometers to drive."

They had just climbed back inside the car when the rest of the pack showed up. Eric stared in amazement as six huge silver beasts walked slowly toward the car, surrounding it.

"They're his," the constable muttered.

"What? Shut up," Eric said. "Driver, turn this car around and let's get going."

"Yes, sir." Michael started the engine and slowly backed up to give himself room to turn.

The wolves watched intently, their eyes on Eric. Their tongues hung out over sharp teeth and strong jaws, all eyes red with fury. The one in back gave ground slowly to the wheels of the automobile. Eric glanced at the constable, who was pressing himself against the back of his seat in terror, and pulled out his gun. He was thankful he sat on the side of the backseat covered in shadow, so no one could see his own fear.

"I think there are too many wolves in this forest," he said, and rolled down his window halfway.

He stuck his gun out and took aim at the nearest wolf, taking care to squeeze the trigger gently. The shot rang out in the quiet night and the bullet hit the wolf in the shoulder. It howled in pain and stumbled away from the car.

Instantly and in unison the others attacked. There were two wolves in front of the car. First one, then the other leapt up on the hood of the car and smashed against the windshield, splintering the glass in front of Hans and leaving a spiderweb of cracks. Michael screamed, his voice high.

Two more wolves hit the left side, snarling and biting at the window next to the constable. The fifth wolf leapt at Eric, who nearly lost the arm holding the pistol. He was lucky and jerked it back just before the jaws would have severed it from his shoulder. Instead, the wolf hit the half-opened window, breaking it, and slid down the side of the car. Although it must have felt great pain, it immediately got to its feet and renewed its attack, climbing onto its back legs and sticking its snout inside the window to get at Eric.

"Drive! Drive!" Eric shouted, hitting at the saliva-coated snout with the barrel of his pistol.

Michael, eyes wide and mouth open, slammed the car into gear and put his foot down on the accelerator. The Mercedes jumped forward and the two wolves on the hood slid off. The rest of the pack chased after the car, growling and running as fast as they could, until finally there was too much distance for them to follow. As Eric watched in the rear window, they slowed and watched the car disappear, their mouths panting in the cold.

"Damn it to hell!" Eric said. His uniform had been torn and the back of his hand was bleeding slightly where he had fallen. The side window would not close, and the night air suddenly felt bitterly cold. "I've never heard of such a thing. Wolves attacking a car. What kind of creatures do you have here anyway, constable?"

"Creatures of the night," the constable muttered.

They rode in silence for a few minutes before Eric spoke again. "Well, we can't drive all night in this car the way it is. We will have to return to the village and get it repaired. When we get there wake up whoever you have to and get them on it immediately." He looked back over his shoulder furiously. "Tomorrow we're going to that castle, no matter what road we have to take, and we're going to see this count, no matter how long we have to wait."

He almost went on because he wanted to talk about what had happened, how insane it was, even how scared he had been, but he used all his will and forced himself to shut his mouth. It would not be seemly for the commanding officer, even of a group like this one, to show fear. Not to the boy, definitely not to the fat constable, and certainly, without a doubt, not to Hans.

18

The howl of a wolf came echoing through the huge, moonlit windows, making Rebecca shudder and wrap her arms across her chest again. She felt confused, and the effect of the wine had increased her sense of vulnerability and helplessness. She was being led into something that was frightening and yet fascinating, and she could not stop it from happening. At the same time a pleasant fatigue came over her, relaxing her and making her almost sleepy. The cry of the wolf had startled her, giving her a momentary rush of adrenaline.

Alexander stepped over to the window and pulled on the long, heavy curtains. Darkness filled the room instantly, and he seemed to disappear into it as the night was shut out. The countess saw the look of apprehension that appeared on Rebecca's face and stepped in front of her.

"Are you cold?" she said.

"No," Rebecca said. "Actually, the fire is very warm. But that howl, was it from a wolf? It sounded so . . . so penetrating."

The countess smiled and put her arms around Rebecca. As soon as she touched her, Rebecca ceased thinking of the wolf, or even of the count. The relaxation that she had been experiencing returned.

Maria held her close and put her lips next to Rebecca's right ear, smelling the sweetness of Rebecca's skin, the clean aroma of her hair. She listened to Rebecca's heart beating heavily in her chest and to the blood racing through her veins.

"You mustn't be frightened, Rebecca," she whispered. "Dear Rebecca. You are safe here, safe always with us, for as long as you wish. Always safe. Always. We will never let anyone harm you." She spoke the words over and over in a soft monotone. "Never let anyone or anything harm you, just as long as you are with us."

Rebecca listened to the soothing words gratefully. The countess continued whispering in the strange, rhythmic, songlike pattern, her lips so close to Rebecca's ear that her tongue was almost inside it. Her breath was very hot as it blew against the soft skin of Rebecca's cheek.

"Do you understand, Rebecca? We love you. Rebecca, do you understand?"

Rebecca's arms slid downward off her breasts and dropped slowly to her sides. Her eyes glazed over. She became aware only of Maria's voice.

"Put your arms on the mantel behind you, Rebecca."

Rebecca's arms came up again automatically from her sides and rested on the mantelpiece.

Maria moved her body gently, touching Rebecca. "We love you, Rebecca," she said again, her voice now even softer. "Do you understand?"

"Yes."

Maria brushed her lips against Rebecca's cheek, just below the bottom of Rebecca's earlobe. Then she moved upward and kissed her again, and this time her lips pressed at the outer edge of Rebecca's ear.

"We love you, Rebecca," she said again.

Rebecca stared straight ahead as the voice droned in her ear repetitively.

"We love you, Rebecca, and we want you. Want you to stay. Want you to be with us. We want you. We want you. I want you to stay. Do you understand?"

There was a long pause before Rebecca answered softly, "Yes."

Maria felt Rebecca tremble, and her own heart beat tympanic rhythms in response. She wanted to taste the tender flesh yet again, to sink her teeth into it and drink the sweet, hot blood. Gently she slid her hands down Rebecca's naked back, feeling the way the spine curved slightly, caressing the curve that flared nicely at her hips. Her fingers danced lightly across Rebecca's hips, touching here and there. Maria breathed heavily.

With a studied grace she brought her hands around Rebecca's sides, her soft palms never losing contact with Rebecca's smooth body. She looked into Rebecca's eyes, saw her helplessly reaching for pleasure, and smiled. Maria paused for a second, then bent forward and kissed Rebecca. As their lips met, Maria brought her hands upward, holding Rebecca's full breasts lightly for a few seconds. She broke the kiss and looked again into Rebecca's eyes. This time she saw a wildness coming alive in Rebecca's soul.

Maria smiled to herself, and with her long, slender fingers she squeezed Rebecca's hardened nipples. At the same time she leaned forward and kissed Rebecca again, this time deeply.

Rebecca's lips trembled slightly, then parted. Maria met her tongue and then quickly broke the kiss. Urgently she put her lips to Rebecca's ear and whispered, "Who was she, Rebecca? Who was your first lover?" As she spoke Maria began to pull lightly on the dark burgundy-colored nipples.

Rebecca's eyes fluttered. "She was . . . her name was Helen. We were best friends. We loved each other . . . in school." She moaned.

Maria kissed her again. "I am Helen," she said. "And I love you."

Her fingers worked magic. Her right hand moved down. The warm palm sliding across Rebecca's flat belly, staying just a moment over the navel before moving down farther. Her long fingers curled in the soft hair between Rebecca's legs, teasing and torturing.

"Yes . . ."

"Do you love me, Rebecca?"

"Yes . . ."

"Do you want me, Rebecca?"

"Yes." Rebecca was breathing heavily, holding herself up by her arms on the mantel behind her.

Excitement mounted in Maria. She felt her teeth extend fully inside her mouth as she contemplated sinking them into the velvety skin of Rebecca's neck. She kept her lips over them to hide them a bit longer and touched Rebecca again. Rebecca whimpered softly.

"Put your arms around my neck, Rebecca," she said.

Rebecca's entire body trembled as her arms lifted obediently from the mantel behind her. They swung forward in a wide arc and lowered onto Maria's shoulders.

"Find the clasp at the back of my dress, Rebecca."

Rebecca's fingers searched the material until they touched the tiny piece of metal.

"Unfasten it, Rebecca."

Rebecca tugged slightly, making the two halves come free. Maria stepped away for just a moment and shook slightly so that the folds of her gown fell down her body, landing in a heap on the floor. Rebecca's eyes cleared and widened slightly at the beauty of Maria's body in the firelight. Maria stood silently for several seconds, posing, then stepped forward again and pressed her body against Rebecca. As their breasts touched, Rebecca gasped.

Maria touched Rebecca's wetness and began to stroke her gently until she cried and shuddered. Maria leaned closer and whispered again into her ear. "Does that feel good, darling?"

"Yes. Oh, yes!"

Maria pushed her back against the mantel. "Put your arms back up again," she said, and Rebecca spread herself out as she was told. "Put your head back, Rebecca."

Rebecca leaned backward, resting her head on the mantel, giving her neck full exposure.

"Do you like this?"

"Yes." Rebecca's chest rose and fell quickly as she breathed.

Maria leaned forward, placing her lips on Rebecca's throat. She wanted the girl herself now, but there was still the agreement. Rebecca had to want this, too. She had to soar into the heights of sexual ecstasy for it to work.

"Good. I can give you even more pleasure," she said. "More pleasure than you have ever had before. If you will stay here with us for a while, pleasure beyond your imagination will be yours."

Rebecca's whole body was trembling. She closed her eyes and whimpered softly.

Maria knew exactly what to do. Two hundred years of learning had taught her to take mortals to the brink and back over and over until they began to sink into a whirlpool of pleasure so intense it stole all their reason.

At the same time Maria, too, swam on a rising tide of pleasure. She could smell Rebecca's blood in her veins and it was driving her mad with desire. She enjoyed the feeling of the soft young skin and the electric thrill of their hardened nipples pressing firmly against each other.

In the shadows the count was watching, she knew, and that also pleased and excited her. It brought out the exhibitionist in her.

Rebecca was on her toes, almost dancing with a wild, primitive abandon. Her head rolled back and forth and she groaned continuously. Then all at once her eyes shot open and she was suddenly gasping for breath so hard that it looked as though she might faint.

It was time for the count to take Rebecca.

But Maria wanted to take something for herself first. She quickly bent forward, placing her lips on Rebecca's taut neck. Her needlelike fangs slipped over her lips. Taking a deep breath, Maria softly punctured the sweet skin and drank deeply of the blood as it spurted into her mouth. Rebecca cried out helplessly with the shock of pain even as she sailed away into a mind-numbing orgasm.

Maria felt a hand on her arm. She lifted her head from Rebecca's neck, and then all at once she was pulled away so strongly that she had to step backward several steps very quickly to avoid falling over. She leaned against the side of the table, panting and rubbing blood from her lips with the back of her hand.

The count had stepped in front of Rebecca. He was now completely nude, too, and his sinewy body glowed in the shadows of the fire. He began thrusting into Rebecca violently. She screamed and begged him not to stop.

Maria watched and thought of Richard, still awaiting her. She smiled, and her right hand moved slowly across her belly and downward into the soft black curls of her own nether hair.

The count bent his head forward, placing his mouth on Rebecca's neck. Rebecca was impaled from both ends, laughing and crying, begging for more. The count measured her readiness. He waited for her mind to become a complete blank, for Rebecca to become lost in a crashing sea of lust.

A few minutes went by and she began to weaken in his arms. Immediately he pulled his head back from her throat and looked into her eyes.

"You are going to let go completely now, Rebecca," he said softly into her ear. "Come fly."

Rebecca bit the back of her arm while every muscle trembled like an aspen leaf in the dry winds of autumn. At the same time Alexander let go himself and pumped into her the mysterious liquids that would change her forever. The sticky wetness rushed into her, filling her with a burning ice that glowed both hot and cold. It rapidly spread upward through her body, claiming her with frost and fire. Rebecca's eyes opened wide as she felt a cold fist encircle her heart, and then everything went black.

Afterward Alexander laid Rebecca down gently on the table and leaned against it. He stood motionless for a full minute, and the countess examined his body in the firelight, enjoying his perfect maleness. Finally he turned to her. "She is ready," he said.

Maria nodded. "We shall come back in a couple of hours."

He gave her a smile tinged with irony. "Of course," he said. "Let us go find Richard and see how his day has been."

✳

19

Rebecca moaned softly. She felt wonderful. She had slept deep and dreamless for the first time in weeks. For a moment she lay still, luxuriating in the pleasure of a slow awakening.

She remembered every detail of what had happened and felt a little ashamed of herself. Oh well, it would be a story never to tell her grandchildren. *These Europeans are so decadent!* she thought. Rebecca looked around and saw the count and countess standing by the fire and talking softly. Each wore a long flowing robe; his was dark red, hers cream colored. With a start she realized it still was the middle of the night. Then she looked down and saw that she was still naked, lying on top of the table. Suddenly shy, she wanted to get up and leave.

Her two lovers stopped talking and looked at her. Something was different. Then it hit her. It was her eyes! Even though her eyelids were down, covering her pupils, she could still see around the room as easily as if they were wide open. Fear welled up in her and she tried to open her mouth to say something about it. But her jaws would not part. Neither, it seemed, would her lips. She struggled to sit up, to bend an arm or leg or even to roll over, but she could do nothing. A long, slow scream roared silently through her.

The count and countess came over to her and stood next to the table. Maria gently stroked her cheek, as one would comfort a baby.

"There, there," she said. "You are all right, Rebecca. Do not be frightened."

The count looked at his wife, who returned his glance and hid her worry. Then they both looked back down at her.

"She's right, Rebecca," he said. "You are fine. It is just the staging process. It does not last long."

Staging? She thought the question and was surprised when they answered as if she had spoken aloud.

"Yes, Rebecca," Maria said. "Your body is preparing itself. It is part of the process. We have all gone through it."

"It takes only a day or so, Rebecca. It's sort of like a cocoon. You will undergo a metamorphosis and come out a butterfly."

"Yes, yes, a butterfly! What a charming metaphor, darling," Maria said. "A beautiful butterfly. With eternal life."

Rebecca felt herself on the edge of madness. *Butterfly? Eternal life?*

"Yes, darling," Maria spoke quickly. "You will live forever. Like us. It will be wonderful, you'll see."

I don't want this.

Again the look shot between the two of them. The count looked down at Rebecca this time and spoke. "It is just different, my dear. That's all. We all undergo a moment's hesitation, a pause at the wonder of it when we face it as reality for the first time. But think"—he parted his arms in a wide gesture—"you are joining an elite group! Soon you will have powers and experiences beyond your imagination!"

Rebecca looked at him, then at Maria. *What do you mean? What kind of powers?*

There was a brief hesitation when no one spoke. Finally it was Maria who broke the silence.

"Rebecca, think of how much fun we have had this evening. Don't you think it has been marvelous? Yes, yes, I know you do. You looked so beautiful, so exquisitely sensuous, so incredibly sexy. Were you not pleased with the way you looked?"

Rebecca stared at her in shock, her mind grappling with what Maria had said.

Maria smiled at her. "You should feel pleased, really. You are beginning a change that very few ever get to experience. Believe me, you look even better now, already! Soon there won't be a man on earth who will be able to resist you, who won't desire you, even worship you."

"Yes, Rebecca," the count said. "She's right. You are changing for the better, even though I would not have thought it possible. You are changing into a woman even more beautiful than before. But you will change more. You will become as beautiful as a goddess."

"Yes, a goddess," Maria echoed.

"And what does a goddess need but a pedestal, so that she may be worshiped properly?"

"A pedestal indeed! She shall have one, too."

"Alexander, pick her up now, and let us place

her where she belongs, on the pedestal in the great hall."

Pedestal? What are you talking about? What does this mean?

"It means, Rebecca," Alexander said solemnly, "that you are about to join us in a special new existence."

I do not understand.

The two of them looked at each other. Then Maria said, "You must explain, Alex."

He nodded and turned back to Rebecca. "Rebecca, Maria and I are vampires."

There was a minute or two when all that came out of Rebecca was a jumble of disconnected thoughts, full of fear and confusion.

Vampires?

"Yes, Rebecca. We have chosen you to join us because we know that you are one of the few people capable of making the change and enjoying what it means."

Rebecca's mind was blank.

"Yes, darling, it will be wonderful," Maria said quickly. "You'll see. An introduction into your new life. Come, Alex, let us do it right now!"

"Has Gregor brought out the mirror?"

Maria nodded, and the count slid his arms under Rebecca and lifted her off the table. Rebecca felt as solid as marble and she was certain it must take tremendous strength to carry her. She wondered at his ability. Was it possible that she, too, would soon possess that kind of strength?

Alexander carried Rebecca into the great hall. There was one huge mirror at the far end, and she saw herself in it, though the other two were invisible in the glass. She watched herself floating in air down the length of the hall and then up onto the pedestal. The count and countess stepped back, admiring her, and Rebecca allowed herself to look into the mirror.

Was it possible? Was that really her? They were right; she was being transformed into something of wondrous beauty. The tiny imperfections with which she had learned to live had vanished, leaving an idealist's version of the female form.

Rebecca's eyes raced up and down the figure in the mirror and her confidence grew as she examined every curve, every turn of cheek, chin, throat. She stared long and hard at the upward curve of her breasts, convinced finally that they now could not possibly fit her frame better. Her ribs, before slightly prominent, had softened and nearly disappeared; her waist had become even smaller, and her hips were taking on an impossible roundness that belied even a thought of angularity.

And her legs! Her legs had always been her proudest feature, but now they looked as though they belonged to Venus herself. Eventually she realized that they were watching her inspect herself, and she looked at them, slightly embarrassed.

"It is all right, Rebecca," Maria said. "You should see the beauty that is yours. We do not usually keep mirrors around, since vampires do not cast a reflection, but since this will be your last time to see yourself in a mirror, we had Gregor bring out this old relic. Enjoy the vision of loveliness that you are becoming."

How long?

"Not more than a day, I should think. Don't you, Maria?"

"I agree, dear. You are progressing wonderfully. The best we have ever seen."

Rebecca stared down at them, standing at her feet. *Like Pygmalion.*

"Pygmalion?" Maria said. "Oh, yes, of course. How droll, my dear."

"An interesting analogy, but not entirely accurate, Rebecca," the count said. "After all, Pygmalion's statue had no personality while he was sculpting her, and in the end she became only who he wanted her to be."

"That's true, darling. You are already an adult human, with all the personality, needs, wants, and thoughts that come with it. So while these will change, still, they will be colored by your already formed persona."

Change, yet remain the same? Are you then creators or destroyers?

"Neither, dear," said the count. "We are merely the conduits for your transformation."

Transformation is inevitable, then?

"If something happens is it not inevitable that it did? Or at the very least, that it would have?"

Or is that just an excuse for doing whatever you want?

The countess laughed. "Brava, Rebecca."

"But it is an interesting point, Maria," Alexander said. "If there is nothing new under the sun, as they say, then is it not true that everything that could happen is merely waiting to happen?"

Waiting to be.

The count clapped his hands. "Exactly! See, you are already beginning to think like a superior intellect."

Or a corrupt one.

He shrugged his shoulders. "Corruption is in

the eye of the beholder. After all, the very word comes from the Latin for body, no? Once in the body one is already corrupt, by definition."

Sophist.

"Ha, ha, Alex," Maria said. "This is wonderful. You shall have one to match wits with for eternity."

Rebecca suddenly felt a wave of sadness. *Eternity?*

The countess looked at her husband, then up to Rebecca. "Do not be too alarmed, dear Rebecca," she said. "There are always options."

What options?

"Never you mind," Maria said, and spun around. "I do believe we are all getting a bit too morbid. Shall we not have some fun instead? Rebecca, I have a surprise for you."

The count, too, seemed suddenly filled with mischief. "Yes, it is a perfect time, Maria," he said.

Maria stroked Rebecca's porcelain foot once, then looked up at her. "It is Richard," she said.

Richard?

"Yes, darling. He is here in the castle. I must confess to you that we were not entirely honest with you earlier. He actually never left at all."

Rebecca looked back and forth between them in wonderment.

Is he . . . a vampire?

The count looked embarrassed. "No, Rebecca," he said.

Rebecca considered what he said and, more importantly, the way he said it.

Why have you made me a vampire, and not him?

Maria looked to her husband, a sly smile dancing on her lips. He avoided both their stares.

Why?

"It is the way we are made, dear," Maria said. "Only the fluids of a male vampire can inaugurate the change, in either a male or female, to make another vampire. When he made love to you and bit you at the same time, the necessary ingredients were placed in your blood to make you a vampire. Alex enjoys women making love with other women, but he cannot bring himself to penetrate another man."

Again Rebecca stared at them. It was too much to take in.

Where is he?

Maria smiled and clapped her hands once, and from the shadows Gregor appeared with Richard.

Rebecca would have gasped if she were able. Strangely enough, for the first time she realized that she was not breathing at all. But she ignored that for the moment and stared at Richard, who was being led toward the base of her pedestal.

He was completely naked and carrying a tremendous erection. His hands were bound behind his back, and a chain held by Gregor was attached to an iron collar around his neck. He glanced madly between the count and the countess, not seeing Rebecca at first.

"Have you missed me so terribly, Richard?" the countess said.

"It would appear so, my dear," the count answered.

"Why . . . what are you doing to me?" Richard said, his voice dry and cracking. "I need . . . I need you, you know that. What are you doing?" He was gasping for breath.

Rebecca felt a pang through her heart, and at the same time she felt something inside her shift slightly.

Gregor led Richard between them and stopped at the base of the pedestal.

"Why, Richard, you are so sweet," Maria said, stroking his cheek with the back of one hand. "I've missed you, too."

"I need you. Please," Richard said.

Maria glanced upward at Rebecca and sent her thoughts directly into Rebecca's brain. The force of her will was so strong that it caused the words to stab painfully at Rebecca's mind. *Do you see, then, how weak he is? Already you are much stronger than him.*

"Would you kneel in front of me, then, Richard?" she said, turning back to him. "Kneel and show me how much you love me, how much you depend upon me?"

Instantly he was on his knees, kissing her feet. She allowed him to continue for several minutes, glancing occasionally up at Rebecca, before stopping him.

"Lie on your back, Richard," she said.

He lay down as commanded, his erect cock lifting slightly off his belly. She stepped over him and lifted her robe, then slowly sat on him, taking him inside her. She moved rhythmically over him, and Rebecca watched his face contort with pleasure. Maria bent forward and sunk her teeth into his neck, and he spasmed heavily as she mixed her saliva with his blood and drank deeply. Finally he collapsed and she stood up again, wiping her lips clean. Then she looked back up at Rebecca.

One of the great joys, Rebecca, is using mortals for our pleasure. When you come down off that dais, the two of us will have a wonderful time together. I'm sure.

Rebecca looked at Richard and wondered if it

was true. He did seem strangely weak and useless to her, although his body was attractive. Perhaps Maria was right.

Maria put her hand on Rebecca's calf. "Now for the fun part," she whispered. "He'll be coming around soon. Watch!"

Sure enough, within a minute Richard groaned and sat up painfully on the cold floor. He looked confused for a few seconds until he saw the count and countess, and then his face showed his remembrance and shame.

"Oh, no!" he cried.

"Why, Richard," the countess exclaimed. "Whatever are you going on about? Did we not just, the two of us, have a moment of wonderful pleasure?"

He looked at her, the hatred on his face already beginning to melt into desire. His male member, too, began to quiver slightly.

"There, that is better. Did you like making love to Rebecca as much as you do to me, Richard?"

For an instant his face showed his confusion. "Rebecca? Where? Where is Rebecca? Where is she!" He jumped to his feet and reached for the countess but Gregor pulled on his leash and he instantly fell backward onto the floor.

Maria put her hand on the porcelain ankle and looked up. "Don't you think this looks like Rebecca, Richard?"

He followed Maria's gaze and his eyes studied her. He became excited and he got to his feet, slowly this time, and walked to the pedestal. "It does," he said. "It does look like her. When did you have it made?"

"Last night. Before she left."

"Left? Rebecca left?"

"Yes, Richard. Rebecca left. She has gone from you forever. She does not love you anymore."

"No!"

"Oh, yes, Richard. It is true. Your Rebecca is gone."

He broke down, weeping. "No, it cannot be true."

Maria patted him on the head. "It is all right, Richard. You still have me. And we shall be together as long as you last."

Richard looked at her, and again the lust showed on his face. "I want you," he said.

Maria smiled sweetly, then looked up at the gray beginnings of dawn in the front windows. "I'm afraid not now, Richard. Later, perhaps. Tonight. Gregor, please take Richard back downstairs."

Gregor nodded and half dragged Richard away. Alexander and Maria watched him go, then turned back to Rebecca. Alexander glanced up at the windows before speaking.

"I'm sorry, dear," he said. "There are some drawbacks even to being immortal. A price for everything, eh? We must go now and avoid the sun. But do not fear, you will be all right until the transformation is complete. We will see you again at sunset."

"Yes, darling, until sunset," Maria agreed, and then the two of them flew away down the hall behind Rebecca into the darkness, leaving her alone on her pedestal in the great hall.

20

It was quiet in the great hall. Left alone, Rebecca stood on her pedestal and stared at the large front doors. The sun came up outside, filling the world with light, some of which leaked in through the arched windows or through the tiny cracks between the huge doors. The brightness did not hurt very much, but all the same she was becoming increasingly aware of it. Occasionally she felt a twinge here or a spasm there, reminding her of the changes taking place inside her.

How odd to be standing here, naked on a pedestal in the main hall of a medieval castle. It is what Richard said he would do to me, when was it? Only a day or so ago?

She thought of Richard, how he had looked up at her with adoration, believing her to be a statue. Maria and Alexander were right. Men would worship her. She glanced in the mirror again, saw once more that her beauty had become dazzling. Strangely enough, her delight had settled somewhat. It almost seemed funny. She would have laughed if she could.

Again she thought of Richard. He had disappointed her. Had failed her, really. He had been seduced by the countess . . .

As was I.

. . . And turned into something bizarre and out of control. Rebecca pitied him, and then she despised him, and then she pitied him all over again, and she wanted to weep. She could not weep, of course.

Another spasm hit her, this one deep in the pit of her stomach. Her legs were changing as well, becoming light and strong inside the porcelain cocoon. A burst of energy raced from her ankles to her thighs, and Rebecca ached to try them out, to run through tall grass. She was thrilled with the power growing in her.

She thought about the count again. Why would he be so squeamish about turning another man into a vampire? It seemed rather stupid, really. After all, he had most certainly committed every other abomination in his career, and it seemed unfair to deny the change to other men.

Instantly a wild rage filled her, overtaking her like a high wind on the ocean. She wanted to scream. She wanted to jump down off the pedestal and kill somebody. Anybody. She could start with Richard and then maybe go on to the count himself. He had taken her lover and taken her as well.

Now he would not give her Richard. She remembered how Richard had begged and pleaded on his knees, and her anger subsided. He had been rather disgusting to watch. She began to fall into a deep depression.

There were whispers swirling around her. She had tried to ignore them earlier, but they came more and more often. Old whispers in languages long dead telling tales she could not understand. Rebecca sighed and looked downward.

To her surprise Gregor was standing at her feet looking up at her face. As quickly as it had come, her depression lifted and she studied him curiously.

"Rebecca?" he said. "I know you can hear me, even though you cannot speak. Not yet, anyway."

He looked around as though expecting to see someone else, then leaned forward and spoke again, his voice urgent and low.

"I know you can communicate with them telepathically when you are in the cocoon. They are very good at reading minds. Not perfect, mind you, but very good.

"Did she tell you?" he went on, studying her face closely. "No, I don't think she would have. I will, though. I think you deserve to know, need to know, because it will matter as to what you decide to do.

"Soon you will be a full vampire and you won't think the way you do as a human. You're almost there, it appears, so maybe it's already too late. But I'll tell you anyway."

Gregor hesitated. He looked down and absently stroked her feet, seeming to choose his words. Rebecca suddenly realized that she knew he was going to tell her about himself and Maria, and she was struck by what that meant. She was well on the way to becoming a vampire.

Finally he looked back up at her.

"Rebecca," he said, his face earnest, "it's about Richard. About his role. You see . . ." He swallowed hard. "I was once like Richard. And Richard will become what I am today.

"Yes, I know you understand," he went on. "I was Maria's lover before she became a vampire. Before Count Viroslav stole her away from me and made her into a vampire. I met her in Kraków. She had fled Russia with a scoundrel who had left her penniless. I picked her up out of the street and gave her food and money. I saved her life and then fell in love with her.

"My family despised her, of course. I came from a well-respected and financially empowered Polish family. They despised all Russians, and when they saw how destitute she was, they forbade me to have anything to do with her.

"I ignored them, even when they threatened to cut me off without any money. Perhaps the power she has now was dormant even then, before she went through the change. I don't know, but it is possible. Anyway, it worked on me.

"I could not live without her. I stole money from my father's business and we sneaked out of town late at night.

"We left Poland two hundred years ago. There was a fair outside Budapest, and Maria begged me to go. She met Count Viroslav then, and he brought us here. Only for the night. Just for one night."

Rebecca watched, fascinated at the way his previously inexpressive face was filled with the emotions of his memory.

He composed himself and went on. "The count took us in. Very cordial he was, too. Welcomed us with all the graciousness of his class and wealth. He called for a full meal and plenty of wine, and we ate and drank until the early hours of the morning.

"But it was for her that he did this. He came to

our room when I was asleep and carried her off." Gregor looked down, shaking his head. "What I did not know was that she had already become his, even before we came to this castle. But I don't think, cannot think, that she would have chosen this . . . this curse, for all eternity!

"Oh! I'm so sorry to say that. It was stupid of me. Actually, it is not so bad at all, if you are a vampire, that is. That is my problem. He would not, will not even now, make me into one. Maria keeps me here, keeps me alive with her own power through lovemaking, but sometimes I fear it has become more out of a sense of duty than anything else.

"I know what you are thinking. What it would take for me to become one." He shrugged his shoulders. "But I cannot leave, and what else have I? I love her now as much as I ever have, and staying here as their servant is almost worse than leaving, or dying. Almost."

He emitted a sigh from the depths of his soul. "But that is my problem. I am telling you this because you must not do this to Richard. I am trapped in this half human state for eternity, unable and unwilling to leave, though it is torture to remain. Richard, too, will willingly become like me, for when he sees you as a full vampire, beholds your stunning beauty and grace, he will sell his soul to remain with you."

Gregor stood silent for a few minutes. When he spoke again it frightened her.

"Rebecca," he said, looking up again. "You must kill Richard. You must kill him as soon as you are out of the cocoon. There will be only a few minutes before you lose your human heart entirely, once you break free. In those few minutes you must strike out with all your new power and strength and kill him. Kill him, Rebecca, and save him!"

Gregor had been grasping her ankles. Now he let go of them and backed away, wiping his forehead with the back of his hand.

"You are marvelously beautiful, my dear," he said. "I am becoming enraptured with you and I know what you are, what you are becoming. Richard won't have a chance. Kill him."

He disappeared into the shadows.

21

There was a pounding on the front door, and when Gregor opened it, Eric and his men pushed him aside and angrily strode in and paused by the base of Rebecca's pedestal. Rebecca was in the middle of a disjointed half circle of men. They stared up at her and she felt the eyes of each one. It made her feel like a whore, or a cabaret dancer, which strangely was neither good nor bad. Of course it was not quite the same as being a physical woman, but it had an amusing aspect to it, standing naked in front of a group of men, teasing them and yet untouchable.

Her sexual attractiveness was increasing rapidly, that was obvious. The youngest even had the beginning of an erection. And that was while she was standing here as solid as marble!

She had thought Gregor would send them away immediately and was surprised when he did not, then became alarmed when he told Eric that he had seen Richard. She could see Eric's enthusiasm grow, and she cursed Gregor for his betrayal.

She found she could hear Eric's thoughts even as she could feel his tension and excitement. She visualized the warm, red blood pounding through the chambers of his pounding heart and imagined the arteries in his neck pushing against the skin.

Then Gregor spoke again. "Why, he's here, sir."

"What! Where?" Eric exploded.

"Yes, yes, I'm quite certain he's the same as the one in your picture." Gregor looked at the snapshot one more time, then handed it back to Stryker, who grabbed it from him and put it in his shirt pocket.

"This man is a criminal," Eric said.

"Really? I'm not surprised. The countess offered both of them shelter, and he thanked her by attempting to steal her jewels. We caught him dead in the act and locked him up in the old castle dungeon."

Eric took a deep breath. "Where is the girl, then?"

A strange half smile formed on Gregor's lips. "That's the really ironic part of all this," he said. He looked up at Rebecca and pointed to her. "You see, sir, the girl looked exactly like a distant relative of the countess. This statue is of that woman, the duchess of Cornwall, from a hundred years ago. The woman had actually been brought up here in this castle, and posed for this sculpture. Anyway, the statue has been here ever since, and when the countess met the unfortunate couple on the train—"

"Yes, yes, but what about her?" Eric interrupted. "Where is she now? Is the girl here as well?"

"Well, no, actually. I'm afraid she was traveling with this scoundrel, unaware of the fact that he was a thief. When we apprehended him she was really quite distraught. Apologized over and over, very ashamed, you know."

Eric was beside himself. "Yes, but where is she now?"

"The countess felt sorry for her and gave her money to continue her journey. She was traveling back to America, I believe. Though why she came this direction, I cannot say."

"Because she was fleeing the law, you idiot." Eric stomped his feet.

His disappointment was obvious to everyone in the room. Looking down on him, Rebecca thought, *He would have gone after me all the way to America if he could.*

Eric paced back and forth. "Are you certain she has left the country?"

Gregor gave him a strange look. "Well, not really. Just that she is no longer here."

Eric looked at his watch. The only train that day was not far off. He had to make it. Then an idea occurred to him that was so obvious, he was amazed he had not thought of it sooner. Rebecca was not likely to leave Richard. She was too loyal. This servant was obviously lying. She was probably hiding in the castle, or at least nearby.

But there was no time to search for her. He would have to make her come to him.

"Well, sir," the servant was saying, "as soon as the count returns I am quite certain he will turn the man over to you. After all, the count is officially the upholder and preserver of the law in the province."

Eric waved his hand dismissively. "We cannot wait that long," he said. "We have the proper papers to take custody of the man, and we wish to do it immediately. Please bring him here, or better yet, take us to where you have him."

"Oh, sir, I—"

"Now!" Eric displayed all the anger of an outraged SS officer.

Gregor glanced among the men, noting Hans's size and strength. "Well," he said, seeming to respect their authority, "if you do have the proper papers. . . ."

Eric nodded at Hans, who gave the custody papers to Gregor.

Rebecca watched Gregor pretend to study the papers, furious at him and wild with frustration at her inability to move or to prevent what was about to happen. She knew why he was handing Richard over to the enemy and was angry with him for presuming he had the right to make that decision.

Damn you, Gregor! If I could . . . When I can get down from here, you will pay dearly for this!

"Well, sir, these papers seem to be in order. Constable, do you agree with this procedure?" Gregor said, turning to the village policeman.

Eric glared at the constable, who nodded very quickly.

"Then, sir, I guess the proper thing to do would be to go ahead and turn the prisoner over to you. If you will come with me, I will lead you to him."

Gregor turned on his heels and led them down the great hall to the stairs that went down to the dungeon.

Betrayer! Rebecca screamed inside her shell. Did Gregor not know what would happen to Richard once the Nazis got their hands on him? Was he ignorant and well-meaning, or just plain stupid? Perhaps he had meant well by warning her earlier, but this was too much. Surely he did not think she would ever do anything to harm Richard, no matter how much of a vampire she became.

Bastard!

She glanced up at the windows. It was still too early for twilight. The count and countess would be sleeping still, holed up wherever they went during sunlight hours. Useless to her, impossible for them to stop this. But would they stop it anyway? Was this all some sort of plot they had cooked up and instructed Gregor to enact?

In spite of herself Rebecca squeezed her fingers together as hard as she could. Nothing happened, not even a tiniest part of an inch worth of movement. She groaned and shouted angrily in her mind and tried to move her right leg. Again nothing.

If I could get down, I don't care what it would mean, I'd . . .

Suddenly she saw herself killing Gregor, and she was more than a little surprised at how good that felt. Her anger, righteous at being betrayed, filled her with satisfaction. Gregor would learn not to cross her. He would know what it meant to enrage a . . . enrage a what?

A vampire!

Rebecca realized they were returning from the dungeon, climbing the stairs back to the great hall. Her ears had picked up the sounds they were making, though she knew they were just beyond range of mortal hearing. Fascinated at this power in spite of her anger, she concentrated harder and followed their steps on the stone as they came up and out of the stairwell into the great hall.

She found that she could easily differentiate each set of feet as they walked, something she would never have been able to do before. She heard the heavy clomp of Hans first, then the deliberate stride of the captain, followed by the shuffle of the constable, the precise steps of Gregor, then the teenage boy, and finally the fifth set, the walk she would have known anywhere, anytime, even without super-hearing. Just as Gregor had said, they were bringing Richard.

Richard! No!

The men walked the length of the hall, stopping in front of the doors. Richard was dressed in his old clothes, looking exhausted and sickly. As he passed the pedestal he looked up at her.

"Rebecca?" he said.

Gregor laughed and the rest of them, except Eric, joined in.

"Look," Gregor said, "the poor fool actually thinks it is his girlfriend. In his state he is not much danger to anyone, I would not think."

"Never mind," Eric said, also staring up at her. "Let us be off. We have work to do and a long journey ahead of us. I do not want to waste any more time."

Rebecca could see in Eric's mind that he was already thinking of Berlin, and then to her surprise she saw herself in his mind! Then she knew that he was taking Richard to make certain she followed.

Well, dear Eric, I will follow. You can be certain of that.

Stryker turned to Gregor. "Tell Rebecca that we have taken her lover back to Berlin. He will stand trial for her crimes."

Hans grabbed Richard by the elbows and pushed him out the door. The rest followed, with Gregor remaining at the threshold until the car had driven away. Then Gregor closed the door and turned back to Rebecca.

"I'm sorry, Rebecca," he said, staring up at her. "But it was for the best. I have done him a favor. He cannot become one of the chosen few, and so he is better off in the mortal world. No matter what happens to him, at least he will not live in the eternal damnation that I have."

Rebecca looked down on him and felt ice in her veins.

It did not have to be like that. That was not the way.

Gregor looked up at her curiously for a few seconds, then reached up and patted her foot. "You'll see. Alexander and Maria will explain it to you when they awaken. It really is for the best. You'll see." Then he turned and walked away.

Rebecca watched him disappear behind her. When he was gone she thought again of Richard, and then of Eric.

How could she have ever been in love with Eric? She tried to recall the feelings that had accompanied her involvement with him. There was a time when she had actually loved him. Her memories drifted back to the warm spring evenings when they had walked through the parks and along the boulevards of Berlin.

Rebecca remembered holding his hand and gazing up at him as they walked. He had talked of the coming new age and the glory that would be Germany's, and she had half listened and not really thought about his words.

She remembered his body, lean and strong. When they first made love he had taken her forcefully, more so than any of her previous lovers, and she had found it very exciting. For a moment she was back in his room and he was pushing her back down on the bed, smothering her with kisses.

"Eric," she had gasped, "is it all right? Is it safe here?"

"Who cares, my love? I want you, and I will have you now."

That answer had caught her off guard, and before she knew what to think he was practically tearing at her clothes. She thought it wonderful to be the cause of so much passion, and when he stripped her and held her down on the bed, pinning her arms against the mattress, she had sighed and given herself completely to him.

It had not been the only time like that.

Again and again he had made her love him, each time more intensely. But somewhere along the way what she had believed was passion had become violent, and even that she had accepted for a long time. He had taken her to see forbidden acts in the seamy nightclubs of the city, places that were discreetly tucked away in back alleys and up outside staircases. There she had seen things that had shocked and sickened her, and yet still she had not refused him when he came to her with ropes. She had become afraid of him, of his anger when she tried to say no. It was easier to give in.

Easier, Rebecca thought, even when he had taken her to his parents' attic and stripped her naked, then hung her by her wrists from the ceiling. . . .

The dream! It was in the dream, and the countess was there. She saw it all. She knows everything about me! It was she who decided to make me into a . . . vampire. Because she knows me! Am I truly like this?

Then she felt something on her cheek, and

looking up she saw that the sun had passed behind the right turret at the front of the castle, throwing the great hall into a false twilight. It was still early, but nighttime was coming, and with it would come the count and countess.

Rebecca squeezed her right fingers again and to her surprise and excitement they moved. She tried the fingers on her left hand. Those would still not move. Undismayed, she kept up the pressure until she could feel the slightest bit of strain against the outer shell. She tried the right fingers again and this time was rewarded with almost instantaneous movement. It was beginning to happen.

If I am to be a vampire, I shall have my way.

Rebecca worked both hands, shifting from one to the other when the movement became painful. Ever so gradually she increased the arc that her fingers would move, and slowly spread her knuckles apart. After nearly a half hour she was able to make both hands flatten out completely. Pieces of the shell cracked and broke free, falling softly down to the base of the pedestal.

For a moment she paused and looked up at the heavy glass over the door. The sun was setting. She realized she had been working on the shell for more than an hour, but instead of becoming tired, her energy level was higher now than it was before she started. She began to push and pull on her arms, working to make them swing. Within another twenty minutes the first cracks came around the shoulders, and she began to feel movement in her shoulder blades. Excited, she pushed herself harder and soon was swinging her arms in complete circles. Now she could use her hands.

She began to push and pull and hit and pound on the shell that covered her body. With each crack, each weakening in the fabric of it, her need to be free increased. The circle of broken pieces of hardened skin increased around the base of the pedestal.

The sun dropped behind the mountain at a little after six o'clock, and Rebecca climbed down. She stood in the center of the great hall, all pieces of dead shell gone from her. For a few seconds she stood on her tiptoes, listening hard to all the sounds around her and reveling in the newfound intensity of her senses. Then she slowly swung her head around and looked into the huge mirror.

She could not see herself.

She moved her hands up and positioned herself deliberately, making sure she was directly in front of the reflecting glass, but still she could not see any part of herself. For an instant she felt a sense of loss and almost cried.

But just as quickly a deep cynicism raced to the front of her thoughts. She laughed sardonically and then, with a sensuous grace that would have surprised any of her previous lovers, she placed the tips of her fingers on her chest and slowly moved them down across her body, swimming in the incredible erotic sensitivity that the feeling brought to her skin. She put her head back, feeling her hair brush across her bare back, and let her fingers move farther down across her belly to the tops of her legs. She felt herself opening and sighed, long and hungry.

All at once she was aware of someone else in the hall. She straightened and looked around. It was him. She saw him even in the shadows where he tried to hide.

"You're free," Gregor said. "You've done it. You've made the transition perfectly. Congratulations! Alexander and Maria will be so pleased. I, too, am very pleased and happy for you. You are beautiful."

Rebecca stared at him, seeing into him in a way she would never have considered possible before. His thoughts were so obvious, so easy to know. She saw that he was unsure and a little wary, though he was trying to mask it. She smiled and walked slowly toward him.

"You are incredibly lovely," he said. "The change has worked magnificently on you."

Rebecca walked right up to him and put her hand on his shoulder. She could feel his heart pounding in his chest.

"Am I, Gregor? Tell me how beautiful I am," she said, her voice a caress of softest velvet.

Gregor swallowed, and to her supersensitive hearing it sounded like an avalanche.

"Your hair, it's so rich and lustrous, it almost shines on its own," he said. "And your skin, it is as clear as perfect alabaster."

"Would you like to feel how soft my skin is, Gregor?" she said, her eyes wide open.

Gregor smiled and his left eyelid twitched. He delicately put his hand on her left shoulder. "Wonderful," he said. "It is wonderful."

"What about my lips, Gregor? Do you like my lips?" She turned them up to him and closed her eyes.

"Yes," he said. He brought his own lips down to her.

But before he could kiss her, Rebecca squeezed her right hand against his collarbone. She was astonished at how fragile it was. Like a small stick that she could snap in her fingers. She wondered what that would feel like.

Gregor winced in pain and jerked his head back. "Stop it!" he said.

She gave a quick tightening of her fingers and heard a satisfying crunch. Gregor screamed in pain.

Rebecca let go of him and watched him drop to the floor. "You should not have given Richard to the Nazis, Gregor," she said.

"Stop it, Rebecca. You don't know what you're doing. It happens sometimes with new vampires. The sudden sensation of power is overwhelming." His face was a mask of agony.

"Is it?" Rebecca said. She walked slowly around him, stretching her legs like a dancer. "How would you know, Gregor? You're not a vampire, are you?"

Gregor pushed himself away from her with his feet. "Rebecca, please. You have suddenly been given tremendous strength. You must learn to control it."

"Like you controlled the Nazis, Gregor."

"It was for the best. He would never have left this castle, and that is not really what you want for him, Rebecca."

She increased the pace of her circumnavigation slightly. "Is it? Is that what I really wanted, Gregor? You're telling me what I want now, Gregor?"

He knew it was his last card when he played it. "Alexander and Maria will be here soon, Rebecca. In a few moments. They've gone off to feed, and then they'll be back. You'll feel better once you talk to them."

Rebecca suddenly stopped. "When will they be here?"

"Not long. They're usually back within the hour. Ten or fifteen more minutes, I should expect."

Her eyes became hard, and when Rebecca smiled it was with her lips only. "You'll be dead by then, Gregor," she said, and raced toward him.

✳

22

Alexander and Maria had just finished feeding. Although the accident had been more than thirty-five miles from the castle, they had felt it and flown there as soon as they awakened. Now they stood up slowly, wiping the blood from their lips and surveying the scene of wreckage that lay around them. The small truck had come around the corner too fast and tipped over. Both the driver and the helper had been thrown from the wreck, but one had a fractured skull and the other two broken ribs. Neither victim had put up much of a fight.

"There will be no trouble," Alexander said. "Look, the truck was on its way to Poland. When they are found the cause of death will be attributed to their injuries."

Maria suddenly shivered.

"What is it, my dear? You are not worried about these two, are you?"

"No. No, it's not that. Something else. Something has happened at the castle. Let us go back there."

Her husband looked at her and frowned, then turned his head back in the direction they had come. "All right," he said.

Both stood still for a few seconds, concentrating, and then there was a sudden updraft and they were gone.

They came down on the rooftop of the castle a few minutes later, descending silently in the night. Their feet lightly touched the tile, and they raced to the front wall and peered down.

"The main entryway is wide open," Maria said. "Where is Gregor?"

"I do not know."

"Come." The count walked quickly across the roof to a door and opened it, then entered the stairwell and disappeared down the stairs. Maria looked back once over the turret and followed him, matching his speed.

They came around the bottom of the stairs together into the great hall and stopped in astonishment. The wreckage was everywhere, beginning with shattered pieces of the pedestal thrown against the wall. Paintings were torn, chairs were broken, and even the huge chandelier lay in a thousand shards of glass across the stone floor.

The count walked to the front of the hall and saw Gregor's body. He bent down and stared at it, and Maria, who had not seen the body until Alexander went to it, stopped in shocked disbelief. For several seconds she remained silent, and then she let out a long and bitter cry and followed her husband to the corpse.

Gregor lay against the stone steps that led up to the castle doors. His neck was twisted at an impossible backward angle, and his throat was torn apart. Gregor's back had obviously been broken as well. The pain had been burned onto his face just before he had died.

Maria lay Gregor's head gently on the steps and then looked at her husband accusingly. "Are you happy that you have turned her into a vampire?"

Alexander stood up and looked again at the broken pieces of dead skin on the floor. He surveyed the rest of the room, then turned slowly and faced Maria. His eyes turned flat and cold, and when he spoke his voice sounded emotionless and distant.

"Remarkable," he said. "The initial effect of the change must have hit her very strong. I have never seen such a reaction. The Germans must have come for her boyfriend, and she blamed Gregor."

"She killed Gregor. He loved me more than anyone else ever has. Even more than you, Alexander. You know that, don't you?" Maria demanded. Her eyes blazed with fury as she spoke. Her hands were pressed against her hips and her feet were rooted in place.

Alexander's own eyes became slits. "You fantasize too much, Maria."

"Stop it!" she screamed. "You know what I say is true!"

"It is not," he said, his voice deliberately calm.

But his placid tone made her even more angry. "I could kill her myself for that."

"But you won't."

Maria walked around the room, kicking bits of debris and stamping her feet. Finally she went to the front and stared out the doorway.

"You really don't care, do you?" she said, not looking at him.

"About what? Gregor? I've never liked him, Maria. You know that. I have always been jealous of your relationship with him. If you want me to feel sorry for his death . . ."

"Don't talk like that, Alexander. You don't care that it hurts me to see Gregor dead. To lose Gregor makes me feel I have lost my last link with whatever it is I once was."

"There are others, Maria. You are being melodramatic. You can take the boy, if you wish. Share him with her."

She turned and sneered at him. "You are disgusting."

Alexander shrugged his shoulders and chuckled. "Perhaps."

"It is not funny."

His face grew serious again. "You must get over this, Maria, and help me find her."

"I cannot believe you. You still do not understand what it means to me to have Gregor dead."

"Because you were planning on running away with him?"

She glared at him.

"It would have been foolish, the two of you out in the world. A vampire and her servant, imagine it. Did you really think you would live long in this century on your own? The two of you would not have lasted two weeks away from here."

The fury drained from Maria and was replaced by a look of infinite sadness. "You did not try to stop us, though, did you, Alexander?"

"Come along, Maria," he said. "Let us go find her before she does something more destructive. We do not wish to lose her."

Maria looked down at Gregor's body once more. "All right."

He looked at her warily. "And Maria, you won't kill her, will you?"

Finally she looked up from the wreckage around them and let out a long sigh. "No," she said. "I won't. For you, I won't. But you know how I feel. For me the pleasures of vampire life are edged in tragedy. I have always feared this sense of futility. Since I became a vampire I have had the power of life and death over others, heedless to their suffering. Now that same power has been used against me. I am lost."

They stared at each other for a moment, then Alexander turned away.

He waved his hand dismissively. "You're becoming maudlin," he said. "Come. We haven't much time. She will have gone to the village to find her lover. She does not understand the delicate balance we have built up here with the local people. We must bring her back here, but we must not bring the entire village down upon us," he said.

Maria spoke softly, still staring at his back. "It will have to be done quietly."

"What do you want?"

"Help me with his body."

Michael, the young man assigned to drive Stryker, was standing by the car in front of the jail, smoking a cigarette. Every now and then he would glance at the brightly lit windows across the street and mutter a curse of dejection. It was cold outside, and he would much rather be in with the constable and the two Germans, enjoying a hot meal.

The shrill cry of a train whistle sounded, and a moment later the black engine of the Berlin 542 became visible, puffing white clouds of steam in the distance. Michael tossed his cigarette on the ground and ran across the parking lot. He leapt up the shallow stairs to the front door of the inn and opened it, and the three men inside looked at him.

"The train?" Stryker said.

Michael felt like saying "obviously," but instead he said, "Yes, sir."

"Good." Stryker wiped his mouth fastidiously on an embroidered cotton napkin, then tossed it onto the table and stood up. "Come, Hans, let us retrieve the prisoner."

They all went back across the street to the jail. The constable fished a ring of keys from his pocket, selected one, then unlocked the door and opened it. Hans stepped inside and grabbed Richard by the arm. Richard blinked and cried out at the pain in his joints as Hans half dragged him out to the train platform.

The stationmaster came running out of his office with their luggage, which he put on the platform next to them. He stood up and saluted them, then stepped back a few feet and watched with them for the train. Stryker stared at him and saw that the man was hoping they would be gone as soon as possible. Frowning, he turned away and faced the constable.

"Thank you, Pietre," he said, allowing the man the honor of being addressed on an equal basis for the first time. "You have been of much help to us, and we are grateful." Stryker considered giving a small speech on the virtues of good international relations, then discarded the idea. To hell with these people. *In a short time they will all be working for us anyway*, he thought.

He turned to Hans. "Come, Hans," he said, "we have a long journey ahead of us back to Berlin."

Hans lifted Richard by the arm and dragged him onto the train. The constable saluted Captain Stryker, and taking the cue, the boy lifted his hand as well. Stryker smiled slightly and saluted them back. Then he raised his hand to the engineer, and the engineer nodded. The wheels began to turn and slowly the train pulled out of the station.

Eric had requested and received a private car. It had been added at the back of the train, and they went there immediately. Once inside, Hans chained Richard to an iron stool. Eric locked the door, then pulled back a small curtain and looked out the window at the darkened countryside racing by. Satisfied, he shut the curtain and sat down on the small sofa that stood along one wall.

"Hans," he said. "Please fix me a cognac. And something for yourself, as well."

Eric felt magnanimous. It had been a weird experience, and truthfully not one he would wish to have to go through again. In fact, he hoped he never saw Romania again. But it was over now, and he could mark it a success. Or at least it would be a success when Rebecca turned up. He had no doubt that he would see her again.

Hans poured the drinks and handed one to his captain. Eric smiled, and they clinked the glasses together. He swirled the golden liquor in his glass, then sipped it.

"I think the rest of our journey should be uneventful," he said. "And with luck we will be back in Berlin by late tomorrow."

* * *

Michael and the constable watched the train leave the station. When it had disappeared from view, the constable turned to Michael and said, "Put the car away and then you can go home. We can be thankful this affair is over. They're a nasty piece, those Nazis. Let's just hope they stay in their own country from now on."

Michael saluted him. "Yes, sir," he said. Although the constable might be glad to see the end of it, to Michael it had been the most exciting thing he had been a part of for quite some time, and he was not ready to quit playing soldier. Still, a soldier follows orders, and anyway there was really nothing else to do. He walked back to the car and climbed in behind the wheel.

The Mercedes' powerful engine started up immediately, and Michael touched the dashboard one more time, enjoying the rich feel of the leather. He flicked a switch, bringing on the twin headlights that swept the road dramatically. Tomorrow the car would have to be returned to the headquarters in Tipslitch, but for tonight he was still custodian. He drove it all the way through the village, stopping at a darkened barn past the last house where the car would spend the night safely. Once inside he shut off the engine and sat still, smelling the car for a moment. Then he opened the door, climbed out onto the straw-covered floor, and shut it again forcefully. The metal clanged loudly and the sound echoed in the vaulted old building.

Michael glanced once around the car. He thought he had seen something in the splintered moonlight that spilled through the cracks in the old wooden walls. Something that did not belong there. He looked again, his eyes carefully scanning the montage of light and dark for something he did not want to find.

Then he saw her step forward. She wore a little black dress and her golden hair hung over her shoulders. His heart began slamming against the inside of his chest.

It was the American girl from Captain Stryker's photograph. The one they had been searching for. Michael told himself that was impossible, but he knew that it was her nonetheless.

She had been up at the castle the whole weekend. Michael knew that no one ever did that. And not come away unchanged, anyway. Suddenly all the tales of his childhood came roaring back into his memory, and his stomach felt as though it were full of old sauerkraut.

He remembered his grandfather telling him that they were supposed to be beautiful, those who entered the dark world up there at the castle of Count Viroslav. This girl certainly was beautiful.

"What have you done with him?" Rebecca said, stepping forward.

Michael's eyes bulged. She was the most exquisitely ravishing woman he had ever seen. Her face and figure were astonishing in their perfection, more than even his late adolescent imagination could have dreamed up.

But in spite of her beauty and desirability, there was something about her that frightened him. Something in the way she moved that made her seem deadly, and his skin turned cold. She stepped forward, never taking her huge eyes from his, confidently moving closer and closer to him.

"You're . . . you're her. The fugitive," he stammered.

"My name is Rebecca, Michael. You came and got Richard this afternoon, you and the Germans. What have you done with him?"

Now she was standing directly in front of him, looking up into his eyes. He could see down the front of her dress, which excited him, though the excitement was tinged with terror. His rational brain was telling him that she was tiny and harmless, but the other part, the part that knew where nightmares came from, was screaming for him to run.

Michael's throat felt too dry to speak.

"Where is he, Michael?" she said again.

She put her hands on his shoulders and stood on her toes, and moved her left leg inside his left leg. It glided up and down gracefully, hypnotically. She pulled him close to her and he stared at her lips, watching them come to take his mouth.

She kissed him, soft at first, then long and passionately, and her leg moved upward against his groin. He was losing control, could feel the twinges turn into a steady hardness in spite of his fear. He felt himself rising and he whimpered softly.

"Tell me, Michael," she murmured as they rose slowly off the floor together. She kissed his chin and then his neck. "Where is he?"

Michael gasped for breath, barely aware that he was floating. He felt her hands on his belt, felt it come loose, and felt his pants fall away. She took him in her hands and squeezed gently. He felt her lips on his neck again, and felt twin points of heat and light push into his throat.

"The train! They took him on the train to Germany!"

With a fury unnamed, Rebecca bit down as

hard as she could and jerked her head back, tearing skin and flesh. The blood from his ruptured arteries spilled out into the night as his body spasmed heavily. In seconds he was dead. She dropped him onto the cold floor and with a whispered curse was gone.

There was a knocking on the door, and the constable got up to answer it. It was getting late and he was tired, so it was with some irritability that he lumbered to the front door and unlocked it. He muttered to himself as the door rolled open that this had better be important. But as soon as he saw who was standing at the threshold, he stepped backward in fear.

"Good evening, Constable," Count Viroslav said, stepping inside. The countess stepped in behind him, and the constable put his hand to his chest.

"Good . . . good evening, Count Viroslav. And Countess," he remembered to add.

The count cut him off with a wave of his hand. "You came to my castle this afternoon when I was out, did you not?"

"Well, yes sir, I did. I came with two German police officers. As I told you they were looking for—"

"I know who they wanted, Constable. They could have had them, but there is a certain question of form that I like to see followed here in our little community."

The constable began to speak very quickly. "Yes, sir, of course; I'm sorry if you were offended, because that was not my intention, but your servant said it would be all right and it's just that—"

"Have they left yet?" the countess said.

The constable turned his head toward her, struck by the power of those beautiful eyes. Like everyone in the village he had lived his whole life under the philosophy of keeping his head down, making the village work, and never interfering with anything that went on at the castle. He had been taught that philosophy at his mother's knee, who herself had learned it from her mother, and her mother before that, as far back as anyone knew. It had worked, too, until tonight. He cursed himself for breaking the rule, testing the limits. Now the castle had come to him, and the ancient whispered tales that they all lived with had become real.

The count looked at his wife, who looked back at him. A thought seemed to flow between them and then they looked back at the constable.

"Your driver, the boy you had this afternoon," the count said. "Where is he?"

"Michael? Why, probably at home. He took the car to the garage, and then he was off for the rest of the evening."

"Garage? Where is it?"

"The old barn, actually. At the edge of town." The constable was white-faced now. He suddenly realized that tonight evil had come to him looking for answers, and that meant things were out of control. Something was out there in the darkness disrupting the delicate balance of power forged over centuries, and Michael was probably its target. Its first target.

The count opened the door and motioned for Pietre to go. He did and the three of them walked quickly down to the barn. It did not take long to discover Michael's body lying by the right front wheel.

The count turned to Pietre. "I think, Constable," he said, his voice full of menace, "that your young driver did a very foolish thing tonight."

"Yes, he got himself into a lot of trouble," the constable answered, not yet understanding but leaping to conclusions ill thought out.

The count stared hard at him. "Your driver took the car out for a ride by himself. It was the first time he had been in possession of it, and it went to his head. He drove out of the village, along the cliff road, much too fast. Do you understand me?"

The constable's face showed that he did. He looked from the count to the countess and back to the broken body of the boy. Tears filled his eyes, but he nodded slowly.

"Good. When your report is read by your superiors, they will see no reason to investigate it then, will they?"

"No. No reason. I'll take care of it."

This time the count smiled and nodded. "I'm sure you will," he said, and looked to his wife. "Come, Maria, there is nothing more we can do here."

They walked out of the barn together and disappeared into the woods.

"She will have gone after the train," Maria said once they were out of sight.

"Yes, she's probably there by now."

"Should we go, too? To stop or to help her?"

The count stopped and turned toward his wife. There was no one around now. They were away from the last light of the village.

"No, I think it is time we went home. She is doing what she needs to do, and doing it logically if somewhat rashly. But those two Nazis are fools, and she won't have much trouble. Then she'll come back to the castle. There is nowhere else for her to go. She's still new at the game, but she will be all right. The constable will take care of things here, and no one will put it all together. Let us go home and wait for her."

❄

23

The train to Berlin worked its way steadily
through the mountains. It twisted and turned
continuously between snow-covered peaks,
throwing the travelers back and forth in the small
compartment. At the end of a long grade, an
especially long tunnel swallowed it up and the
whistle screamed painfully. The lights flickered
on and off, turning the last car from light to dark
for several minutes. When the lighting stabilized
Eric raised his arm and looked at his watch, then
swore when he saw that it had stopped.

"What time do you make it, Hans?" he said,
speaking loudly over the noise of the wheels on
the old track.

Hans looked at his wrist. "Mine, too," he said
in surprise. "A new watch, completely stopped."

Eric put his hand back down disgustedly. "Oh,
well, it's late. It must be past three." He picked up
his drink and sipped the last of the cognac. He
held the glass in his hand for a few seconds,
debating whether to have another, then put it

down on the small side bar. No need to get drunk. There was still a lot to do once they got to Berlin.

Eric looked over at Richard, shackled to the iron stool in the corner. He himself felt exhausted, so he assumed the prisoner must feel even worse. It was just as well. An exhausted prisoner was a docile one, and right then all Eric wanted was to finish the assignment uneventfully. Which, with the tiniest bit of luck, is what would happen. The sun would be up in a few hours, and by then they would be well across the border and halfway to Berlin.

Eric turned his head the other way and looked at Hans. Hans, it appeared, was no worse for the wear. Eric stifled a yawn.

"Well, Hans," he said, "we should get this one back easily and both have a success to our credit."

"Yes," Hans said, nodding.

Eric stood up and stretched wearily, then pulled back a curtain and looked out at the shadowy night. "Strange country, though, eh Hans? Strange people. I don't think it would be my first choice for a billet." This was Eric's standing joke. Everyone knew the only billet he wanted was Berlin, close to the seat of power.

This time Hans shook his head.

Eric looked at him. He was an idiot, but incredibly strong and very loyal. For good reason, too, Eric thought, congratulating himself. He had pulled Hans out of a prison on the border of Poland where Hans had been awaiting trial for the murder of seven Poles. Hans, it seemed, had a hobby of sneaking into Poland and killing people, usually during a full moon. Eric had given Hans the opportunity to trade the gallows for an SS uniform. The Poles had complained loud and long, but no one cared much. What was awaiting the Poles was far worse than anything Hans had done so far. And Hans had a talent for killing that could be used by the Nazi party. Eric smiled a ghost of a smile and considered his plans for when he returned to Berlin.

The overhead lights blinked again, then went out for ten or fifteen seconds, and they all sat in complete darkness.

When the lights came back on, Eric swore. "These trains are a disgrace. Somebody had better do something about them soon."

Hans thought about that, then nodded.

Eric glanced at Richard, then did a double take. Something about him had changed. He was still sitting in the same place, still shackled and helpless, but he seemed more alert. The dejection and depression that he had carried were gone, and he was actually smiling. Eric frowned and nervously scanned the car. He saw nothing and heard only the clattering of the wheels on the tracks. But something was different about Richard, and Eric did not like it. He stood up and walked over to Richard.

"Prisoner," he said.

Richard stopped smiling and turned his head toward Eric.

"Tell me something. Where is she?"

Richard looked at the floor and said nothing.

Eric walked over to him and hit him once across the mouth. "Next time I will let Hans hit you. Now, answer my question. Where is she?"

Richard licked the blood from his lips and studied Eric. "You are chasing Rebecca? Even though she told you she does not want to see you again?" He shook his head and chuckled. "You are in love with her and she can't stand you, Eric. You're a fool."

Eric hit him across the mouth a second time. "We'll see who is the fool," he said. He backed away and leaned against the wall, waiting for his heart to slow down. "There's a war coming, you know."

Now Richard looked back at Eric. "I know," he said.

"And you will never get out."

The grin returned to Richard's face. "And neither will you, Eric."

The insolence infuriated Eric. With another quick backward swing, Eric brought his gloved hand out and down and hit Richard on the mouth again. This time Richard jerked backward from the force of the blow, and the trickle of blood on the right of his mouth gushed out of the wound for a few seconds, but he said nothing.

"Where is she?" Eric said again.

Richard looked up. "I do not really know. But I imagine you will see her again very soon."

Eric did not like the tone of Richard's voice or his words. "What do you mean?"

Richard glanced at Hans, then back at Eric. "Your henchman is not the only one capable of destruction, Captain. If you had seen what I have over the last couple of days, you would be far more worried."

"What have you seen?"

Richard smiled. "Strange things."

"You're crazy."

"I might be at that."

Eric glared at him. "Where is she?"

The lights went out again.

"What the—" Eric reached for the Lüger at his waist and unholstered it. He lifted it and put his finger on the trigger, pointing at the darkness. An unseen prisoner was always to be considered a threat, even a shackled one. "Hans, see what the problem is with these damn lights!"

"Yes, sir."

Hans stood up and grabbed the brass railing on the wall, then shuffled carefully forward in the darkness to the door. Eric had hoped the lights would be back on before Hans reached the entrance, but they remained dark. Eventually Hans found the doorknob and pulled on it. A blast of icy wind blew into the cabin, and Eric saw Hans' silhouette like a black hole in the middle of a thousand stars. Then Hans stepped out onto the narrow platform that separated their car from the previous one and pulled the door closed behind him. Again the compartment was without any lights, and Eric and the prisoner were alone.

"Actually, Captain, to be honest I don't know what I thought I was doing," Richard suddenly said. "She's just a girl, after all. And she's not really in love with me, anyway."

Eric spun around at the sound of the voice. He took a breath and got himself under control.

"Yes, well, now you will pay for your foolishness."

"I think, Captain, that I have already paid for my foolishness."

"What do you mean? Do you think that what awaits you in Berlin is a picnic? I told you, you will be swallowed up even before this war begins!"

"No, Captain, I think that it is *you* who are about to be swallowed up."

Eric could not believe what he was hearing. Who did the little shit think he was? He could actually hear the smile in Richard's voice and it drove him wild. Eric was angry enough to hit him again, but the car jerked suddenly and he fell backward against the brass rail, catching the small of his back against it and shouting in pain in spite of himself. He pulled himself to his feet just as there was a change in the movement of the train.

The car was slowing down. Eric clenched his pistol in his fist and shouted into the blackness, "Hans!"

His back continued to throb, and Eric pressed against the bruise to try and ease the pain. Where was Hans? Could nothing be done right here?

"Hans!"

He made his way blindly through the compartment to the front. The car continued to slow, obviously coming to a complete halt, and now Eric could hear the rest of the train pulling away into the night. He felt a slight twitch over his right temple where a blood vessel pounded, and his skin felt clammy.

All at once the lights came back on.

"Well, that's something," Eric said. The door suddenly opened and Hans stood in the frame. "Hans! What the hell happened?"

Hans looked strange, as if he were drunk. His eyes were glassy, and Eric realized that Hans was not standing by himself. "Hans?" he said.

Then the big man's head rolled forward, and Eric thought that his neck was broken. But the head continued forward and fell off Hans' body onto the floor, and Eric screamed in surprise and horror. The rest of the body dropped away next, falling backward into the night, and in its place stood a smiling, beautiful, petite young woman. Eric gulped for air and fought to get himself under control as he slowly realized it was Rebecca.

What he had just seen was impossible. That Rebecca had a part in it was ludicrous.

"Rebecca! What's going on? You can't be here!"

She stepped forward gracefully, still smiling. "Why not, Eric? Why can't I be here?"

There was something about her that was different. It was Rebecca, and yet it was not. She was not the same naive girl he had made love to in Berlin, not the picture of beauty and innocence that had driven him to pursue her into this hell of a country. *Beauty, yes, my God, what beauty,* he thought as he stared at her. It was uncanny. As though someone had taken her best features and added . . . what? What had happened?

Rebecca took a few steps toward Eric, and without thinking he backed away.

"What is the matter with you, Eric?" she said. "There was a time when you could not get enough of me."

He swallowed hard. "You . . . you're different."

"Am I?" she asked coyly, and took another step toward him.

Again he backed away. "What is the matter with you?"

"Matter? Why, nothing, Herr Captain Eric Stryker. I am back with you, as you wished. Did you not chase me halfway across Europe? At long last I have realized how much you love me. What girl could resist such pursuit?"

"Stop toying with me, Rebecca!"

She stopped, gave him a questioning look, then glanced at Richard. "You have captured Richard, I see."

Eric wiped a bead of sweat from his forehead. "Rebecca, I . . . I love you." He frowned as he said it and peered at her.

"Yes, I know, Eric. You really love me." She leaned against a crate. "You always said you did, but I guess I never believed you. Or maybe I just never really understood your love before."

"Before?"

"Why yes, Eric, before I became a . . . well, just before."

"What are you talking about, Rebecca? You confuse me."

"Ah, well, it's all a bit complicated. You see, back in Berlin I never understood the power and seductiveness of evil. Not in the way you did, anyway."

"Evil?"

"Don't be coy, Eric. Of course, evil. You are evil, as is everything you stand for. When you raped me the last day, you showed me your true self. And that true self was evil."

"I . . . I didn't really rape you, Rebecca. I didn't mean it to be rape. I . . . that is, we were always like that, you and me. I was always dominant with you, and you liked it."

"Did I, Eric? Did I really like it?"

"Didn't you?"

She smiled, and he saw the pronounced canine teeth.

"Rebecca! What has happened to you!" he screamed.

"I think you know, Eric," she said, and took a

step toward him. "I've become a vampire. Oh, you probably don't believe in such things, but they are real. And I am here to prove it to you."

Eric's mind began to shred. It was impossible, he kept repeating to himself. With trembling hands he raised the gun and pointed it at her. He jerked the trigger twice and the bullets went wild, smashing into the wooden frame over her head. Eric placed his other hand alongside the first to steady the gun barrel, and forced himself to squeeze the trigger slowly this time, just as his training had taught him. When the gun fired he knew the bullet hit her. He saw the way her body jerked slightly as the bullets slammed into her chest. Yet it did not seem to affect her. She stood silently, smiling at him.

"So you would kill me, Eric? You who are a master of evil would kill me just as I become that which you pride yourself in being?"

"I am not evil," he stammered. "I have only done what is required."

"As will I from now on, Eric. And the first thing that is required is your life."

The gun went off three more times, and she began to chuckle. Eric pulled the trigger until the gun stopped firing and even then he continued pulling the trigger uselessly.

"Why won't you die!" He heard the terrible wildness in his own voice, wildness that was trying to deny what he knew she had become. The word stood at the edge of his consciousness, as though in the wings of some mad theater, awaiting its cue.

"I thought I explained that already, Eric. I am a vampire. You cannot kill me."

Vampire.

The mad theater, he realized, was his own mind.

Rebecca stood serenely, watching him. Finally realizing that the gun was empty, he threw it at her. It bounced off her elegant nose without a scratch.

Hysteria inside Eric bubbled up and spilled over, rapidly becoming uncontrollable laughter. Eric Stryker, captain of the SS, rising star in Berlin and soon to be a department head, was laughing too loudly. Too loudly for a Nazi secret service captain who was a leader of men. Much too loudly. As loudly as he had when he was a small child and put a snake down the back of his teacher's dress. He remembered that now, how funny it had been. Just like now.

Rebecca took another step toward him.

She was his teacher coming to punish him. He laughed even harder. Teacher didn't seem angry. Teacher was smiling, too. It was a funny joke. Teacher put her hands on him. Teacher kissed him.

Eric laughed through it all. He laughed so hard he did not even feel it when she ripped open his throat. And when his head left his body and went sailing out into the darkness, the insanity frozen on his face confirmed what a great joke it all had been.

※

24

"Rebecca?"

She turned around slowly.

"Is it you, Rebecca? Have you become one of them?"

Rebecca walked back into the car and stood in front of Richard.

"Did you come to save me, Rebecca?"

Rebecca studied him. He looked exhausted and nearly emaciated.

He has weakened so quickly, she thought. *Would I have been like that if I had not become a vampire?*

Richard was staring at her, not quite accusingly but not in a way that made her very comfortable, either. For a moment she felt human again, full of guilt for having killed. Her emotions tumbled down a deep slide as she saw herself in his eyes, and the thrill she had been having with her vampire powers threatened to desert her.

"Did you kill Gregor, Rebecca?" he asked. "The way you killed those two men? You were very angry. It was you in the statue, wasn't it? I could tell; I don't know how, but I knew it. What was it

like in the statue, Rebecca? What is it like now?"
He searched her face for a response. "Did you
come just to kill those two men, or did you come
to kill me as well?"

Rebecca closed her eyes and listened to the
sound of his voice. By concentrating she could
force down the thoughts of guilt that had temporarily plagued her, and even ignore them. The
human in her that called to her could be denied.

Immediately Richard no longer seemed as important as he had been just a moment before. It
had been important to kill the people tonight, and
she had assumed that it was because of Richard.
But now she realized that she had not killed them
for Richard at all.

Her mind swirled in a cacophony of bizarre
images and disconnected thoughts, and she felt
momentarily overwhelmed and confused. Rebecca put her hand to her head and steadied herself
against the wall.

I must think slowly.

She had killed those people tonight, and it was
not even because they were bad, or because they
deserved to die. She had killed them simply
because she had wanted to kill them. She frowned
and opened her eyes, and fixed her stare on
Richard. Again she was aware of how dramatically her thinking patterns were changing.

*It is not that Richard is of no importance, or that I do
not care anything for him, it's just that I do not see him
in the same way I did before.*

She thought of Eric, lying dead and dismem-
bered on the railroad tracks outside. All of a
sudden it was difficult to know whether she felt
angry or happy about that.

"They will be angry with you for killing Gregor," Richard said.

Rebecca almost laughed. It was impossible for anyone to be more off the mark. They would not be angry with her. Couldn't he see that? They would no more be angry with her than she would be angry with them if they killed Richard. He was like a pet or a possession. A thing. He was pathetic, too. A full-grown man who could do so very little for himself. A man who had allowed himself to be tied to a stool by a couple of half-wits, helpless without her coming to rescue him.

She looked at him and something came into her mind like a distant echo. Something that Gregor had said to her about Richard. He had said it before she had made the complete transformation and now, like everything else about that time, it was slipping away from her. Her new form and powers were simply too fascinating. Richard's world seemed to her like a dream from which she had just awakened. It was like looking down a long tube at what she had been. Not quite gone, yet no longer there.

Richard's voice was wary. "Are you angry at me for what happened? With the countess, I mean?"

The countess. There was someone who understood the magnificence of power. That is what made the countess so wonderful, so thrilling, so . . . sexy. Incredibly sexy, as was the count. Why had she not understood these things before?

"I'm sorry if you are," Richard said. "I guess I could not help it. They were just too much for me. But then," he looked at her slyly, "most vampires are."

Rebecca was surprised. He had given her his

most beguiling smile. She had always liked that smile; she remembered that he had used it on her the first time she went to bed with him. She laughed, and he laughed, too, but his laugh turned nervous and soon he quit.

"Do you think I am beautiful, Richard?" she said at last.

He raised his eyebrows. "Beautiful? Yes, of course. You were always very attractive, but now you are exquisite."

She nodded. Then she walked all the way around him, studying his shackles. They were ridiculously weak. She reached down and grabbed the chains with both hands and gave them a tug. With a loud snap they came apart, and Richard was free. He stood up, rubbing his wrists, and stared at her.

For a moment neither of them spoke.

Then Rebecca put a hand to her head and brushed back a lock of blond hair. It was a simple gesture, innocent and seductive at the same time.

"What's it like?" Richard said.

She knew what he was asking but said, "What do you mean?"

"You know, being a vampire."

"Like nothing you can imagine." She said it in a curt manner, not really meaning to be sharp with him and yet somehow unable to speak casually. For a moment she felt like a freak and hated it. Then the feeling of insecurity was gone and she was again in control. "It's wonderful, Richard. I can do anything I want."

"Except get a suntan."

Anger raced through her. "You don't know who you're talking to," she said in a voice that was as cold as the bottom of a cave. She felt gratified to see a spasm of fear shoot across his face.

"My God, you really are one, aren't you?"

She ignored the question. Taking a moment to collect her thoughts and calm down, she walked to the doorway and looked out at Eric's body. "He raped me, Richard," she said finally.

"I'm sorry."

"Why are you sorry?" Again anger welled up inside her. "There was nothing you could have done about it."

He looked at the floor. "I'm still sorry, Rebecca. For the pain it caused you."

"Well, he won't do it again." She suddenly laughed. "Nor will anyone else, for that matter."

"Is that why you killed him?"

"What do you think?"

"I . . . I guess I'm not sure. If you killed him for revenge, I could understand."

Again a long silence filled the railroad car. Rebecca stared out at the night.

"I enjoy it, Richard," she said finally. "I like the feeling it gives. Everything is heightened. I can't quite control the intensity of my feelings or desires. I guess that's really why I killed Eric. I just got so angry at him that I slipped into high gear, and the next thing I knew . . . well, he was dead. Can you understand?"

Rebecca turned around and walked to him. She saw the wary look on his face, which made her sad, and then angry, and then sad again. She put her hand on his cheek and stroked it. "Do you like my beauty, Richard?"

"It's magnificent. You are truly stunning, Rebecca. When I look at you it does something to me, puts me in a completely strange frame of mind. If it wasn't that you . . ." He caught himself too late.

A look of pain shattered the happy smile on Rebecca's face. "You mean if it wasn't that I am a vampire, don't you? Well, I am, and that's all there is to it!" She spun around and furiously pushed over a small table, sending the lamp and papers on it flying across the floor.

"Rebecca!"

She spun around again, facing him. "What? What do you want, Richard?"

"Rebecca, I'm sorry I hurt your feelings. It must be dreadful, what you're going through."

She felt his pity and refused it. "Dreadful? Not at all, Richard. On the contrary, it's magnificent. I only wish you could become a vampire, too."

"Me? A vampire?" He shook his head. "No, I don't think I would want to."

"And be with me forever? Didn't you once say that?"

"Well, yes."

She smiled. "It's all right, Richard. You can't become a vampire, anyway. Alexander won't allow it."

His face darkened. "Alexander. He's behind all of this. He's taken you away from me."

"Not entirely, Richard. Not if you don't want it to be that way."

"What do you mean?"

"Well, it's sort of complicated. But it's possible for you to stay with me. Not as a vampire, but as a human. For literally as long as you want. Like Gregor," she said quickly, and was again struck by the memory of Gregor's own warning to her, and then by the fact that Gregor was now dead by her own hand.

"Me and Gregor? Waiting on the three of you?"

"No. Gregor has . . . left."

He did not ask her for an explanation, for which she was grateful. Instead he seemed to be considering her offer.

"Do you still love me, Richard?" she said softly.

He looked at her, and she was again gratified to see his expression. With the slightest concentration she found that she could actually enhance the effect she made, and now she put all her willpower into looking as seductive as possible. It worked.

"Rebecca, yes. I do still love you. As always." He put his arms around her and kissed her, long and lovingly.

Rebecca reveled in the erotic sensuality of the kiss and felt herself soar with passion. Every part of her body glowed with desire. Finally she broke the kiss and held his face in her hands, looking at him.

"What would you do, Richard, if you found you couldn't leave me? Because the sex was so good."

"There's no such thing. It would only be because I love you, Rebecca."

Rebecca looked up to his eyes for a second, reading them, and she could see a faint sheen on his forehead. It made her smile and she dropped her eyes to his throat, studying the throbbing artery on his neck.

Is it really possible that biting a neck can be erotic?

The thought made her feel perverse, and yet it excited her. She became flirtatious and challenging. "Really?" she said, dropping her hands and moving away from him to lean catlike against the chair where he had been tied. "I made love with the count, Richard. And I made love with the countess, too. Up until that point I might have agreed with you. There's nothing like it, I promise you."

His eyes widened. "Are you trying to frighten me, Rebecca?"

She was silent for a second, thinking. Then, "Richard, I want you to make love to me. I want us to be together forever. It can be that way, if you want it. Make love to me now, and see if you want it. If you do not wish to be with me, you may leave, but if you decide you want to share my love, then come to the castle."

He stood still, staring at her. Rebecca closed her eyes and again concentrated on being a picture of beauty and sexuality. She made the lights in the railway car go off one by one, until only the one over her head remained shining. Then she opened her eyes.

With a grace of movement unknown to her before, she splayed her fingers along her hips and slowly brought her hands up her sides to her shoulders, then reached behind her neck and unzipped the black dress she was wearing. With little more than a shake of her wrists the dress dropped to her ankles, and she stepped out of it. She was wearing nothing underneath.

Her slender fingers moved back across her shoulders and then lightly down her front to her breasts, which she caressed and held for a few seconds. Her nipples became taut, and she teased them lightly, closing her eyes and moaning at the same time.

"Richard," she whispered. "I want you."

She slid her fingers down across her flat stomach, resting them briefly on her hips. "Richard, make love to me. Take me now!"

Then her hands sculpted her own thighs and

her fingers moved inward to the thin, downy hair between her legs.

"Richard!" she cried hoarsely.

He came to her, tearing off his clothes as he did. He grabbed her in his arms and kissed her, and she felt his tongue discover her long canine teeth, but he did not back away. She felt his erection on her belly, and then she levitated herself slightly until she could look him in the eyes; then kissing him again, she slid downward onto him.

They remained frozen like that for an eternity where all thoughts were banished and time did not exist, giving each other pleasure that neither knew existed, and then they both exploded in sexual climax together.

They tumbled to the floor together, laughing.

"Rebecca! That was incredible."

"I think there's more," she said, crawling on top of him.

"No, no," he said, still laughing, "I couldn't . . ."

But she showed him he could.

Rebecca stood at the doorway to the railroad car, looking back at Richard. They were quiet with each other now, the time for making love having passed, and neither was certain what the other was thinking.

Rebecca worried because she knew she had to go back to the castle, and she could not think of exactly what to say. She had felt the call coming first from Alexander and then from Maria, gentle at the start and then more insistent. They were warning her it was dangerous to be away too long.

"I love you, Richard," she said. "Deeply. And

need you. In a strange way, I think perhaps even more now than I did before.''

He nodded. "I know what you mean. I think I feel the same. But would we have to stay with them?''

"I don't know. Maybe for a while. It will be all right, Richard. You'll see.''

A troubled look came over his face. "But what does it mean, Rebecca? Can we really love each other throughout eternity like this? Or are we pretending, indulging in a sexual frenzy? Are the countess and Gregor happy?''

Rebecca took a deep breath. "I have to return to the castle, Richard. It must be your decision to come with me.''

He nodded. "I know.''

Rebecca stepped out onto the platform behind the car, tensed slightly, and flew off into the night. Richard watched her go.

"Can the damned truly love?'' he said to the darkness.

米

25

"She has killed the German, her ex-lover," Alexander said. He and Maria were sitting by the fireplace in the music room.

Maria stared into the flames licking upward. "Yes, I felt it too."

"She is a willful one, is our young Rebecca."

For a long time Maria said nothing. Finally she raised her eyes and stared hollowly at her husband. "Is she then 'our' Rebecca, Alexander?"

"What do you mean?"

"You know."

He got up and walked over to the fireplace, then turned and leaned against it, facing her. "Not really," he said.

"I mean that you have picked and chosen young women over the years, and I was always expected to play along."

"You never seemed to mind. And anyway, there were always enough young men for you to take pleasure in as well."

"Yes, you're right. You have never denied me anything that you had the power to grant me,

Alexander. In your own way I suppose that passes for love."

"I've always loved you. More than anyone else."

Maria laughed bitterly. "You're a vampire, Alexander. If you ever knew how to love, you've forgotten long ago."

"Of course I do!"

"Really? And just what is love then, to you?"

He shifted his stance but did not answer.

"See what I mean?"

"Stop cross-examining me, Maria. Is a dictionary definition of the word what you want?"

"No, not at all. That is just my point. You don't feel anything anymore, so when you attempt to express a feeling, you are at a loss."

He strode angrily across the room and looked out a window. "Maria, stop this. You're upset about Gregor and you're trying to hurt me to compensate."

"Perhaps, Alexander. But I'm still right. You have been a vampire so long that all the human in you has finally disappeared. I just realized that is what happens."

"Now what are you talking about?"

"That you think you've become a vampire when you come out of the cocoon. When I came out I was so thrilled with the new powers that I lost myself in them, and thought, 'So this is what it is like to be a vampire.'

"I was wrong, of course," she went on. "I had only just started becoming a vampire."

"Maria . . ."

"No, let me finish, Alexander. Please."

Alexander returned to her and sat down in the chair.

She continued. "The physical transformation was complete. So physically I was a vampire. But for a long time I still thought like a human, so for a while I had the best of both worlds. The heightened sensuality of a vampire with the emotions of a young woman made existence a never ending thrill. I enjoyed the pleasures as much as you did with everyone we brought home. I don't deny or regret it.

"But I realize now that the decay of my soul also began when I came out of that cocoon. It was not apparent to me, or at first even profound enough to notice. But it began, and over time it increased until somewhere I lost the ability to experience the pleasures for their own sake. I still enjoyed them, but it was different somehow. Compulsive, maybe. Anyway, there was a desperation about it all.

"That's where I relied on Gregor. Gregor loved me, Alexander, as only a human can love. Early on I loved Gregor, too, and was disappointed when you would not make him a vampire. But now I realize that if you had made him into a vampire, then he, too, would have begun the spiritual decay that I as well as you have undergone. Then he would not have given me that link to human love that I still so desperately need.

"I'm telling you all this now, Alexander, because I am only just understanding it. The process of my own spiritual decay was so subtle and has taken so long that I was unaware of it, as I think you are, until tonight when I saw Gregor lying dead on the floor."

"You loved Gregor more than me?" Alexander said.

"Stop it, Alexander. Don't indulge in petty jealousy."

"Are you saying then that you don't love me?"

"Oh, I suppose I do, Alex," she said, giving him a sad smile. "At least as much as one vampire can love another. Which is to say, I see the world through the same corrupt vampire eyes that you do."

He was silent for a moment, then stood up. "You are weary, Maria. It happens sometimes, just from having lived so long."

"Lived? Don't you mean 'existed'?"

"Whatever. My point is, don't become maudlin; it is dangerous."

"You're not listening to me, Alexander. I'm telling you I do not wish to go on any longer."

"Maria, don't say that."

"It's true. I've finally seen what happens to you once you become a vampire, and it sickens me. I will not continue."

"Maria!"

"Don't try to dissuade me. You have Rebecca now. She is still new, and who knows, perhaps like you she will always want to be a vampire. But when you made me a vampire, you made me a solemn promise that if I ever wished to end it you would not prevent me."

"Yes, Maria, but please consider this. You do not have to do anything immediately."

"Yes, I do. If I don't I will be seduced by the subtle arguments of the vampire, the subtle pulls of soul decay, and I'll just continue on into ever increasing unhappiness."

"No, Maria. It's not like that. This is just a temporary mood you're in. I'm not unhappy. I like being a vampire."

"I know you do. But I'm not certain I am capable of loving anymore, now that Gregor is dead. Any more than you are."

"I am capable of love!" he protested.

"Really?"

"Of course!"

"And you love me?"

"Yes, I do."

"Then fulfill your promise to me and do not interfere with my passing."

He stared at her. "You've tricked me."

She shook her head in exhaustion. "No, Alexander. I've just told you what I wish and asked you to respect that wish, as you promised you would."

He stared into the fire, and she watched the expression on his face change gradually into acceptance. "What will you do?"

"Take Gregor's body to the tower and wait for the sunrise."

"It is truly what you wish, Maria?"

She nodded. "Yes, Alexander. My time is now."

26

Rebecca felt as though she weighed no more than the air itself, and she moved through it six or seven feet off the ground as though she were swimming. It was exhilarating. She smiled as the wind blew her hair behind her and whistled in her ears.

She followed the tracks back to the village, enjoying the way the twin steel bands beneath her gleamed in the moonlight. In minutes she was back at the same station where she and Richard had originally disembarked.

Rebecca dropped down gracefully and walked the short distance into the village. A dog, crossing the street, suddenly saw her and froze. It growled softly in the back of its throat and the fur along its back rose. It shivered with fright, then backed away. She heard a clicking sound to her right and looked up, realizing it was the old clock in the square. It was nearly four o'clock. Dawn was a couple of hours off.

She remembered the pain she had felt yesterday from sunlight and shuddered to think what it would be like now.

No one was on the streets of the small town. Rebecca passed the barn where she had killed the boy and glanced inside. She saw that his body had been removed, and nodded. That would have been Alexander, she thought, cleaning up after her. She giggled.

She wanted to get back to the castle now. She began to move quicker, not quite flying yet moving her feet so fast that they seemed to blur.

In seconds she had left the town and entered the woods. An owl hooted from far away. Her ears picked up other night forest sounds, but she ignored them and hurried on.

A few miles farther she met the wolves. There were six of them, standing in a semicircle and waiting for her. She walked to the center of the group and put her hands on her hips, then grinned at them. Looking at them, it seemed hilarious that they could frighten anyone. Instead they seemed like so many puppies. They each bowed their heads to her.

"Come here," she said, and patted her leg with her right hand.

They all walked over to her in a line, wagging their tails, and formed a tight circle around her legs. She pulled on their ears and scratched their necks, laughing, and suddenly realized that as she touched each one she could read its thoughts. They were idolizing her.

Realizing that she understood them completely, each one clamored for her attention. One by one they got on their hind legs and tried to hug her with their front paws, licking her face and neck.

Finally she pushed them off and walked away. Time was passing, after all.

"Go on, then," she said, and first one, then the next and the next began a long mournful cry of sadness. She walked away, holding her ears.

She reached the broken bridge seconds later. With a leap she crossed the river. She moved on until she came to the edge of the forest, where it gave way to the grounds of the castle. There she stopped and looked again at the stone structure. There were lights on in the great hall and in some of the adjacent rooms.

They would be waiting for her. Rebecca felt as she had as a teenager, when she had come home too late. She shrugged her shoulders unconsciously and stepped onto the lawn. The dew on the grass felt cold, and for the first time she remembered she had not worn shoes to go out; they just had not seemed necessary. Rebecca glanced to the sky and saw that the moon had set. She felt so much better now than she had when she had first come out of the statue. She was a little tired, but who wouldn't be after a night like that?

After all, I was "born," made my first kills, had good sex, and ran around half the countryside doing it.

She laughed out loud, then stopped when she realized her voice was a little shrill.

It was time to go in. Rebecca took several long strides to the open front doors and entered the castle. The great hall was empty, though candles and electric lights burned everywhere. She walked past the rows of armaments and peeked into the music room, half expecting to find them in there.

But it was empty and she continued on into the dining room, and from there into the library. Finally she found the count in a small side chamber by himself, sitting on an old wooden throne and staring at the floor. For a brief moment his face looked strained and wrinkled, and Rebecca was reminded of his great age. Then he looked up and saw her, and the lines disappeared.

"There you are, my darling," he said, smiling. "I was beginning to worry about you. You are still new to the game, and I was afraid you might get caught out after sunrise. Fortunately you didn't." He rose from his chair and came over to her, then put his hands on her shoulders and kissed her lightly on the mouth.

"I did all sorts of things tonight, Alexander," Rebecca said. "I feel changed."

"You are changed, my dear. You have become one of the special people. Welcome."

"Thank you," she said, and he kissed her again.

"There is a place for you to rest during the daylight hours beneath the castle floor. It is hidden and you will be safe. For security we sleep separately, but there is nothing to fear. You are safe now. The door is here, behind the throne." He gestured at it and the throne slid around, exposing a narrow door and stairs leading down into darkness.

Rebecca nodded. Then she looked around. "Where is Maria? Has she gone to sleep already?"

Alexander did not answer her, and she repeated her question. Finally he said simply, "Maria is up in the main tower."

"The tower? Why? What is she doing up there? Isn't that unsafe?"

Alexander looked at her sternly, and Rebecca

was aware of how quickly he could change. Instead of the vulnerability she had glimpsed a few seconds before, he showed the fierceness of a vampire again. "Maria is quite capable of taking care of herself. I will explain it all later. You must not worry about her."

Then his expression softened and he put his arm around her. He gently urged her toward the clandestine stairwell. "Come, let me show you where to sleep."

Rebecca went along with him, still wondering why Maria had not hidden herself as well, but letting herself be led by Alexander. They went down the winding stairs, pulling the door closed behind them, to a large room filled with caskets. One candle burned in the center of the room, but it was all Rebecca needed to see around her. Alexander showed a casket to her and motioned for her to crawl into it.

She suddenly felt exhausted. The casket seemed wonderful now, and even though it was still a little while before dawn, she did as he indicated, crawling lightly over the side and slipping down onto the soft cushions. Alexander disappeared, presumably off to his own coffin. She yawned once and closed her eyes.

Suddenly a wild thought entered her head. Rebecca's eyes flew open and she sat upright. Without a second's pause she leapt from the casket and raced back up the stairs. The throne moved away in front of her and she tore across the room and back out into the great hall, heading for the northeast turret.

Cold air blew through shafts in the circular walls designed for archers defending the castle. Rebecca reached the bottom stair in seconds, and began to climb. Round and round she went toward the top, and climbed the nearly hundred-foot tower in seconds. As she came to the top, the first faint predawn glow appeared in the mountains to the east.

Rebecca stopped suddenly.

In the corner sat Maria, her face masked with sorrow, holding herself tightly with both arms and staring at the lifeless body of Gregor lying next to her.

"Maria!" Rebecca said. "What are you doing? Alexander said you had come up here, but why?"

Maria raised her head with obvious effort and smiled at Rebecca wearily. She shook her head. "It is over for me, Rebecca. I no longer wish to be a vampire."

"Maria, no!"

"I wanted you to become a vampire because Alex wanted it," Maria went on. "Now you are. Go back to the coffin he has prepared for you. Enjoy yourself for as long as you wish. I have for over two hundred years. That is more than enough for me."

Maria sighed and looked again at Gregor. "I have seen that the only man who loved me was Gregor. Now I have grown weary of the game. I only wish it to stop." Behind her the light on the horizon grew slightly brighter.

"Is it because I killed Gregor?"

Maria shook her head and the smile on her lips was a twist of pain. "No, Rebecca. I am actually thankful to you for doing it, as I am sure Gregor would be. You do not understand, of course, but that is how I feel."

"But how can I be what you have been? I need you to stay. I want you to stay."

Maria looked up at her. "You will be fine, Rebecca. Alexander will show you many things. You are about to have a tremendous adventure."

"If it is so tremendous, why are you leaving it?"

Maria considered the question. When she spoke her voice quavered slightly.

"Rebecca, my lover is dead. My true lover, that is. It is a terrible thing to lose the one who loves you. I have been sitting up here remembering the very first time I saw Gregor, and trying to recall the feelings I had that night.

"As I told you, I was suffering and on my own in Kraków, and Gregor provided for me. But what was so amazing to me, then and now, is that he never asked anything of me. Perhaps he should have. Maybe I would not have taken him so much for granted.

"That first night, he took me back to his house and had me sit by the fire. I was wet and shivering and very hungry. He tossed more logs onto it and knelt to stir them up. As he did so I caught him glancing at my legs, and I thought that he was going to make me have sex with him. I decided then that if he did I would kill him. For you see, my bitterness had changed me, and I had by then learned to mistrust everyone.

"But to my surprise, without a word he left the room. I huddled by the fire, which began to roar upward, and put my hands to its warmth. When he did return a little while later, it was with a tray of food. In spite of my earlier resolve, I was so grateful that I wept.

"With the tenderest look I have ever seen, Gregor brushed the hair from my eyes and raised some food to my lips. I licked it from his hand like a grateful puppy.

"He brought more food, and I ate until I was full. Then he let me sleep unmolested on the sofa. For several days I stayed there on that sofa, until the trouble began with his family. They, of course, thought I was a vixen wanting to steal his money and use him.

"It made me angry that they saw me that way, and although I could understand their suspicions, still I took it out on him. I flirted with him and eventually seduced him. I slowly became the thing they thought I was.

"I left him in Kraków, confident that he would pursue me. And of course I was right. He found me days later in Budapest and agreed to go anywhere I wished. His love for me was his doom, and my abuse of that love was my own. For you see, I had met Alexander by then and was swept off my feet. Alexander was everything Gregor was not."

Maria smiled wryly. "I just did not realize what that meant. I did not want Gregor to leave; I only wanted him to be there when I decreed he should be. And knowing how selfless his love for me was, I made sure that he stayed on at the castle, catering to Alexander and myself.

"I guess in my own way I did love him. Perhaps I was of the vampire mentality long before meeting Alexander."

Rebecca shuddered. "Am I of the vampire mentality also, Maria? Is that why you two chose me?"

But Maria did not answer. The glow from the predawn had increased to nearly yellow, and its effect made them both stiffen suddenly with pain.

"Maria! Come away from this. You must return

below. Don't allow this horrible death to take you!"

Maria closed her eyes, taking a few seconds to control the level of pain she was suffering. When she opened them again she gave Rebecca a sad look but said nothing.

Rebecca covered her eyes from the stinging needles of luminescence and backed down the stairs involuntarily. "Maria!" she cried. "Come!"

The dawn seemed to come quicker and quicker as the sun neared the horizon. The light became like fire, burning them. Again Rebecca retreated farther down the winding stairs. Then the topmost red tip of the sun popped over the horizon and the entire structure became a burning hell. Rebecca screamed in pain.

"Maria! Please come with me!"

Maria took a deep breath and in her agony spoke her final words. "Go, Rebecca! This is my moment. You must hide yourself. Go now and flee. But remember this, and never leave Alexander by himself. I would have done this before, but I waited until I found you. Go!"

Rebecca's eyes were closed to slits. They were bulging, puffy, and beginning to bleed. Nearly blinded by the hateful brilliance of the rising sun, Rebecca saw Maria slowly climb to her feet.

Maria raised a hand to Rebecca, then took a deep breath and stepped in front of the open window, taking the full light of the rising sun. She screamed once more and burst into flames. Rebecca watched in horror as the sun burned Maria's hair, her clothing, and her skin, and then she was gone.

Racked with a pain so intense it shut off her

emotions and made her think only of survival, Rebecca shut her eyes and raced back down the stairs. Unable to see as the blood flowed freely down her cheeks, she was forced to hold her hands in front of her and feel her way along the stone walls. Not until she had entered the hidden stairs and pulled the door closed behind her did the searing on her flesh stop. Weak and battered, she crept down into the cool darkness to her casket. As soon as she was there, she tumbled into its dark safety and slept deep and dreamless.

Outside the sun passed slowly overhead.

※

27

Richard opened his eyes. In spite of his intentions, he had fallen asleep after Rebecca left. With an effort he got to his feet and climbed down from the railcar onto the tracks. At first the bright sunshine seemed warm, but a dry wind blew down on him from the snow-capped peaks and he shivered. The brilliant light reflecting off the pristine whiteness of the snow dazzled him. For a few minutes everything that had happened over the last two days seemed nothing more than a bad dream. But he knew that it was not a dream, and he breathed deeply to make the cold mountain air clear his mind.

Richard put his hands in his pockets and began walking down the tracks back toward the village. He listened to his feet crunching on the sooty pebbles between the railroad ties and went over in his mind the entire time he had known Rebecca. He remembered their first date, the first time they had slept together, and how they had fled Berlin together. To keep the focus and strength necessary for what he had decided to do, he needed to remember all the reasons he loved her.

From far off came the clear chimes of a mountain church. Richard walked quickly, not certain how he was going to accomplish it, but certain that he must.

It took him until midafternoon to get back to the village. Shortly after three o'clock he stumbled up onto the station platform, exhausted, thirsty, and disheveled. He got a splinter in his right hand from the old wooden planks and stopped for a moment at the edge of the railing to remove it.

The stationmaster looked out the window at the wild-looking young man and immediately picked up the phone and called the constable.

"He's here on the platform, Pietre!"

"Who? Who are you talking about?"

"That boy. The American boy. Standing here looking like the very devil."

"Have you spoken to him yet?"

"No."

"I'll be right there."

Pietre put on his coat and strode out of his tiny office, turning in the direction of the station. This was not something he had expected. He had spent most of last night covering up the murder of young Michael, doing as he had been told to make it look like an automobile accident. He had just finished filling out a blizzard of official reports, and that without any breakfast or even coffee. His consolation was that at least it was over. The damnable count and countess had led him to believe that it was over. And now this. Angrily he stepped up onto the platform and stood in front of the boy.

"What are you doing here?" he said.

Richard looked up at him. "I need your help."

"What happened to the Germans?"

Richard shrugged. "They're gone," he said. Then again, "I need your help."

"Stop saying that!"

"But it's true."

Pietre took out a handkerchief and wiped his brow. It was awfully hot for this late in the year, he thought. "I cannot help you," he said.

"You must. You have no choice."

Pietre barked a short laugh. "Ha. No choice? It is you, my young friend; you have no choice. You are in very big trouble."

"Then why don't you arrest me?"

"You speak very bravely. Perhaps I should. But why don't you just move on, go back to your own country, your own home? This is no place for you."

Richard stared at him for a few seconds before speaking. "The Germans are dead."

The constable turned pale.

"They were killed early this morning on the train. The car was loosed from the rest of the train, and in fact it is still sitting on the tracks."

Pietre's heart pounded in his chest. He thought of the trouble this would cause, and his fear made him angry. "Damn you! Who killed them? You?"

Now Richard laughed. "It was the vampires, Herr Constable."

Pietre stepped backward. "What vampires? There . . . there are no vampires," he stammered.

"You know what I am saying is true. I can see it in your eyes. I repeat, I need your help."

Pietre heard voices and looked around. To his

alarm a small crowd was beginning to gather on the street. "Come," he said, "we cannot stand here talking. Come with me."

He led Richard through the throng of people back to his house. There he gave Richard food and clean clothing and again cautioned him to leave as quickly as possible.

"I need your help, Constable," Richard said wearily. "They must be killed. They cannot be allowed to propagate."

The constable bent over his desk, busily filling out forms. "They do not increase their numbers," he said without looking up.

"What? How can you say that?"

"Anyway, they cannot be killed. Only they can kill themselves. They do it every now and then, no one knows why, but their numbers do not increase."

Richard was silent until the constable finally looked up at him.

"Go," he said. "Go back to America. We are who we are. Do not try to correct our balance. If it is evil you wish to correct, do so in your own country. From what I hear you have more than enough of it there."

"No. Rebecca . . . my girlfriend. She has become one of them."

Pietre looked back down at his desktop. That meant there was a new countess now. The old one must have killed herself. "Then I am sorry for you, and for her. But there is nothing that can be done."

Richard exploded. "Coward! Well, I'm going to do something," he shouted, and stalked outside, slamming the door shut behind him.

The streets were deserted. All the doors in the

village were locked tight, all the windows covered. It might have been a ghost town. Richard looked at his watch. It was just before four o'clock. He had to get moving.

The barn was open at the end of town. Richard went into it and found a hammer and saw, and crafted three stakes out of wood from a pile in one corner. His mind raced, considering plans and options yet unable to repress the humiliating and frightening memories that reminded him he had been their victim once and he would have to be very clever and lucky not to be one again.

By the time he stepped back out onto the street, high clouds had covered the sky, obscuring the late-afternoon sun and turning the world a sickly gray. The wind had grown stronger and colder. Richard looked back down the street and again saw no one.

"What the hell," he muttered to the empty town. "If you won't help me, you can at least lend me one of your cars."

A black pickup truck stood by itself in front of a closed hardware store. Richard walked over to it, looked around once, and tossed his tools in the back. It only took a minute to hot-wire it. He backed it away from the curb and then turned it around and drove out of town. No one came after him.

The truck was not very fast, but it held steady. As Richard turned north and entered the forest, the wind scattered dead leaves everywhere. He followed the road as best he could, climbing upward to where it crossed the gorge.

The road was unpaved for most of the way, and twice he drove off it when swirling leaves hid the way completely. Both times he had to backtrack carefully to find the dirt path before he could continue in the right direction.

When he finally reached a bridge, he stopped and looked at his watch. It was four-thirty. He looked up at the sky over the river and saw that the early winter darkness was already beginning to descend.

The wooden planks in front of him seemed shaky, but there was no choice. He eased out the clutch and let the truck crawl slowly across, listening to the planks rattle beneath him. When he looked down he could see rushing water through gaps in the framework, but he continued until he came down onto the other side. The tires touched solid ground, and he realized he had been gripping the wheel with all his strength. He wiped his forehead with the back of his hand, then continued.

When the path came to the line of trees that marked the beginning of the castle grounds, Richard stopped the truck. The wind was much stronger, buffeting the small vehicle with icy blasts. Richard looked to his right and saw heavy storm clouds being blown in from the east. To the west the storm front was nearly to the horizon, and he could see the yellow ball of sun hanging, as though stuck momentarily between clouds and earth. Then it began to slide downward.

Richard dropped the clutch and slammed his foot onto the accelerator. The truck let loose a blast of smoke from its tailpipe and lurched forward onto the paved drive. Richard raced to the front of the castle and braked hard at the stone entrance. He turned off the key and jumped out of the cab.

Breathing hard, he reached in the back and

picked up the hammer and three stakes, then walked around the front of the truck and bounded up the steps to the huge wooden doors. He stopped at the entrance, took a deep breath, and glanced once more toward the west. Half the sun was already below the horizon. Heart pounding, he grabbed the handle of the door and pulled it open.

Rebecca opened her eyes. She could not move yet, but she was fully awake. This was obviously the way it worked. The sun must be nearly set, she decided. When it was completely down she assumed she would be able to arise. Arise and . . . and what? And go eat? Feast on blood? There was no doubt that is what she would have to do. It did not bother her; in fact she was quite hungry. To her surprise, the thought of drinking some hot, rich blood did not disgust her; it raised her appetite enormously.

She thought briefly of Richard, of how easily she had seduced him. There was no doubt he would be along soon. He could not do otherwise. The look in his eyes when he gazed at her told her that.

She thought of the count. Count Alexander Viroslav. She wanted to love and to serve him now. Then she thought of Maria. It was sad, of course, but after all it was her choice. Then a thought occurred to her. With the countess gone, long live the countess! Countess Rebecca Viroslav. That's what she would be, of course. It was wonderful.

Rebecca started to smile and realized she could not move even those facial muscles. Well, it would be night soon.

Her vampire hearing picked up the sound of the truck, then the front door being opened. The noise frightened her, and she whimpered softly at the frustration of not being able to move. It was almost as bad as being the statue.

She heard footsteps and recognized them as Richard's. She felt better knowing it was him. He would fill the gap left by Gregor, and that was good. They needed someone, a mortal, to do the little things that they could not. Especially during the daylight hours.

There was a crash, then the sound of doors opening and closing. What was he doing up there? Rebecca listened intently, marking his progress around the level above. He was looking for her. For her, or for them.

Was he out of his mind? Alexander would be furious that Richard was even trying to find them. He had made it very clear to Rebecca that this place was their secret. If Richard wanted to stay here in good favor, he was going to have to learn his place, that was all there was to it. His footsteps moved down the hall and into the small throne room overhead.

An image of what had happened in the railcar earlier flashed into Rebecca's mind. Was he as angry? But that was absurd! He had no idea what he was dealing with if he had some naive thoughts of revenge.

She tried to move, still could not. It could not be much longer.

Then, incredibly, she heard a scraping sound. It was the throne being moved! How could he have possibly found that? But he had, and now she heard his steps on the stairway, moving slowly down into the darkness.

Rebecca looked around. If Alexander caught him who knew what might happen. Then it occurred to her that she had moved her eyes. Moved a muscle. That meant it was almost time.

"Rebecca."

It was Richard! How had he found the casket room?

"Rebecca, it's Richard. Where is the count?"

Did he think she would tell him? She heard his footsteps, counted them from the entrance to the room, and then suddenly he was standing by her casket and looking down at her. He held a small candle in one hand and something else in the other. It was a stake!

"Rebecca, where is he?"

She tried to move, tried to shout. This could not happen! Not like this! But without thinking she moved her eyes up in her head, and he followed the tiny gesture.

"In there?" he said. Then he nodded and his face became hard. Determined, he moved out of her range of vision.

She listened to his footsteps fade slightly as he moved away from her. Damn him!

Alexander! My love, he is coming for you!

Ten steps, twenty, then he stopped. Rebecca heard him put the stake and hammer down and then the long, slow creaking as the casket lid was opened.

Alexander! Alexander!

Then came the sound she dreaded. A heavy clink, and a horrified Alexander screaming in pain. The awful sound echoing all around the chamber. With tears in her eyes she listened to Alexander's cries of agony as Richard drove the stake into him.

Suddenly she was aware that the sun was down. All at once her powers returned and she was filled with strength. Alexander, too, must have come back, but too late. He had come back only to die.

The sound of his death struggle cut into Rebecca even as she leapt from the casket and put her hands to her ears to block it out.

"No! No, Richard! Stop!"

But Rebecca knew it was too late. She felt a hot, searing blast race through the darkened room, followed by an icy wind, and she knew now that not only Maria but the count, too, was gone.

28

Richard stared silently at the few bits of dust lying on the silk material inside the coffin of Count Viroslav. It had been easier than he thought, killing the vampire. He had not been certain that he had the strength to pound a stake into the chest of someone, even if that someone was a vampire. That had worried Richard and slowed him down. Then when he had placed the point of the stake over the heart and raised his hammer, he had seen the eyes open. His timing had been just right. A few seconds later and the vampire would have been on him. Then things would have undoubtedly gone quite differently.

But it had not happened, and Richard was victorious. He had killed the evil creature who had haunted this region for centuries. It should make him feel wonderful, but he only felt weary.

And there was still Rebecca. What would he do when the time came with her? Even now he felt tempted to allow her to continue to exist. He shook his head.

I must not weaken.

Richard turned around to go back to the other room, the one where Rebecca's coffin was, but to his surprise there were several doors along the wall of the cavernous room, and he was not certain which one he had come through. He had been in such a hurry, he had not paid attention when he entered. He retraced his steps across the floor the best he could and chose the most likely door.

Rebecca was leaning against the casket waiting for Richard. She was aware of a gnawing hunger. She was also aware that the only thing that would satiate it was blood. For a few moments she was tempted to get that blood from Richard. But what was she going to do? She had been left alone, a neophyte vampire in a foreign country, her two mentors dead and gone. She needed Richard and even still wanted him, yet at the same time she knew there was not much else she could do, at least for the present. By herself she could not make Richard a vampire.

But there was also the question whether she even should make Richard a vampire. Even if she could figure out a way. She reasoned that she already knew Richard and he knew her, at least knew her pre-vampire, and more importantly already knew that she was a vampire.

But what was Richard thinking? He had just slain Alexander. Did he mean to be a vampire killer? Did he wish to kill her as well? She was not afraid of him, now that she was awake and out of her coffin. He could not harm her as long as she was awake. But if he caught her during the daylight hours, what would he do to her? She would have to determine his plans.

There were footsteps in the next chamber again, returning toward her. Without a second thought she pulled loose the ties of her dress and let it fall to the floor, making certain that her radiant nudity would be the first thing he saw. She stood silently and waited.

For a few seconds the shadows hid everything. Then her eyes widened in fear as she saw that it was not Richard who stepped from the black shadows that filled the castle's nether levels, but someone whom Rebecca had never seen before. A tall, extremely handsome man with jet black hair, thick eyebrows, and arresting blue eyes now stood gazing down at her. His skin was olive colored, as though he had a deep tan, his lips thin and cruel. But his chin was strong, matching the bulges of his shoulders and chest that were apparent even through the black cloak he wore. He seemed enormous to Rebecca. He was at least a foot taller than she was. He took one step forward into the candlelight and stopped.

"Who . . . who are you?" she said, and heard her own voice waver slightly.

"You do not know me, but I am who you have become. I am the ultimate creator of your line. I, in fact, made your dear departed count who he was for these many centuries. I am the Black Prince."

Rebecca said nothing. The Black Prince stepped in front of her. He lifted his right hand and casually stroked her forehead, brushing a lock of hair back. Then he caressed her cheek and finally dropped his hand back to his side.

"You are wondering what has happened to Richard," he said. "Do not worry; Richard is lost right now, wandering around the many circuitous halls and chambers down here. I made certain he would remain that way for a while."

He raised his hand again and spread his thumb and fingers apart, making a vise. With a smoothness that accentuated his enormous strength, he placed them on either side of Rebecca's neck and lightly touched the skin of her throat. Then he bent down and kissed her lightly on the lips. Her whole body tingled. It terrified her, yet she felt herself being seduced by that one kiss. Unable to move, Rebecca received his kiss without complaint.

When he broke the kiss he brought his hand down her chest, touching her breasts, stomach, and sex. Rebecca felt the hand burn deep into her womb.

"I wish to see you like this whenever I come here," he said.

His hand further pressed against her, and this time she saw visions of fiends and demons dancing with the naked souls of humans. She watched them moving through roaring fires laughing maniacally, and she gasped. He withdrew his hand slowly, and the vision vanished.

Rebecca clung to the side of the casket, gasping for breath.

The Black Prince regarded her silently before speaking again. When he spoke his voice was calm, authoritative. "Your Richard has removed my tenant from my castle, Rebecca. I allowed it to happen, of course, because it was my pleasure. Count Viroslav no longer pleased me. Now I still have you, but the rent is high here. You will need help. I believe you wished Richard to join you, did you not?"

The hunger was growing within her again, now

more fiercely. She wanted blood. And she wanted sex. It struck her that her desires were both simple and monstrous.

"What about Richard? What if I do not choose him?"

The Black Prince shrugged. "Richard has dabbled with something greater than he is capable of controlling. You may choose to let him go his own way, but already he has tainted his path. Whether he would be able to return to his previous world remains to be seen. What is certain is he can never view it in the same way."

"Are there others like me?"

He nodded. "But none currently available, I'm afraid."

The need for blood was now roaring within her. It was so difficult to think. "I . . . I do not know . . ." she said.

"What do you wish? We can find you someone else, make him become the count of this castle, if you wish."

"Can I feed before I make this decision?"

This time the Black Prince shook his head. "No. These decisions can only be made when you are at the edge. Only then can you really know your self, your weaknesses, your needs. This is what being a vampire is all about, Rebecca. It is only now that you will need Richard enough to choose for him to join you, or conversely, to leave you."

Her body quivered, the hunger driving her mad. She tried to think of Richard, of what they had called love previously. He had been devoted to her then. Would he still be? Would he choose this path, if given the opportunity to choose?

She felt her female lips pulsating, felt her stomach rumbling, felt both needs converging.

The sharp fangs, with a life of their own, slipped over her lips. She saw Richard as he had been, dressed in the party tuxedo, then naked before Maria, and finally as he had been in the rail car. She saw the determination on his face as he hunted Alexander in this very room. And she wanted his blood and wanted his body more than anything else she could think of.

"Yes," she cried. "I want him!"

The Black Prince's lips spread into a triumphant smile. "Then behold," he said, lifting an arm toward the shadows behind him, "here he comes. Prepare him for me." The Black Prince disappeared.

Richard stepped from the shadows, carrying a stake and a hammer.

"There you are," he said. "I've been wandering around looking for you, Rebecca."

Suddenly he realized she was nude. His eyes widened at her unearthly beauty and he hesitated.

Rebecca smiled. Her mouth craved the taste of blood now so strongly that she could smell it in him even through his pores. She slowly spread her arms out in a welcoming gesture.

"Come to me, my darling," she said.

"I've . . . I've just killed the count. I do not know where Maria is."

Why was he talking about such things? Talk could be later; now was forever. "She's gone, Richard. It is now just you and me. Together for eternity. Come to me."

"Rebecca, it must stop." His eyes glazed. "My God, you are beautiful."

"Yes, Richard. I am beautiful. And my beauty is

for you. Come to me, my darling." Her fangs grew longer and her eyes more intense.

He wavered. The eyes! They were the eyes he had seen in Maria. So hypnotic, so seductive. "Rebecca . . ."

"I know, darling. But it is all right. Come to me."

He took a faltering step forward, his arms becoming slack, and then another and another. She smiled at him, commanding him with her eyes.

"Come, Richard, join me. We will live forever with each other, and nothing can harm us."

He stopped in front of her and dropped the stake and hammer on the floor. Then he reached for her.

"I want you, Richard, just as you want me." She reached up and undid his shirt and pulled it open. Without stopping she unbuckled his pants and pulled them free and down his legs. She stripped him in seconds, then she stood up again and put her arms around his neck and kissed him. She had become desperately eager to taste his blood.

"Come, take me, my darling," she said, and drew him downward onto the floor.

They sank together and she spread her legs wide apart, taking him into her and holding him tightly.

"Rebecca . . ." he said again.

Her teeth punctured his skin and two tiny fountains of blood appeared for her to lap up. As she drank deeply Richard wavered back and forth, falling quickly into semiconsciousness from the effect of making love to Rebecca and being drained of blood at the same time. His body spasmed over and over and his willpower began to leave him.

Rebecca drank ever deeper, thrilling to the warm, salty taste even while she moved with him. She murmured over and over, telling him endearments, expressing her love. She felt him sinking deeper and deeper, and she sang to him.

Then something jolted her and she opened her eyes. She had nearly forgotten. It was the Black Prince, standing over them.

The Black Prince was now covered in darkness, as though light could not touch him. Rebecca could barely see his body, but she knew most certainly that he was nude also. She could make out his phallus, huge and throbbing, as he began to kneel between the back of Richard's knees. He looked into Rebecca's eyes, smiling in victory, and as she watched his incredibly long white fangs slide dangerously over his lips, some last bit of her humanity revolted.

"No!" she cried out suddenly. Without thinking she jerked her head back and severed Richard's carotid artery.

Blood spouted from Richard's neck, covering her in red. His eyes opened wide very briefly, and he looked at her in surprise. "Rebecca?" he said, and then came the dawning of understanding. "Thank you," he said before closing his eyes.

The Black Prince got to his feet, enraged.

"How dare you!" he screamed. His voice thundered through the entire castle. "You do not break your agreements with me! Only I decide when things change. You do not deserve to inhabit this place. Your time on earth has ended. You will not enjoy the privileges of the vampire. Instead you will come straight to hell with me now!"

He reached for Richard's body, intending to throw it aside to get at Rebecca. But at that instant Richard opened his eyes and smiled at her. He grabbed the stake and put it between her breasts and fell forward on it, forcing it through her heart.

Rebecca felt a brief agony of pain, and then she looked at Richard and saw him die. The Black Prince pulled Richard's body off, then screamed in fury when he saw the stake through her heart.

"No!" he screamed wildly as he saw the consciousness still in Rebecca's eyes. He made to grab for her soul, bending his arm forward like a scorpion, but before he could touch her throat her eyes filled with peace and she slipped out of her body.

❊

EPILOGUE

The Nazis came and went and the castle remained undisturbed. The people in the small village brought up a new generation and filled them with the legends of the place, just as they had been filled with the same legends when they were children.

Since the locals themselves never went out to the castle, they assumed that no one else did, either. Which was true, for the most part. Many years passed before anyone saw a change.

On a bitter cold winter night in 1972, a young Soviet colonel was traveling by train through Romania. He considered himself destined for greatness and normally would carry with him at least one or two aides. But on that particular night he was alone.

He had been forced to take this particular route because traffic on the others had been tied up with a huge shipment of armaments heading for Afghanistan. Although unhappy with the primitive accessories and generally poor repair of the line, he had been overridden by his commander and so was forced to utilize this way. In a generally foul temper, he spent most of the time staring out at the blinding snowstorm and drinking the local vodka, something that he equated to goat piss.

The train began to slow down around five o'clock, creeping through the mounting drifts. By eight it became clear it would have to stop completely. Furious, the colonel picked up his coat and stomped out onto the platform of the small village and followed a rather attractive woman into the waiting room.

He stared at her figure unabashedly, but it was she who turned and smiled at him. "Colonel Zhirinovsky," she said, her dark eyes flashing, "allow me to introduce myself. I am Princess Alicia, and I live in this valley. I would deem it a great honor if you would sit out this terrible storm in my château, which is not far from here. I am going there now," she said, "to meet my husband, Prince Mephisonegro."

The stationmaster says that he went with her.